THE
CHRISTMAS
CRUSH

THE
CHRISTMAS
CRUSH

A Novel

NOELLE DOUGLAS

alcove
press

PUBLISHER'S NOTE: The recipes contained in this book are to be followed exactly as written. The publisher is not responsible for your specific health or allergy needs that may require medical supervision. The publisher is not responsible for any adverse reaction to the recipes contained in this book.

Copyright © 2024 by Alcove Press

All rights reserved.

Published in the United States by Alcove Press, an imprint of The Quick Brown Fox & Company LLC.

Alcove Press and its logo are trademarks of The Quick Brown Fox & Company LLC.

Library of Congress Catalog-in-Publication data available upon request.

ISBN (paperback): 978-1-63-910-888-6
ISBN (ebook): 978-1-63910-889-3

Cover design by Lucy Davey

Printed in the United States.

www.alcovepress.com

Alcove Press
34 West 27th St., 10th Floor
New York, NY 10001

First Edition: October 2024

10 9 8 7 6 5 4 3 2 1

To Mom AKA Accounts
For teaching me letters and how to love them

CHAPTER ONE

If he held his breath, Lawrence Higgins could believe this Christmas would still be perfect. When he exhaled, clouding the winter air, his worries came rushing out, but for the moment, he chose to focus on opening his bakery.

Pink dawn light tinted the cold sky as he started unloading crates from the bed of his old red truck. Glass jars of local honey rattled. He stacked the crates by the back door entrance to Sweet L's Bakery. "You're not gonna offer to help, Sugar?"

Sugar, a big bundle of frizzy white fluff claiming to be a dog, watched him from the warm truck cab.

"I know, I know. You don't work until you've had your coffee."

Beeps from a reversing cube van and its red brake lights broke the quiet semidarkness in the back alley. A hulking man got out and cracked his tattooed knuckles. The older man jumped out of his skin when he spotted Lawrence in the shadows. Lawrence struggled to suppress a smile.

"Whoa, man. You startled me. And I don't startle easy," the driver said. He consulted his clipboard. "I'm looking for Sweet L's Bakery, but, uh, I must've gotten turned around."

Lawrence loved the look on people's faces when they learned he owned a bakery and made all the cookies himself. Sometimes, when he felt extra mischievous, he'd make them take a few guesses about his profession before the big reveal. They'd size up his broad shoulders, strong arms, and long legs and say "firefighter" or "construction foreman." One time someone even guessed "Navy SEAL," which he had to admit still made him proud. No one ever suspected that strapping Lawrence kept his arms toned by hand-mixing all his doughs.

"Where do you think you are?" Lawrence asked, keeping his voice low and gravelly to mess with the guy. "I've got private business in this alley."

The driver visibly gulped and took a step back toward his van, right as Lawrence burst out laughing.

"I'm kidding, pal. I'm Lawrence, Sweet L himself. You must have my flour."

The delivery driver's shoulders dropped as he sighed with relief. "You got me, brother."

Lawrence and the driver made amicable small talk while they carried heavy flour bags into the kitchen. After setting his last bag down with a thwack, Lawrence grabbed a leftover chocolate chip cookie and gave it to the driver. "Here, dude, this is for being a good sport."

"Thanks!" The driver smiled, shook his head. "You had me going there. For a second I thought I stumbled on a Mafia enforcer about to burn down a business that owed money."

Still chuckling at his own prank after the driver left, Lawrence flipped on the bright overhead lights, turned on the radio, then grabbed a ball of gingerbread dough from the cooler. He set the oven to preheat.

Moments later, fragrant dough, sweet with brown sugar, molasses, cinnamon, and ginger, became a smooth sheet under his pin. Even before he baked it off, the dough smelled so mouthwatering, so much like Christmas itself, he wanted to sneak a bite. But he knew it would taste best fresh from the oven. He used all his self-control to resist temptation. Good things were worth the wait.

After the dough reached a perfect, even one-quarter inch, he took out his box of cookie cutters. Rattling away, he dug past stars, angels, and stockings until he located the trusty gingerbread man cutter. The copper cutter used to belong to his nana, but since it was his favorite, she'd given it to him when he turned seven. At that age other kids didn't understand why he wanted to spend every Saturday afternoon baking at his grandma's little house on the edge of town. Most kids in New Hope, Pennsylvania, preferred riding bikes down the tree-lined streets or skipping stones across the creek.

Lawrence used to feel quirky—even strange—for loving to bake, but he had lived for Saturday afternoons at Nana's and always chose them over more typical pastimes. Back then, Nana would take down her recipe binder and let him pick anything he wanted to bake. Now he didn't need to follow a recipe; he had them all memorized.

Whistling along to the carol playing over the bakery's speakers, he stamped out gingerbread men, then placed them in neat rows on parchment paper–lined pans. Sure, the bakery didn't open for an hour and there were no customers to enjoy the seasonal music yet, but it felt wrong to bake gingerbread while listening to the news.

He popped three pans of the cookies into his large commercial oven—the one that cost a fortune—and set a timer to rotate the racks so the cookies would brown evenly. "That's the secret, Sugar," he said to the dog, who'd curled up like a croissant next to the warm oven. "You can't just stick them in there for ten minutes and forget about them. They need to be babied, cared for, spoiled. Like you."

Sugar raised her head and gave him a skeptical look. "Don't believe me? You know there's nothing worse than cookies that are overbaked on one side of the pan and half-raw on the other."

"Talking to the dog again, boss?" Carmen Garcia asked as she hurried into the kitchen, tying her red apron strings as she strode toward him.

Lawrence didn't need to look at the clock to know Carmen was running late, but he also didn't have the heart to nag her about it. He knew his assistant's mornings were pure chaos, since she was the primary babysitter to a bundle of grandchildren. Plus, Carmen reminded him of Nana.

"You were probably getting lonely since I'm late. Again." She popped on her Sweet L's Bakery baseball cap to keep her short, steel-gray hair covered while she worked.

"Don't worry about it, Carm, they'll be on winter break soon, and then you'll really be late." He laughed to put her at ease, and also to cover his own anxiety. Worries came creeping back. His chest tightened. Fear that Carmen would retire to babysit full-time set his teeth on edge, especially this close to the holidays. Without his assistant, the workload would quickly overwhelm him. Running a small business required him to wear many hats, but he couldn't wear them *all* and keep his sanity.

"Maybe you're trying to stay on my good side since I haven't reported you for letting Sugar sneak in here." Carmen loved teasing him about Sugar, even though she knew he never let the dog near the ingredients. He prided himself on running a spotless shop. No one had ever complained of finding white fur on a cookie, and they never would. Sugar followed the rules in exchange for fresh-baked peanut-butter doggie treats.

"You heard the lady, Sugar. Back to the office with you."

With an exasperated sigh, Sugar rose and made her way to the office, toenails clicking across the white tile floor as she went. She might act put out, but soon she'd be snoozing in the nice patch of sunlight from the window that looked out on the corner of Main and Liberty.

The timer rang, drowning out the carol.

"Smells incredible as always, boss." Gingerbread sent waves of deliciousness through the kitchen when he opened the oven door.

"It's that fresh ground cinnamon," he said, gesturing to the stainless-steel electric grinder. Another pricy appliance, but one he believed set his cookies apart from the mass-produced junk at chain bakeries. Thinking of chain bakeries made him even more anxious than Carmen retiring. Chain bakeries could destroy his independent business. A stress ball formed in his middle as he imagined Nana's sadness if Sweet L's failed. "Did you have time for breakfast, Carm?"

"Well, no, now that you mention it, I don't think I did. I forgot about it in the morning rush." Carmen sighed heavily. "Then I took a little detour."

"To where?" he asked, even though he had a sinking feeling he already knew the answer.

"I know you said it's not going to be a problem for us, but I couldn't resist driving past the Sparkle Cookie site."

"And?" he prompted after a long pause while Carmen stared at her red Converse sneakers, part of the informal Sweet L's Bakery uniform.

"Just to take a quick peek." Carmen's eyes shifted behind her glasses. "They updated the sign."

Again she paused. The information she hesitated to reveal hung heavy between them. Lawrence rapped his knuckles on the cold stainless-steel workbench, looked at his own red Converse, currently flecked with flour.

"Looks like it's opening on Christmas Eve," she said at last.

That news sent his nerves straight to the roof. Sparked a few shallow breaths. Somehow he'd tricked himself into believing the mass-market cookie bakery wouldn't really open, that New Hope would keep its quaint charm. That his would always be the best bakery in town. The *only* bakery.

He muscled past the bad news, quickly changed the subject so he didn't have to dwell. "We gotta get you fed. You start the coffee, then plate the Swedish butter cookies. I'll whip you up a little something."

The best way to deal with stress was to avoid it, and the best way to avoid it was to bake. Carmen shrugged her shoulders, then went to fiddle with their temperamental coffeemaker. He took the gingerbread out of the oven, slid the pans onto a rolling cooling cart, then grabbed a few eggs from the refrigerator. Even though he only served cookies at the bakery, he could still bake anything someone might crave.

He whisked the eggs with some vanilla extract, milk, and honey, trying to focus on getting the perfect consistency instead of the fact that Sparkle *also* served only cookies. Sparkle was a social media sensation thanks to a clever marketing campaign that encouraged the hashtag *iSparkle*. People loved filming themselves standing in long lines at the chain's countless bakeries, fighting over the last of the double-fudge brownie cookies he strongly suspected came from a boxed mix.

He'd seen the photos posted online, and he had to admit the oversized cookies looked great in their pale-purple, glittery boxes. Eye-catching. Women wearing trendy clothes posed with cookies in their hands, showing off the latest flavors to millions of followers.

But how could cookies that had to taste exactly the same across a hundred stores possibly compete with cookies made by hand, in small batches, by someone who sourced each ingredient himself? The obvious answer was they couldn't. He believed his cookies were better. But would people still prefer the flashy, photogenic Sparkle cookies to his homemade creations? Would they be able to taste the care he put into each cookie?

Now he'd started overbeating the egg mixture, his speed matching his whirring thoughts. He forced his hand to slow.

He got worked up because cookies were much more than a sweet treat. Edible art, a gesture of hospitality, the perfect gift. In the two years his bakery had been open, people had turned to him for first birthday cookie cakes, colorful cookie bouquets to cheer sick friends, and beautifully arranged cookie platters to serve at their holiday gatherings. He'd even helped his old high school pal, Trey, propose to his sweetheart by piping *Will you marry me?* onto a dozen heart-shaped pink sugar cookies.

He weighed a scoop of oats on his kitchen scale, folded them into the eggs. Added a handful of chopped pecans and some frozen blueberries. Sparkle couldn't recreate his relationship with his neighbors in New Hope. Many of them knew the Christmas cookies were made with Nana's old cookie cutter and loved the stories he told about baking with her.

But as much as they cared about him as a friend, they might still get caught up in the excitement of a new thing. And the tourists who came to New Hope to look at the Christmas decorations in shop windows or attend the tree-lighting ceremony at the gazebo? They might go for the popular brand name they knew over the local guy.

Even a small decline in business could be fatal for a little shop like his. The commercial oven, the grinder, the quality ingredients, the great location on Main, it all came with a major price tag. He could pay his bills at the moment, but it was a house of cards. Pull out enough regular customers and he'd be in trouble.

Nana insisted the seed money she'd given him to start Sweet L's was a gift, yet his biggest dream remained paying it all back, with interest. Success meant showing Nana that she'd been right to believe in him.

"Are you making my favorite baked oatmeal?" Carmen asked, peeking into the bowl. He grinned and nodded, then poured the mixture into a buttered baking dish.

"Give this about half an hour and you'll have yourself a nice, filling meal."

Crinkles sprouted around her dark eyes as she smiled back at him. "I owe you one!"

Remembering the delivery driver's comment about Mafia enforcers, he said, "Want to help me burn down the Sparkle Cookie bakery?"

"I can make it look like an accident," she replied without hesitation, a seriousness in her voice that made him laugh despite his fears.

He put his arm around her, and she gave him a squeeze in return. Of course, he could never really commit arson, so he'd have to find some other way to stop the rival bakery from opening. And he'd have to come up with a solution in the next few weeks.

CHAPTER TWO

"What's the most coffee you can legally sell me?" Elena Voss asked Mel, the barista on duty. Mel rolled her eyes, then smiled, used to Elena's outlandish requests. Begging for shocking amounts of caffeine at the café next to the Sparkle Cookie corporate headquarters was a regular habit of hers. Baristas and customers alike were familiar with Elena stumbling in, a groggy expression clouding her features.

"Same as it was yesterday, Elena. Twenty-five ounces with five extra shots of espresso." Mel tucked a hunk of her rainbow-hued hair behind her left ear. She tapped the register screen, adding caramel syrup to the order without Elena having to ask. "Up late painting again?"

"How'd you guess? Besides needing a near criminal amount of caffeine?"

The barista raised a pierced eyebrow.

"Might be the dried paint smeared on your chin." Mel took a paper towel from the handwash station, dampened it at the sink, and handed it to Elena. "Here, use this while I make your banned-in-all-fifty-states coffee."

"I don't really have paint dried on my face, do I?" Before Mel could answer, Elena ran her hand across her jaw and, sure enough, felt flaky bits of gouache. She started to scrub it off as she stepped out of line. Good thing Mel had said something. She could hardly show up at this morning's strategy meeting covered in shades of green and baby blue. Her boss, Derick Cunningham, would have a field day with that mistake, calling her out in front of everyone.

Steam rose as Mel pulled the espresso shots into Elena's reusable travel mug. *Jug* might be a more accurate word to describe her cup, since it held half a gallon of liquid. She'd designed it herself, using infusible ink to permanently affix a field of flowers on the surface. Too bad Derick had pressured her to add a vinyl sticker of the Sparkle Cookie logo. He expected his team to be walking billboards for the cookie company.

While she waited for the lifesaving liquid, Elena rummaged through her leather tote bag. Her fingers ran over the smooth, circular metal of her compact. She snuck a look in the compact mirror. All clean, and her makeup still looked fresh. Derick demanded the Sparkle employees always be perfectly presentable, and he set the standard himself with nary a hair out of place, even on a windy day.

At least her outfit wouldn't cause any issues at work. She wore a lavender cashmere sweater despite wishing it were a more festive color, like a deep cranberry. Once again, Derick was to blame, since he required everyone to dress in company colors. The light purple didn't bother her in springtime, but it felt downright bah-humbug in December. Besides, she preferred jewel tones; she thought they looked best with her long, dark hair.

"When are you going to paint full-time?" Mel asked, stirring caramel syrup into the coffee, long spoon clinking against the travel jug.

"My dad would freak out. I barely repaired our relationship after I chose a cookie corporation over joining his firm." At the time, working for Sparkle's marketing department had seemed like a good compromise between her artistic ambitions and her dad's obsession with professional careers. Lately, though, it seemed like Derick wanted her to churn out cookie-cutter images for the website. She never got a chance to flex her creativity. A flower without sun or water, wilting away.

"I know all about that problem, believe me." Mel screwed the lid on the mug. "You should've seen the look on my mom's face when I said I planned to work here to have time for my band gigs."

Mel passed Elena the toasty mug, and she wrapped her hands around it. "Thanks, Mel, for the coffee. And for being a listening ear."

"Promise me you'll pace yourself with that. Don't glug it all down at once."

Elena didn't like to lie, so she said, "I'll do my best."

Downy flurries sprinkled around Elena as she trotted from the cozy café to work. The receptionist at the lavender front desk nodded, too harried to say good-morning to a fellow employee when Elena walked in. Elena had gotten used to the chilly workplace atmosphere at Sparkle Cookie, but it still bothered her. Last week she'd brought in eggnog lattes, foamy and spicy with nutmeg, to surprise her coworkers. After a quick "Thanks," everyone had turned right back to their computers, sipping their drinks in silence.

A shiver ran over her. She gripped her coffee jug tighter for warmth. *Yeesh, is Derick planning to increase profits by refusing to heat this place?*

Derick had promised that if this quarter's sales improved over last, the staff would earn a holiday party. There might be a chance to socialize then. Sadness sat heavy in her chest at the thought of numbers on a spreadsheet determining her level of seasonal cheer.

Sparkle Cookie company guidelines forbade decorations for any holiday, or even birthdays, which left the halls looking grim despite their lavender paint. She didn't want the blank walls and impersonal cubicles to remind her of growing up in her parents' house, but they did. How many times had Dad been too busy with work to join them in trimming the tree? Her mom worked full-time at the firm too, and often didn't have the energy after writing briefs all day. Eighty-hour work weeks didn't leave much time for holiday traditions.

Shaking away the painful memories, she put on a smile as she entered the conference room, determined to stay positive. She nodded hello to Derick's assistant, Sarah, and Priya, her only work buddy, as she took her seat at the long oval table. Sarah's fingers waited poised over her laptop keyboard to take meeting notes the minute Derick arrived. Alan from accounting whispered "Hi" before Derick stalked into the room and everyone froze.

Derick wore a slate-gray suit and lavender tie. He seemed to own a hundred similar ties; Elena could only tell them apart thanks to years spent studying color theory. As usual, he wore his blond hair slicked back, shellacked into submission with some product that made the whole room smell like cedar. Something about his manner always reminded Elena of a piranha. *Maybe it's the hangry eyes*, she thought. *Or that sharp grimace.*

"All right, team." Derick shot up the cuff of his dress shirt, glanced at a gold watch. "I have eight o'clock exactly, which means we're starting. Alan, that better not be a yawn you're suppressing. If you can't handle late nights, don't have a newborn."

Alan sat up a bit straighter to prove he was wide awake before he lost his job.

"We've got a major issue brewing with our New Hope location, set to open at the end of the month," Derick continued. "It's a disaster out there. Have a look at this disgusting mess."

Derick clicked a button on his small remote, and an image lit up the large projection screen on the west wall.

What Elena saw knocked the breath right out of her.

She didn't see a mess; she saw magic. A wide shot showed a town right out of a Christmas village: a winding creek running through snowcapped fir trees, a gazebo decked with greenery, and a cheerful main street. Derick clicked again, moving to a closer view of Main Street. Brown and red brick buildings with wide windows, multicolored lights strung neatly around them. A fresh snowfall made everything seem iced, as smooth as a frosted cake.

Through a bakery window she noticed a tree covered in whisks, wooden spoons, and cookie cutters. At the florist next door, red and white poinsettias filled the window, an abundance of flowers. A wreath with the most beautiful silver bow Elena had even seen decorated the door of a bookshop with steamy windows. She could almost smell the pine-fresh air.

Derick said something Elena didn't hear. She yearned to paint that street, paint that town. Her fingers curled like they could grip a brush right now. She imagined a series of canvases she could take out every year to hang on her walls for the holidays. One of winter sunlight streaming on the white gazebo, glittering on the creek. Another of Santa shopping along Main. One of her standing hand in hand with . . . with . . .

Well, she didn't have anyone special whose hand she could hold while strolling New Hope's streets. In fact, she hadn't even been looking for a partner. Everyone on the dating apps or who she met on nights out with Priya seemed like they didn't understand her. They all tried to impress her with flashy professions, going on and on about finance or medicine. She tried to change the conversation, asking if they preferred Monet to Van Gogh. Men met this question with depressingly blank stares.

Dating hadn't even been on her radar lately.

So what was it about that street, that town, that made her want someone she could share a hot cocoa with in front of a stone fireplace? Logs crackling, warmth from the flames. The feeling came from nowhere, and she shook her head, trying to concentrate on Derick's words.

"One of you needs to go to New Hope, crash their upcoming town hall meeting, and convince them Sparkle Cookies is going to be a great addition." He glared around the room. New-father Alan didn't have a moment to spare, and he visibly tried to avoid Derick's gaze. "The meeting is in two days, but I know we can work with short notice."

"They don't want us there?" Elena asked, before she remembered she hadn't been paying attention. She gulped. Priya stared at her with large, horrified eyes.

"Try to keep up, Voss," Derick snapped. She shrank back into her faux-leather conference chair. It wobbled uneasily on its wheels. "They're worried we're going to ruin their small-town, local-business vibe. They've been whining on our social media pages. It's not the image we want. Who's going, or do I have to make one of you?"

Not wanting to seem greedy by leaping at the chance to escape Derick, Elena hesitated. Obviously, Alan couldn't leave his wife and baby, but did no one else on her team want to visit a town straight out of a holiday movie? When Priya didn't make a move, Elena put up her hand. "I'll go."

For a moment Derick regarded her, speechless. He quickly regained his composure.

"I wasn't expecting such eagerness from you, Voss. Nothing much has been coming from you since the #iSparkle idea." Elena ignored his insult. That hashtag had driven social media engagement, and she felt proud of her work. Even her dad had been impressed when she told him. She leveled her gaze right back at Derick until he continued. "Okay. Keep up this level of enthusiasm and you might earn that party for the whole team, Elena. The rest of you, get to work crunching some numbers Elena can throw at these bozos. They need to learn how the economy works."

Anger flared hot in Elena's cheeks at Derick's dismissive attitude toward New Hope. But this was her job, this was how she paid the bills and avoided having to work for her dad. And this job was about to give her the opportunity to visit that beautiful town.

"It's only a forty-five-minute drive from here. Keep track of your miles for Sarah, and she'll reimburse you. And don't screw this up." Derick put his hands on the polished tabletop, glowered across at her. His shoulders hunched in a menacing stance, a viper about to strike. Elena heard Sarah's breath speed up. Priya mouthed *Be careful.* "Don't assume you're getting a free Christmas vacation out of this. If you can't convince those townies to stop dragging us online, you can go upstairs to the CEO yourself and explain to her why you failed," Derick said. All three of her coworkers sat still as statues, afraid to draw Derick's attention to themselves.

Did she feel intimidated? Obviously. Her mouth went dry when Derick threatened a meeting with the CEO. But she also felt something she hadn't felt in forever. She felt the town might live up to its name.

It might offer hope.

CHAPTER THREE

Town hall stood three blocks from Sweet L's Bakery at the southern end of the square, right behind the gazebo. The community Christmas tree had a place of pride in the center of the gazebo. Each year, the day after Thanksgiving, everyone gathered to hang ornaments and string lights. The lights wouldn't be lit until Christmas Eve, though, in a big ceremony headed by Santa, who rode in on a fire truck.

Lawrence had seen Santa arrive in New Hope every Christmas Eve to light their tree since before he could remember. Pictures by the tree of Lawrence and his sister, Lonnie, from babies on up, filled family photo albums. Blue eyes shining, their smiles bright with excitement, cheeks and noses pink from the cold. Nana kept the picture of four-year-old Lawrence on her mantel year-round, in a pretty golden frame. Everyone in the family said the look on Lawrence's face—thrilled innocence—perfectly captured the holiday joy people longed for this time of year.

As an adult, Lawrence knew the magical moment where Santa touched the tree and the lights burst on was part of a carefully coordinated plan by the mayor's staff. First, a town trustee clicked a walkie-talkie to catch the crowd loudly counting down. Next, a second trustee in town hall on the other walkie-talkie flipped the real switch when they shouted "Zero." Still, Lawrence never lost the feeling of wonder when the tree came to life and all the little kids gasped. Grown-ups cheered, and Mrs. Claus handed out candy canes.

Tonight he took the wide stone steps up to the town hall two at a time, balancing a big box of cookies in his hands. He tried to ignore the sense of dread overtaking him that he might miss next year's tree lighting. If Sparkle Cookie ran him out of business, if he had to commute to Philly for work, would he still have time for the tradition? Right now he set his own hours, served his own cookies at the tree lighting. *No one is taking this away from me*, he promised himself.

A welcome warmth greeted him as he swung open the old oak door and stepped into the building. Constructed in 1881, the building hung on to its vintage charm despite the addition of modern technology. Computers at the front desk and a screen outside the mayor's office displaying an events calendar didn't detract from the worn wood floors or exposed beams.

Lawrence hung a left at the desk, went down a narrow hallway adorned with black-and-white photos of New Hope in its early days. Horses, wagons, even the little brick building that now housed Sweet L's made an appearance in the grainy pictures.

"Hey, Lawrence, over here." Pamela, the florist and his mom's best friend, waved him into the spacious main room. Old high school classmates, former teachers, and other business owners filled the space, chatting and sipping cider from Styrofoam cups.

"Hi there!" He gave Pamela a hug. "Mom says I'm supposed to ask you about her poinsettia order. She and Dad can't make it tonight."

"Okay, pick it up from my truck after we finish here." Lawrence passed the cookie box to Carmen, who swooped over with a quick

"Hello." She swirled away as fast as she'd come, heading for a table with a red-and-green plaid tablecloth to set out the cookies on plastic trays.

"You all right, kiddo?" Pamela asked. "You look flushed, but it's freezing outside. Getting sick?"

"Nah, I'm fine. It's just all these layers." He pulled off his cream knit hat, the matching mittens, and unwound the long scarf from his neck. He ran a hand through his thick hair to save it from hat head.

Fine, huh? A bit of a stretch. His heartbeat kept speeding up and slowing down, and his stomach had been clenched in antsy knots all day. Every time Sparkle Cookie crossed his mind, he felt sick. His eyes shot around the busy room until he spotted Carm's daughter, Dr. Isabel Garcia-Peters. At least she could revive him if (when) he passed out.

Despite being surrounded by friendly faces, and even though Mayor Montgomery was stern but fair, waves of unease rolled through him. How could he convince everyone Sparkle Cookie shouldn't be allowed to move into town? His friends were one thing, but they weren't the only ones with a stake. Some outside investors owned property in town and wanted the rent Sparkle could pay.

He saw a couple of executive-type guys in their midforties, sporting button-downs and crisply pressed pants, sitting in the third row of folding chairs facing the podium. They stood out in the sea of comfy flannel and soft sweaters. Lawrence didn't recognize a single one. If he only had to convince his friends and neighbors, he wouldn't feel this gnawing stage fright, but he assumed he had to win over those guys too. He wished he could meet them at the pub a block away and intimidate them with his size instead of having to use his words.

Guys had a way of backing down like that delivery driver when Lawrence stood to his full height of six foot three. He wouldn't ever engage in a physical altercation, but he wasn't against flexing a bit to get bullies to buzz off.

Pamela led him like a skittish puppy to a chair near the middle of the room. She patted him on his shoulder, and he realized his response about being fine hadn't fooled her. Chewing away at his bottom lip, he scanned the crowd, hoping to see his buddy, Trey. He wanted to make small talk to keep his mind off the meeting as long as possible while they waited for the mayor.

No sign of Trey yet. Then his gaze fell on another person he didn't recognize. A very pretty person with wavy hair the color of melted milk chocolate. A light-purple V-neck sweater skimmed over her curves. *Well, who are you?* Her hair slipped off her shoulder as she pivoted in his direction. Quickly he turned away so she didn't catch him staring like a creeper. She didn't look like an executive. She looked like an angel on top of the tree.

A new nervousness took over his body, made his palms sweat. He rubbed them against his knees, the corduroy fabric rough under his hands, in case he got a chance to introduce himself. Maybe she was someone's cousin or friend in town for Christmas. A friend of a friend, perhaps.

Lawrence knew every woman around his age in town, but he couldn't recall ever seeing this one before. And he would remember. He'd only dated one fellow townie. Most of the New Hope girls had been his friends since kindergarten and felt more like sisters than potential lovers. That ex had moved away for college and never come back. Of course, he'd dated around in culinary school in the city, had a girlfriend for ten months, but he'd been out of school for years now.

No wonder I'm nervous. I'm so out of practice it's ridiculous. Time to stop staring or hiding and act like a grown man. He pasted a confident smile—at least he hoped it was confident, not goofy—on his face and looked back at the mystery woman.

Downright gorgeous, prettier than the last time he'd seen her five seconds ago. She smiled at Carmen, her long legs half the height of his petite assistant. Glossy lips parted and she took a small bite of a cookie. *His* cookie. When the flavor hit her tongue, her eyes rolled back. Lashes fluttering as she savored the taste. His chair creaked, and he almost fell out when her eyes opened to rest on him. A bit of powdered sugar clung to her lips; she licked it away.

He nearly leapt out of his chair to get to her. Just as he got to his feet, there was a clamor from somewhere behind him, people shifted, and he couldn't see her. The mayor strode in, followed by the police chief and the town administrator. Lawrence craned his neck, but he couldn't find where she had taken a seat. He sat back down, bounced his legs, flexed his fingers.

"I want to thank everyone for coming out tonight," Mayor Montgomery said, her friendly but authoritative tone silencing the chatter. She placed her hands on either side of the podium. "I know we're anxious to discuss snow removal in common areas, and, of course, business licenses for nonlocal enterprises. We said we'd do snow first, but it looks like we have some out-of-towners, so let's start with business licenses. Mr. Higgins has something to say, if I'm not mistaken."

The room fell so silent it was the quietest thing he'd ever experienced. He had not planned on opening the meeting. He had not planned on giving his speech in front of a beautiful stranger. Thoughts fluttered around in his head; someone coughed to prompt him to speak. The flush flared up again, turning his neck and cheeks hot, and certainly red.

"We have to put a stop to those crooks at Sparkle Cookie," he blurted out, completely forgetting the more diplomatic words he'd rehearsed in his truck on the way over.

"Now why would you want to do that?" asked a sweet voice. He searched for the source. Then, across the aisle, the mystery woman rose, fixed her eyes on him. "I'm Elena Voss, VP of marketing at Sparkle Cookie, and I'm here to convince you our bakery is going to be the best thing that ever happened to New Hope."

Lawrence's shoulders fell, panicked responses rising before his good sense could catch up. "I'm sure your cookies are fine, ma'am, but—"

Ma'am? Why on earth had he called her *ma'am?* What was wrong with him? She couldn't be older than twenty-five. Had he insulted her personally on top of insulting her job? Thus far, he'd called Elena a crook and an old lady. This was going worse than his worst nightmares.

"My cookies are scrumptious, I assure you," Elena said, smiling out at the audience. Her lovely face was already drawing sympathetic looks from the townspeople. He saw Pamela smile back at Elena. He was losing his own supporters.

And the way she said *scrumptious* had him thinking about anything but cookies. He willed his hands to stop trembling, swallowed, and tried again. "What I'm saying is, we already have delicious cookies in town." A few people clapped, led by Carm. His confidence grew. "And we don't need corporate box-mix cookies churned out on conveyor belts. We don't need chain restaurants coming to town, driving up rents for the people who actually live here."

"True, I don't live here, but I think this place is special, and I want to see it succeed too. We all do, right?" Her responses were calm, measured. She seemed unflappable, like an experienced attorney giving a convincing closing statement. Mayor Montgomery nodded in agreement from her place at the podium. "Sparkle Cookie locations bring new jobs. Our proven brand name draws new customers, who will shop at other places in town once they're here."

The heat in his face changed from anxiety to frustration when Elena mentioned driving town business. New customers might help Pamela at the floral shop or the Martinezes' book store, but it would destroy his bakery.

His passion for handmade treats overwhelmed his tact. "They're not going to buy more cookies from Sweet L's once they've filled up on your gar—"

He stopped himself in the nick of time, before he said something else he'd regret. He finally saw Trey in the crowd, who was furiously shaking his hand in front of his throat in a *Cut it out, man* gesture.

"Why do you care so much about cookies anyway, sir?" She said *sir* pointedly, a rejoinder to his *ma'am*. Her eyes narrowed; a fiery expression replaced the sweet one. With triumphant relief, he realized she'd made the same mistake everyone made about him. She assumed he didn't know the first thing about baking. This was his chance to turn the tide in his favor.

In a level voice he asked, "Did you enjoy the cookie you sampled from Sweet L's Bakery?" He already knew the answer. He'd seen her lick those full lips to get every last morsel.

"It was delicious," she admitted, confusion at his sudden change in demeanor plain on her face.

"They're delicious because they use local ingredients, like butter from the Johnsons' farm, or handpicked berries from Betty Sander's sustainable community garden. What makes them special is each batch is made right here. With love."

She scoffed, crossed her arms. "You can't taste love."

"You can absolutely taste the love in my cookies, Ms. Voss." Then he turned her own phrase against her, said each word slowly for maximum effect. "I assure you."

Applause broke out again. All the townspeople knew firsthand the difference his love made to a batch of cookies. Elena's mouth dropped open; her eyes widened. "You're . . . you're Sweet L?"

"My loyal customers call me that," he said. "You can call me Lawrence. Or Mr. Higgins."

She plopped down in her seat, arms still crossed. His chin jutted out, smirking with pleasure that he'd won. Mayor Montgomery said she'd review Sparkle Cookie's business license to make sure all was in order, which might delay the opening. He saw Elena blink away tears.

With those few blinks, shadows from her lashes against her cheeks, all the pleasure of being right drained away from him.

Mr. Martinez slapped his shoulder in congratulations, Carmen shot him a thumbs-up from the cookie table, but he felt worse than when the night had started. He'd gotten his point across, Mayor Montgomery seemed persuaded, but he couldn't shake the certainty he'd gone about it the wrong way.

Then Elena grabbed her bag, hurried toward the door, and the regret set in deeper than it ever had before. With her back to him, he noticed her shoulders were shaking. *No, please tell me I didn't make her cry.*

Weren't people from big corporations supposed to be soulless drones obsessed with the bottom line? Not pretty women with kind smiles and confident manners. A confidence he'd personally shot down.

He looked to her empty chair and realized that in her haste, she'd left behind a leather glove. No doubt he was the last person she wanted to see. He hesitated for a moment, embarrassment from his own actions holding him back, making his limbs heavy.

She could always buy more gloves.

But that wouldn't give him a chance to apologize.

So he abandoned his chair as the topic switched to snow removal, snatched up the glove, and went after her.

CHAPTER FOUR

Icy air hit Elena's face as she pushed open the heavy door. Good, maybe it would cool her cheeks, which were hot with embarrassment. Had everyone in the town hall seen her face go red? Seen the tears fill her eyes? *Never let them see you cry, Elena*, her dad always said. *You can't come back from it. Can't gain the upper hand.* Her boots crunched over road salt as she hurried down the town hall front steps, not even caring if she slipped on hidden ice.

Vosses are bosses, Elena. Dad often hadn't had time to attend Elena's soccer games or science fairs or ballet recitals, but on the rare occasions he had, that was his response when Elena acted disappointed, frustrated, or overwhelmed. Life was a constant competition, and he intended her to win. Sometimes his motto gave her a burst of confidence; sometimes it made her feel misunderstood.

Tonight, it reminded her she'd lost control of the situation.

Her phone buzzed with a text at the base of the stairs. Ahead lay the gazebo, eerily dark in contrast to the shops, which were colorful with holiday lights and decorations. Maybe these people were small-town weirdos, like Derick thought. Why didn't they light the tree in the gazebo, of all things? It looked odd standing there decorated but dark.

She whipped the phone from her bag. As she swiped the screen, she realized she'd lost a glove. Her left hand felt stiff, pinpricks of cold stinging her skin. Report back with GOOD news read a new text from Derick. She fought the urge to toss the phone into a snowbank and run off into the nearby woods. Survival with only one glove and a dressy peacoat might be tough, though. More tears fell at melodramatic thoughts of freezing to death.

Under normal circumstances, Elena could stop tears on a dime. All Dad's instructions over the years had made her a pro at outward composure, able to suppress inner turmoil at any cost. Derick ripped into her at work multiple times a week, in meetings full of Sparkle employees. Elena always remained calm.

Why were tears dripping from her eyes after a little dustup with the town baker, then? Why couldn't she stop them? She'd been embarrassed in work situations before, countless times. No matter how well prepared she was, she messed up sometimes, or Derick ruthlessly critiqued her hard work. Usually she didn't crumple, didn't have a crushing in her chest.

She strode down Main, momentarily blanking on where she'd parked her car. Earlier, she'd been awestruck by the adorable town, drinking it all in like a tourist. Seeing it with her artist's eye, as if painted in watercolors. Brick buildings of varying heights, doors painted rich reds and soft creams. Old-fashioned iron lampposts and benches complete with pretty metal swirls. Everything well cared for, well loved. She'd hardly paid attention to where she'd parked. Ah, there it was, right in front of—

No! Not that miserable cookie bakery she'd found precious an hour ago. The large front window decorated with *Sweet L's Bakery* in arching gold letters, the beautiful tree inside trimmed with baking accoutrements. Okay, maybe it was still kind of precious. She leaned closer to the window to inspect the tree. One of the ornaments was a framed photo of that jerk Lawrence Higgins with his arm around a tiny old lady. His poor grandmother, she guessed. If he weren't number one on her list of rudest people ever, she would be charmed by the way his grandma smiled up at her grandson.

Maybe she felt a shade charmed, despite his dismissive behavior. Maybe she was upset because Lawrence's real-world response to Sparkle Cookie didn't fit into the idealized vision of the town she held in her heart. She certainly hadn't expected some hulking beast of a guy to imply Sparkle Cookie's cookies were garbage in a crowded room. Or make her look like a fool for not knowing who owned competing businesses. She couldn't believe she'd thought he was cute when he first stood up to speak at the meeting.

She'd been struck by his impressive height, his bright-blue eyes, and his cuddly sweater that whispered *touch me* across the meeting room. Unlike his exterior, the bakery didn't impress her close up.

He might be good with cookies, but the storefront could use some major polish. Her tears slowed as she critiqued the many missteps he'd made marketing the bakery. In the window, old flyers from local summer events, yellowed with age, obscured part of the view inside. Made it hard to see the cookies in the case. What would entice visitors to New Hope? A clear view of the cookies from the street was free advertising.

She noticed a piece of plain copy paper taped to the inside of the glass door. Weekly specials were scrawled across it, some almost illegible. The third line had been written with such haste that she couldn't make it out at all. Surely he didn't really sell "squid ookies" on Tuesday. She laughed under her breath, retrieved a tissue from her bag to blot her eyes.

This place needed an overhaul. He wouldn't have to be worried about competition if he put in a little more effort. A small, petty part of herself hoped he never figured that out.

The sound of heavy footsteps on the sidewalk pulled her attention from the window. *Oh please, not him*, she thought as Lawrence

Higgins approached. At least he had the decency to look abashed, like a lumbering bear who'd been scolded for stealing trash. Big shoulders hunched, hands deep in his Carhartt jacket pockets. Eyes downcast.

Vosses are bosses, Elena. You can still turn this to your advantage. She scrubbed her face dry with the back of her gloved hand to hide her emotion.

"Your place is super cute," she said in a tone that sounded smug, a little mean, even to her own ears. In the darkness he wouldn't be able to tell she'd ever been crying. The only light came from an iron lamppost adorned with a wreath and the soft glow of the half-lit bakery. "You must have a loyal customer base. Sparkle Cookie doesn't have that here. However, we do have a sizable marketing budget. You'd be surprised what money can buy."

The words sounded like they came straight from her father's mouth. Superior, meant to throw off the opponent. And it worked. Instantly. His blue eyes widened, surprise plain in them. He'd underestimated her. He'd must've thought he'd won at town hall when she struggled with her emotions. If he'd followed her to gloat, to scare her off her job here, he'd be disappointed.

"And our cookies may not be as folksy as yours—yours really are tasty—but we can pump out a ton of ours per day. Volume is a powerful thing."

He narrowed his eyes at her veiled threat. Annoyance flashed hot on her skin in the cold air when he didn't back down. Then her indignation mixed with a confusing impulse to relent when his gaze fell to the sidewalk. He'd gone from looking angry to seeming strangely hurt with such speed that it threw her. *Fight me back; that I can handle.* Her hard-won calm began to wane and tears threatened to rise again. What was wrong with her? Her throat spasmed against her attempt to swallow. She charged ahead to rush past her unease. She continued before he could get a word in.

"I see on your sign the bakery is closed Sundays and Mondays. And only open six hours on Wednesdays? That's very nice. Great work/life balance. Sparkle is open seven days a week, ten hours a day. Where do people go around here for cookies after five PM?"

"Um, I guess I never asked." His posture stiffened and he pursed his lips. He had a nice mouth; she'd give him that. Just the right size for his face, expressive. Then he laughed, a hollow, uncertain sound. "You've got some confidence rolling into town thinking you can snatch my customers. Most of them have known me since the day I was born. Good luck with that plan."

Her mind raced, searching for a blistering response to his jab, but he suddenly shook his head and threw up his hands. "Anyway, listen, I didn't want to argue more with you. I think we both got a little carried away back there. Passions and all that. I wanted to catch up to you because you forgot your glove."

Nothing he said could've surprised her more. He'd seen her fallen glove? Ran after her in the cold to return it? Sure enough, he held it out to her. Elena could escalate an argument in her sleep, but this decent gesture sent her reeling. The glove looked ridiculously small in his hand. The sight derailed her train of thought, and for once in her life she didn't want to summon a crushing reply. Still, she couldn't let herself soften merely because he'd shown a shred of kindness. A smile played at the corner of his lips, then faded when she didn't return it. She managed to say, "Yes, we obviously both have strong feelings about baked goods."

He held tightly to the glove for a second as she attempted to tug it from his grip. "Mine are probably a little stronger. This is my life's work. You must have something you love more than anything else."

Painting. But she said, "You're right. Sparkle's success is my life's work."

"Thrilling." Now he was the one who sounded patronizing.

She yanked her glove harder right as he freed it. The force of her own motion made her stumble back a step. Away from him.

"Whoa, are you all right?" As he reached out a hand to steady her, she swiped her arm from his reach. For a split second she wished she could let him catch her. A foolish, fleeting desire to know what his touch felt like. She shook her head to chase out this unwelcome thought. Keeping the upper hand meant taking care of yourself, refusing help from your adversary.

"Perfectly fine." She recalled the smartass way he'd told her to call him Mr. Higgins. Irritation prickled anew at that embarrassing memory. "Good night, Mr. Hopkins."

She turned toward her car as he mumbled, "Higgins. It's Higgins, Elena."

He remembered her name? "Sorry, Larry," she said, because even if a small part of herself wanted to give him a break for remembering her name and returning her glove, she couldn't afford to. Not with Derick breathing down her neck. This time he didn't correct her, and if he continued standing there while she got into her car and drove off, she didn't look back to verify.

She had to concentrate on the drive and on how to spin this night to reassure Derick. No room in her life for anything else.

CHAPTER FIVE

Lawrence stood on the chilly doorstep to his bakery, stunned. Frozen in place, and not by the arctic temperature.

Had he just gotten into a second disagreement with Elena Voss? They'd known each other less than an hour. Did that break some kind of record? An abnormal ratio of disagreements to acquaintance by any measure. He'd had entire relationships with less conflict. To be fair, he often hadn't been invested enough to fight with a girlfriend or date, choosing to let them have their way to avoid a conflict. Why waste energy arguing with someone he didn't see a future with? Not that he saw a future with Elena. And this was nowhere close to a romantic partnership, of course. Never would be.

A business relationship, acquaintanceship, whatever. Since when hadn't he been able to handle a little healthy competition in the workplace? He'd seen his fair share of cutthroat behavior in culinary school. A fellow student had once sabotaged Lawrence's broth for a practical exam. They'd dumped every spice in the kitchen into the pot, which made the chef grading the exam throw up. Lawrence kept his cool then and would do the same now. He didn't let stuff like that get to him.

Then why did he want to chase down Elena and attempt to explain himself a third time?

Elena didn't seem like the type to be persuaded. He couldn't shake the feeling he had her all wrong. Didn't have her at all. Was she a vulnerable person trying her best, driven to tears by a grouchy baker? Or was she a vicious, career-driven type who only lived to increase the bottom line?

Perhaps he'd misread the whole evening and she'd actually been shaking with rage when she ran out of town hall. She might've been on the verge of throwing hands, for all he knew. Although, based on the size of her glove, he wasn't sure she could do much damage.

He began to doubt his own memory of the altercation at the meeting. Had he actually seen tears? If she hadn't been crying in the first place, he didn't need to feel guilty. Maybe he had simply imagined he had the ability to make her care, seen tears where none existed. Not bringing her to tears meant he hadn't needed to make it up by returning the glove.

He hadn't noticed a single teardrop on the street a few minutes ago, he knew that much for certain. Instead, she'd practically backed him into a corner with her assertive criticisms of his business model and boasts about Sparkle's superior methods. He should've kept the glove. Did someone that calculating even get cold?

Well, he felt plenty cold now. In fact, he didn't know why he continued to stand on the street on this moonless night. Before hypothermia had a chance to set in, he unlocked the front door, jingling the bell above it as he pushed into the front of the shop.

Sugar ran from the office to greet him, eager to head home for a long night's sleep after a busy day of napping. "Sugar, where were you when the scary lady told me everything that's wrong with me right outside our own bakery? Snoozing away, I bet. Why didn't you rescue me with your cuteness and calm her down?"

He ruffled Sugar's fluffy white topknot, mussing her frizzy curls. Sugar panted, not knowing why they were up in arms but willing to support him.

Someone knocked. For a second, he expected to see Elena. Ridiculous. Why would she come back? She'd made her point. Eloquently. Instead, he saw Trey. He waved him in.

"What's up buddy? Did you make that poor girl cry back there?" Trey stomped snow off his boots. Chunks of ice landed on the cheeky doormat that read *bite me* with a big cookie beside it. A gag gift from Nana. "First new woman we've seen around these parts in a decade, and you manage to scare her away in two seconds flat. If you're betting on me and Iris asking you to join a throuple, I'm sorry, you're a great guy, but we're not interested."

"Iris already puts up with enough being engaged to you. Give the poor thing a break." Lawrence wouldn't impose himself on any woman at this point in the evening. The apology he'd concocted while running after Elena hadn't made it past his lips. She'd thrown him off his game and managed to irritate him enough to make him forget his manners again.

He went to the counter, grabbed a pair of peanut butter cookies big as dinner plates, and gave one to Trey.

They both took healthy bites at the same time. The perfect amount of crunch from the crispy top sanded with sugar, and then the moist middle melted on his tongue. Sensational. Eating his feelings seemed like the best option. Might as well enjoy something tonight.

"Where is Iris, by the way?"

"Hanging out at her sister's. Nobody is getting any rest in that house with the twins. Scared me off children for life, those two." Trey shook his head, brushed cookie crumbs off his plaid jacket. Sugar trotted over to lick up the crumbs, snuffling at the worn wood floor like a truffle pig.

Lawrence made a crack in return about babies being difficult and said he could barely handle Sugar. Secretly he thought Iris's nephews were the cutest things he'd ever seen. Their parents dressed them in matching pj's and sailor suits. Who could resist that? He figured Trey might be bluffing too, since he'd seen his best friend's eyes go googly when Iris held the babies.

"I didn't come here to point out you have no game." Trey grinned. He leaned back against the counter while Lawrence gave him a warning look. On a typical night, he loved nothing better than trading barbs with Trey. This time, he felt sensitive in a way he didn't want to think too much about. Trey flipped his locs away from his face and looked Lawrence in the eye. "Sorry, bro, all joking aside. I do have something important to tell you."

"Why do I get the distinct impression it's not good news?" Lawrence reached for another treat, a chocolate marshmallow sandwich cookie with a thick layer of fudge frosting between the cookies. He couldn't handle more bad news without some carbs. Trey let Lawrence finish the cookie—it only took two bites—before he went on.

"I know you saw those dudes in the suits up front. After the meeting broke, I wanted to head over here to check on you. I was worried you might be eating raw flour and crying into your sugar."

"Ha. Ha." Lawrence did have to crack a little smile. "I can't afford to replace sugar I melt with my tears."

Sugar the dog perked up, held out a paw. Lawrence took her warm foot. "I could never melt you, sweetie."

"This is about money too. These guys were all standing in a tight little circle, talking to each other in the lobby. I heard one say Sparkle is going to attract more chains in no time. Another said local landlords will start increasing rents every six months if they're smart. I had to give you a heads-up."

"I appreciate it." He and Trey always looked out for each other. Yet Trey's words didn't quite hit; Lawrence's mind was somewhere else. "You know how tight things are around here as it is. With any luck, my landlord won't go for that strategy. Just in case, I gotta be on my A game. Drum up some new customers. I need to get them loyal before Elena comes in and steals them all."

"Who's Elena?"

Lawrence cleared his throat, washed his hands, then began to busy himself boxing up the day's unsold cookies. He'd drop them off at the retirement home in the morning. "I mean the Sparkle Cookie representative."

"Ah. I didn't catch her name." Trey eyed him suspiciously, traced his fingertips along the countertop. He had the mercy not to press Lawrence on the Elena issue. "This is good. You've got to formulate a solid road map to head this off at the pass."

"I'm sure I can, man." Did his voice sound confident? He hoped it did. Where would a small local bakery find new customers? For the first time in two years, he began to doubt his focus on New Hope, wonder if he should cast a wider net. But how? Recipes, flavor, those were his thing. Business models and marketing strategies—those were definitely not his thing, as Elena had thoroughly brought to his attention.

"You look like you need a beer." Trey knew him well. A beer and a game of pool would get his mind off the anvil of problems about to drop on his head.

"You're buying." Lawrence clipped Sugar's pink leash to her matching collar. "Want a pub burger, baby?"

"I know I do." Trey clapped his hands on Lawrence's shoulders. Lawrence noticed how tense he'd gotten and did his best to unclench his muscles.

A few hours' relaxation would help. It had to. Some brilliant idea would come to him. He would save the bakery. He did his best to laugh along with Trey while he locked up. Tried to squish down the premonition that a greasy burger at the hole-in-the-wall bar at the edge of town would only add heartburn to his unenviable situation.

No matter what, he wouldn't worry about his bakery for the next few hours. Or Elena. He knew there was something more to her than cold and calculating, underneath her bluster. He'd seen it in the heat in her dark, beautiful eyes when he'd challenged her, when he'd asked her what she loved more than anything. She'd said Sparkle after a brief hesitation. But whatever had first come to her mind unbidden was what she really loved. Her lips parting, then closing—the truth lay in that unspoken word.

In that quick breath of time, her eyes had given her away, their hands inches apart, her small glove stretched between them. If instead of letting go, he'd held on, what would've happened?

CHAPTER SIX

The entire drive back from New Hope, Elena fumed, replaying their arguments a thousand times, coming up with a million cutting remarks she could've used to subdue him. She almost missed her exit, she'd been so preoccupied by her ongoing imaginary verbal battle with Lawrence.

And she couldn't *stop* fuming, because now more than thirty-six hours had passed and it still dominated her thoughts. She found herself blocking the register in the coffee shop, giving Mel an unsolicited, detailed description of the fight. A bean grinder's rattling whir interrupted her, but she picked up without missing a beat the second it stopped.

"Is he attractive? I mean, yes. But I'm not even sure guys built like Michelangelo's *David* are my type. Obviously, they're, like, everyone's type. People have been gawking at that statue for five hundred plus years for a reason. What difference does it make even if he is my type?

"I told Derick I made some good inroads—which I did—but there's still work to be done there. All thanks to Lawrence Higgins

36

and his little passion project. I'm not the least bit worried about their mayor reviewing our business license. Legal handles that and they never screw up.

"Anyway, to answer your question, yes, he is very good-looking. You did ask, right? And he might be pretty nice under different circumstances." She squeezed her glove in her pocket, a habit she'd recently developed. "But, as I said, these aren't different circumstances, and I'm just giving you all this information so we can figure out how to destroy him."

A hand tapped her shoulder in sharp beats. "Lady, are you going to order or what?"

Mel raised a finger to silence the customer in line behind Elena. Elena glanced over her shoulder, gave the man a half smile in apology. He didn't return it.

There was actually quite a long line in the café, which made sense, given it was seven in the morning on a workday. Voices hummed around her. A woman with a baby in a stroller tapped her watch pointedly, glaring at Elena. "Let her finish, okay?" Mel said, voice raised to be heard above the disgruntled din. She shook her head and whispered, "People are in too much of a rush these days."

Elena held out her travel jug. "In sum, it doesn't matter who he is as a person. Or what he looks like. He's an obstacle."

Mel tipped her head to the espresso machine, and Elena stepped out of line. The waiting customers didn't cheer, but Elena sensed they wanted to, their relief swelling. Another barista appeared at the register while Mel pulled the espresso shots. "Even I have to admit it would be hard keeping a cool head around a dude who looks like he was carved out of marble by a master sculptor. And I don't find men attractive period."

"See, Mel, I knew you'd get where I was coming from. It's a problem to be solved, and I can solve it." *Vosses are bosses*, Elena thought, squeezing the glove again. She had to stop doing that. With each squeeze, she pictured Lawrence holding the glove.

She held out both hands for her travel jug. Mel smiled at Elena's paint-stained fingernails. She'd done her best to clean off last night's colors. Hopefully, Derick wouldn't notice. "Looks like you've been using a lot of blue. What are you working on?" Mel asked.

"Nothing," Elena said too quickly.

Mel smirked. She pulled a lever to aerate the milk, a hiss of steam rising around her bemused face. She returned Elena's mug after mixing the ingredients. "And what color are this obstacle's eyes, by the way?"

Elena took a long sip of the steaming-hot drink. A river of super-sweet coffee rushed over her taste buds. She swallowed. "I haven't the least idea."

"Sure." Mel wiped her hands on her apron.

It wasn't Elena's fault Lawrence had an inspiring eye color. And she hadn't been painting his eyes like an obsessed stalker. They happened to remind her of the color cyan, that perfect mix of blue and green. She'd needed to replicate it in the tropical water of a seascape she'd started last month and almost scrapped because she couldn't find the right hue.

It didn't mean anything. She found inspiration in all sorts of random places. Once, she'd spent weeks mixing colors to match a patch of rust she'd seen on a broken-down car. She didn't find the car attractive.

"Okay, Elena. In the meantime, stare a little to the right of his face so he thinks you're looking at him but you're not. To protect yourself from the glare of his beauty."

Elena playfully rolled her eyes. "Solid tip. I'll be fine, though. I'm concocting a strategy as we speak."

"Enough speaking," Mel's coworker barked. "We just got twenty-one mobile orders!"

"I better go back to the register before these people riot," Mel said. Elena thanked her and departed the café for work.

Today it didn't bother her as much that no one had time to say hello. She rushed to her cubicle, tossing her coat on the desk and then powering on her computer. She needed to find another opportunity to visit New Hope. Opinions on New Hope's village social media page and recent comments under Sparkle Cookie posts weren't terrible, but they weren't great either. She had to do a better job of convincing them Sparkle would benefit the town.

When the screen lit up, she got to work, searching for a way to persuade or downright bribe the residents of New Hope. She sent an email to the New Hope village secretary asking if Sparkle could get a table at an upcoming holiday craft fair. That could work. If she handed out samples of their top-selling cookies, she could rope in potential customers by the bucketful.

The event would be held in the high school gym. Elena felt certain she could wow them with a flashy display. Maybe freebies besides cookies as well. Lavender key chains with the Sparkle logo or lavender pens with cookie-scented ink. She knew the supply closet was well stocked with options she had helped design.

Her intense focus on a document proposing the plan for the fair caused her to jump at the sound of her message alert piercing the mostly silent office. The village secretary had already replied.

Dear Ms. Voss,
Thank you for your interest. However—
Uh-oh. This didn't sound good. Her heart sank as she read on.
—due to the extreme popularity of the event, we are already fully booked. Vendors interested in next year's fair are encouraged to submit applications by August 31.

Had Higgins gotten to the village secretary, telling her to block any cookie competition? She wouldn't put it past him, but maybe the event really was that popular. She rubbed her temples, then went back to searching for another way to bring cookies to New Hope. The New Hope Public Library website listed a holiday open house on their events calendar. Elena loathed cold calling, yet it seemed to be the best option for offering to bring cookies.

She didn't have to be nervous. Who would turn down free cookies?

Her heart thumped twice as fast as the rings on the other end as she waited to be connected to the library. She had to channel her dad's self-assured tone three times before she got transferred to someone who could actually make a decision.

"Business office," a no-nonsense voice said after picking up on the first ring.

"Hi, my name is Elena Voss, I work for Sparkle Cookie, and we would like to offer a sampling of free cookies for the library to serve at the holiday open house."

"Thanks, but we have a local guy who handles the treats. Have a nice day."

Click.

Higgins. Who else? He had a cookie monopoly on the town of New Hope. Too bad for him she had the zeal of an antitrust legislator and would break his hold no matter what it took.

Time to switch tactics. She widened her search range to surrounding towns, sipping her coffee as she scrolled results. Sugar and caffeine coursed through her veins, heightening her sense of urgency. Her foot tapped a constant rhythm against the desk, her leg bouncing along.

Home Baker's Quarterly, a regional magazine, advertised a cookie swap at an inn ten minutes outside New Hope. Fingers metaphorically crossed, since her hands were busy, she checked to see if she'd missed the registration deadline for this option too. She closed her eyes for a second before plucking up the courage to read the details.

You can never have too many cookies! Join us at the picturesque Snowcap Inn to trade your best holiday baked goods with friends and neighbors. Simply bring five dozen of a single flavor of cookies to swap. Participants receive a commemorative mug. All are welcome, hot cocoa bar provided.

Elena clapped her hands in delight.

"We don't clap in here, Voss. It's not part of our corporate culture," Derick said, appearing out of nowhere to hover by her desk. "Pretty wishy-washy results from your incursion into New Hope. I expected more."

Incursion? Was this a hostile cookie takeover? Derick had a talent for making even the most innocent things aggressive. Not that she minded a bit of aggression when it came to proving Lawrence wrong. She swiveled her chair to avoid the odor of Derick's s too-strong cologne.

"Cookie swap?" he asked, staring at her computer screen. "What's the point of that?"

Now was one of the times her dad's instructions came in handy. She didn't squeak at all when she answered Derick. "To both increase goodwill in the New Hope area and create word-of-mouth buzz for our cookie creations. You can expect to see a thirty-five percent improvement in New Hope attitudes to Sparkle Cookie with this approach."

Total nonsense; she didn't know where she'd come up with that bogus number. Could an attitude be measured in percents? Perhaps with a formal poll? An idea sprang to mind. "I'll be handing out surveys with our cookies to gauge reactions to our samples."

"Now you want me to give you freebies?" Derick looked down his too-straight nose at her. She suspected no actual human could have such precise, cold features. Either he'd had cosmetic surgery or he was really an android.

"We gave samples away at that music festival over the summer, and Sparkle Cookie shops within a twenty-five-mile radius reported a nine percent jump in sales." That fact was true, though she couldn't believe she'd remembered it. A kernel of knowledge from some cramped spreadsheet or colorless slide months ago that stuck in her subconscious.

"You're going to get me fifteen percent. I want the New Hope location to post our biggest opening yet. It's the holidays, people want cookies. This is easy stuff, Voss. If you can't do it, someone else will." He walked away without giving her a chance to respond.

She took a deep breath when he disappeared from view. Derick's demands and too much coffee left her shaking all over. *I can do this; I can make this successful.* The odds were against her that the cookie monster, Lawrence Higgins, would skip out on a cookie event practically in his backyard.

Attempting to summon the confidence she'd had after talking to Mel, she promised herself Lawrence wouldn't throw her off her game a second time. A whole workweek to prepare would be more than enough to show New Hope her cookies were as good as their hometown boy's.

And if not? No, she couldn't think that way. Victory only.

CHAPTER SEVEN

Sugar paced the office floor like she knew Lawrence had a big idea to share and was offended he wouldn't let her in on the secret. Lawrence checked the paper calendar he kept on his scratched oak desk. Paper calendars were old school, but without them he was hopeless, missing appointments, forgetting to make orders until the last minute. He set his teacup on the desk, where it would be sure to add a new ring to the many already scattered across the scarred surface.

Yes, if he worked overtime, he could juggle it, make time for a new venture. Despite Elena's crack about Sweet L's limited hours, he knew a mountain of work went on behind the scenes, before the first customer walked in the door. Today alone he'd completed a stock check, written out the baking schedule for this week, juggled his own schedule to allow Carm a late start tomorrow, and test-baked his new recipe for candied orange ginger cookies.

Carm's late start tomorrow would make it tight, but it might be okay. He needed it to be okay.

Don't stress about the roadblocks, he told himself. He scrolled through the contacts on his phone, tapping on the one with a picture of an elderly woman with a mass of white curls. The phone rang and rang. It took Nana a while to get to her house phone. She didn't like cell phones and she always left her cordless phone on the kitchen table, even though he bugged her to keep it handy in case she needed something.

"Hi, pumpkin," she said when she finally answered. Nana loved the "new" technology of caller identification. Her favorite thing was answering as if she'd been expecting your call all day.

"Hi, Nana Banana. What are you doing this morning?" Nana got up with the sun, so Lawrence never had to worry about calling her too early. Outside his window, he saw Pamela, the florist, place a few miniature evergreens in red-and-white-striped pots outside her shop's front door. Mr. Martinez salted the bookshop's front step, then came over to scatter some on Lawrence's step. The bookseller's breath came out foggy as he worked. Lawrence lifted a hand in thanks. He'd make sure to pop over with a paper cup of coffee for Mr. Martinez later. New Hope Main Street was slowly waking up.

"I got some steps on my treadmill. I'm already at four thousand three hundred and one."

"That's incredible, Nana."

"I love this step counter watch you got me. Except for when my shows are on and it buzzes to make me get up to walk around. Nag, nag, nag." Nana chuckled. He heard her turn down a morning news program. She never minded if Lawrence interrupted. "What about you, pumpkin?"

Without meaning to, he let out an enormous sigh. Sugar came over and rested her head on his knee. He ran his fingers through her fur, and she looked up at him with thoughtful eyes. "You know, the usual. Busy. We have special orders every day, which is good. A lot to get done, but that's good. All good overall, I'd say."

"Yes. Sounds like everything is quite good." Nana went quiet. Lawrence suspected she was waiting for him to confess what wasn't good. He took a sip of his English Breakfast tea.

"Do you think, on top off all the holiday orders, the holiday craft fair, the library open house, and regular stock, I can swing bringing a few dozen cookies to a cookie swap event? *Home Baker's Quarterly* sent out an email a few weeks back saying they were sponsoring a swap nearby at Snowcap Inn."

"Cookie swaps are lovely, dear. My pals and I used to have them all the time, back when your dad was a little one. I always brought dozens of my almond crescents, and that beautiful crystal platter Grandpa got me. We'd have eggnog—and yes, it was spiked, your nana wasn't always an old bird—chat and trade cookies. By the end of the night, we'd have listened to the *White Christmas* soundtrack about twenty times and I'd go home with a platter full of fifteen different varieties of cookies."

Lawrence smiled as Nana reminisced. He pictured her in her frilly apron, the one with holly-and-berries fabric, toasting the holidays with her closest friends. Creamy eggnog with a splash of brandy. "I bet those almond crescents were the first to be snapped up."

"You'd be right. Are they still a best seller?"

"Everyone in New Hope puts them at the top of their special orders in December." Crumbly but never dry, the cookies dissolved on the tongue, leaving behind a subtle almond flavor and mellow sweetness from a dusting of powdered sugar. When he was a kid in Nana's kitchen, shaping the lumps of dough into crescents had been his favorite part. Nana let him get creative and come up with almond alphabet cookies or almond hearts. The funky shapes didn't always turn out well, but Nana insisted experimentation was an important part of innovation.

"You do have your hands full over there. Why do you need to do the swap?"

Lawrence explained he wanted to entice new customers. He left Elena and Sparkle Cookie out of it, and he didn't mention the threat of rising rent either. Sugar wagged her tail when he scratched under her chin to keep himself calm.

"I'm sure anyone who tried your cookies will become a loyal customer."

"Our cookies, Nana."

"Now, you've taken my recipes and run with them. They're a whole new thing thanks to your talent. What would you say if I came to the bakery for a spell, helped you make a few batches? My morning is clear. I have an eye doctor appointment after lunch, but I know we'd be done by then."

Lawrence wanted to whoop with joy. He hadn't called her expecting to gain a free assistant for the day. He wouldn't say no, though. Nana helping would make the day smoother and easier in a dozen small ways. Instead of Carm having to rush from the front of the house to the back to balance walk-in customers with packing orders, she could focus on the front while Lawrence packed. And he could take breaks to bake with Nana.

A hundred-pound weight floated off his body. He felt eight years old again, excited to spend the day tweaking recipes, munching cookies, and goofing around with Nana. "I'll come get you in a few minutes! Thanks so much, Nana Banana."

Nana might be eighty, but she could turn out five dozen cookies like it was nothing.

"No, no. You stay there and work. I want to start up the sedan. Can't let it sit around in this cold."

"All right. You toot the horn when you get here, and I can walk you in. There's salt down, but there could be hidden icy patches."

"You worry too much. I've been tromping around New Hope winters since the Stone Age. Still, I guess it can't hurt to have an escort. I'd hate to slip and break something before the senior center Christmas Eve dance. I promised Mr. Simmons I'd dance the waltz with him."

"Trey's grandpa?" Lawrence exclaimed, plopping down his teacup in surprise. Tea sloshed over the sides. "Am I going to end up related to my best friend?"

"Goodness, what a romantic imagination you have. Let's see how the dance goes. What if I step on his toe and scare him off?"

Lawrence knew all about scaring people off. He couldn't believe Nana would ever make a bad impression. The whole of New Hope found her delightful. Her social calendar booked up weeks in advance. He jotted a note on the pad next to his laptop: *Ask Nana for advice on interpersonal skills.*

After his disastrous first encounter with Elena Voss, he doubted he'd get a second chance. Not that he wanted one, per se. He wanted . . . he wanted to be more poised in general. Elena had simply shown him where he was lacking. He wouldn't improve for her, since he would never see her again. He'd do it for himself.

"I can't wait, Nana." They said their goodbyes for now, and he hustled out to the kitchen to keep working.

CHAPTER EIGHT

"How did dinner with your parents go?" Elena asked Priya. The two stood side by side at a long counter in the copy room. The counter was made of Sparkle Cookie lavender laminate. At night, when Elena closed her eyes to fall asleep, she saw that color. Never saw the swirl of colors on her newest canvas or the rainbow of colored pencils she kept in a cup on her nightstand. Didn't even see cyan eyes. Sparkle lavender all day, every day, led to Sparkle lavender all night. She swore her dreams had a lavender hue.

"Things are still bad with my brother." Priya arranged a stack of cardstock, tapped it on the counter to neaten it. "He got another speeding ticket—my dad had to take away the keys to his car. I tried talking to Kiaan myself after dinner. He didn't pick up my call, the brat."

Priya's seventeen-year-old brother caused no end of drama for the Patel family. Over the years of working together, Elena had come to realize that Priya both adored Kiaan and was seriously annoyed with him most days.

"Since I moved out last year, we haven't been as close. There are six years between us, but we always had fun with each other. He can be total a clown and crack me up like no other. I used to let him get away with stuff Mom and Dad wouldn't, like watching TV late when they were out or extra sweets."

"I'm sorry to hear he's making bad choices. Doesn't he realize everyone is worried for his safety?"

Priya's face scrunched with frustration. "I feel like a wise old woman of twenty-three, but kids these days. He won't listen to anyone. Do you feel like you aren't close with your brothers since leaving the family home?"

Priya handed her the stack of cardstock. Elena lined it up on the paper cutter grids, then began making clean slices to quarter the stack. She searched her memories for a time she and her brothers had been close. When they were little kids, before Dad's expectations got in the way? She couldn't remember. "We were all busy with school and extracurriculars—we hardly saw each other most days. My dad wouldn't accept anything less than As, and he encouraged us to take AP classes in high school. My older brother was salutatorian, which made Dad try to get me and my middle brother to get valedictorian. Oliver did, I didn't. Another disgraceful salutatorian." Elena laughed.

"Man, I thought my parents were intense about school, but that is next level." Priya's yellow-gold bracelets jingled as she fiddled with them, then looked Elena in the eye. "Wasn't that a hard way to grow up? I mean, obviously you're super successful for your young age. It was worth it, just . . ."

Priya's voice trailed off; Elena shrugged. She usually loved working in the copy room thanks to the small vent in the ceiling that blew genuinely warm air. She swore her cubicle ran even colder than the rest of the frigid office. Right now, the heat felt uncomfortable. "Sometimes," Elena said.

All times. However, she didn't want to have such an intense conversation at work. If she and Priya went to dinner again soon, Elena could go into more detail then. Not that she wanted to bad-mouth her dad. In her heart, Elena knew his drive came from his humble background and wanting his kids to have better.

"What do you think of the surveys?" Elena asked, glad she could shift Priya's attention from family history. Elena fanned out the cards.

"They turned out really pretty. I love what you did with the boarders."

"Thanks! The QR code was a good idea." Elena still owed Priya a coffee for helping her brainstorm how to best engage customers with the survey. With Priya's addition of the QR code, customers could either fill out the paper survey or complete it online for a ten percent discount off their first cookie.

"Are you worried Derick is gonna flip about the discount?" Priya asked. The addition of the discount had been Elena's idea.

It was pretty much a given Derick wouldn't like the idea of los-ing a few cents, although most people who came for the discounted cookie would end up buying more at full price in the same transac-tion. Elena plucked up her courage and said, "Hey, I'm VP of mar-keting. This is my call."

She and Priya both giggled at the wobble in Elena's voice when she spoke. "You tell 'em, girl boss. Better to ask forgiveness than permission."

Elena high-fived Priya. They left the copy room and made their way to the test kitchen one floor down. A wall of windows offered a glimpse of the bakers at work. All wore immaculate white coats, hairnets, and gloves. With mechanical precision they moved about the kitchen, ripping open packages of mix or cracking the lids off tubs of frosting. All Sparkle cookies began with the same base ingredients, produced in a few factories across the country and shipped to Sparkle locations on a weekly basis.

Elena found the "test" in "test kitchen" misleading, since the bakers didn't have much freedom to develop recipes. Most of the add-in flavors were a corporate decision from the higher-ups, who based their choices on intensive market research. Elena aggregated data each week to present to Derick, who later repeated it to top management like he'd done all the legwork. The bakers here were some of the best money could buy, even though they had little leeway when it came to producing new types of cookies.

"I don't think the guy on the left has blinked once since we've been standing here," Elena whispered. Priya nodded in agreement.

Elena opened the test kitchen door. Sweet vanilla buttercream frosting scented the air, almost masking the sterile smell of the bleach used to clean surfaces every thirty minutes. Fluorescent lights glinted off stainless-steel workbenches, leaving flares in Elena's vision.

"No civilians past the red line," a woman in black-rimmed glasses declared. Elena and Priya both stopped in their tracks, looking down at the floor at the red line two feet inside the door. The tip of Elena's black leather boot was a hair over the line. She pulled her foot back at once.

"We're here to pick up five dozen sample cookies for an event," Elena said, speaking loudly to be heard over a stand mixer the size of a small car.

The baker pushed up her glasses, then tipped her chin to a row of four large lavender paper shopping bags. They were arranged on a workbench just outside the red zone. Elena stretched a hand out.

"Excuse me!" Glasses Baker shook her head, a look of disgust in her eyes. "No stepping *or* reaching across the line. As I said one minute ago."

Elena put her arms by her sides and gave Priya a pleading look. Priya mouthed, *What now?* Glasses went back to spreading frosting on a tray of cookies. No one else in the kitchen even looked their way.

Time to channel her dad. His courtroom authority. "My email stated the samples were to be given to me at three PM. It is now 3:02. Please remand the cookies to my custody. Immediately!" The final word came out at a terrifying volume, because someone shut off the giant mixer right as Elena shouted it.

She stood her ground, suppressing the instinct to apologize for her abrupt manner. It seemed to earn Glasses' grudging respect. The baker left her cookies and came over to hand Elena and Priya two bags apiece. Dozens of cookies were heavy. The rolled paper handles bit into Elena's palms.

"Five dozen sample-size caramel macchiato cookies, individually wrapped and boxed. Plus one extra for your inspection. Sign here." The baker held a clipboard out. Elena took her time signing it in her best penmanship. She didn't want to lose the advantage she had gained with her unintended outburst by hurrying.

"Thank you," Elena said, then an overhead buzzer rang, signaling something to the bakers, who all marched off to the cooler. Elena and Priya fled.

"That kitchen gives me the creeps," Priya said as soon as the door swung shut. "Kitchens should be warm and homey, not stark and cold."

"You'd think being around cookies all day would make people happy."

They went to Elena's desk to check the samples. Elena's cookie came in a pretty square lavender box emblazoned with the Sparkle logo. The only difference between hers and the ones for the swap was that her box had *VP Approval Sample* stamped in black letters across the logo. She opened the box, Priya peering over her shoulder. Inside sat the cookie wrapped in lavender cellophane. Lovely, but all wrong.

"What's the matter?" Priya asked. "They did a good job with the packaging, right?"

Lawrence's words from the town hall meeting about the love in his cookies came back to her. She'd told him you couldn't taste love, even though she knew it wasn't true. She didn't need to see the other cookies at the swap to know hers would be the only ones that looked corporate. Mass-produced.

"The packaging is exactly the way it's supposed to be." Elena slid a paint-stained fingernail under the cellophane seam. She broke the cookie in half and shared with Priya. They both munched away, Elena nodding her head. Caramel macchiato was their best seller, a strong cookie across all markets, even accounting for regional preferences.

The sample cookie had the correct ratio of caramel buttercream to chocolate coffee cookie. The caramel drizzle was both beautiful and predictable. All sample-size cookies sported three lines of drizzle and no more. Tasty, moist, a perfect cookie.

What did it lack? How could she put it into words?

"I have to infuse these with some love," she said at last.

"That sounds a little weird, Elena. Don't make out with the boxes or anything like that."

"Ew, no. Nothing like that. I want them to be less off-the-rack, more holiday." A spark of excitement flared inside her. At last, a chance—a small chance—to do something creative at work. Normally, by late afternoon she stared bug-eyed at spreadsheets, begging the clock to advance to six.

"I'll let you get to work," Priya said. She smiled as Elena grabbed her tablet and stylus.

After murmuring a goodbye to her friend, Elena got right down to business. In her design software she sketched her idea, a festive, fun, and best of all, personalized addition to the Sparkle samples.

Optimism made her fingers quick, the stylus swooping over the screen in elegant arcs and loops. For the first time in ages, she didn't notice the cold or the harsh overhead lights. Sparkle Cookie's soul-crushing office disappeared, leaving just her art. Instead of sitting in a gray-walled cubicle, she could be standing in a sunlit studio or painting on the banks of the river in Paris. The rest of the world didn't matter or exist when she felt this inspiration.

She couldn't wait to see how her project turned out. Or to see the look on Lawrence Higgins's too-cute face when he realized she'd returned for round three, ready to throw down. He wasn't the only one who could bring the holiday spirit. Not that she expected to see him again. But if she happened to, she intended to walk away with a clear victory.

CHAPTER NINE

Amid red and green Christmas card envelops, the plain white letter-size envelope with his landlord's return address stuck out like a sore thumb. *If I put this straight in the trash, I can pretend this isn't happening.* Lawrence wished he hadn't stopped at the mailbox on his way to Snowcap Inn. Going out of his way to drum up new customers was enough of a stretch for one afternoon. What if he unrolled the truck window and let the envelope blow out on the highway? He pressed the button, lowered the window. Wind whipped in, bringing him to his senses. Ditching the notice had the potential to make his problems worse. He couldn't afford an increase, much less back rent.

Once he parked the truck, he couldn't handle the anticipation any longer. His hands tingled, his fingers clumsy as he tore open the envelope. Blood rushed in his ears as he unfolded the page and saw his worst fears in black and white.

Dear Mr. Higgins,

Please be advised of the following change to your rent. A monthly increase of $480 effective January 1.

The landlord had the gall to end the letter with the phrase *Happy Holidays and New Year.* Just great. He wadded the letter into a ball and threw it on the passenger-side floor, next to a discarded hamburger wrapper he'd been meaning to dispose of for the last week. With any luck, 120 customers who wanted to spend four dollars a month on cookies would attend the cookie swap.

Concerns about the rent relented as he carried his cookies up the cobblestone front drive to the Snowcap Inn. He'd seen the stately building from the road many times, but the three-story white clapboard structure had been mostly hidden by soaring pine trees. Their crisp aroma traveled on the light breeze stirring their branches. The sounds of the road were muffled by the trees, making the songs of a few brave, frost-proof birds audible. How could he panic on this clear, bright day? The sky full of white clouds like spun sugar. This place seemed designed to relax the mind and body, to instill a gentle sense of retreat.

He passed a hand-painted sign staked in front of the steps, informing visitors that a horse-drawn sleigh departed every two hours from the back porch. That sounded cool. He felt as if he'd stepped back in time. Evergreen-colored shutters, fuzzy boughs of pine over the double doors, and a weathered, antique Santa statue with rosy cheeks completed the idyllic entrance.

"Welcome," said a cheery woman around his mom's age sporting a pink Santa hat at a jaunty angle. She wore a gold name tag with *Marilyn* in block letters. "Are you from the snowplow company?"

"Uh. No. I run Sweet L's Bakery in New Hope." He held up the boxes of cookies as proof. "I'm here for the cookie exchange."

Confusion crossed Marilyn's face. He gulped, worried he had the wrong day. Wasting five dozen fresh cookies was not what he needed right now.

"Oh, of course you are, dear. You didn't strike me as the baking type. Silly me." The lady's face turned as pink as her hat. She cleared her throat. "Let me show you to the reception room."

Lawrence tried not to gawk at the fancy upholstered chairs around the wide fireplace or the expensive-looking oil painting above the mantel. They walked down a wallpapered hallway, passing more original art and elegant brass sconces with flame-shaped light-bulbs. He shot a look behind himself to make sure he wasn't track-ing in snow on the plush runner rugs over the polished wood floors.

Should he have dressed up a little? Soft jeans and a gray Henley seemed too casual in comparison to the classy surroundings. His eyes slid to Marilyn, who he noticed wore a sweater covered in rein-deer. Okay, he wasn't crazy out of place. And for some reason women always seemed to like this shirt, though he couldn't figure out what made it special.

He wavered when they got to the ballroom, wishing again he'd at least worn a collared shirt. Through glass-paned French doors, he glimpsed the reception tables with white cloths arranged in a semi-circle around a twelve-foot Christmas tree. A tartan ribbon garland swooped over the branches; light glinted from crystal ornaments. A silver star topper crowned the tree. He followed Marilyn into the room.

"Here's a nice, hot cup of cocoa for you in the souvenir mug, and this will be your table," she said.

Lawrence set down his boxes, and Marylin gave him a green mug wearing a knit sweater. Why? Maybe to keep the drink warm? He raised an eyebrow at it. Was the cup better dressed than he? While Marilyn tutted and fussed around, helping him open boxes, he caught sight of his swap neighbor.

Part of her, at least. The best part, by the looks of it. She was leaning over the table to reach something, her magnificent ass front and center in a flattering purple sweaterdress. His lips parted; his jaw muscles slackened. Long legs in patterned tights. He didn't mean to ogle, but his eyes forgot how to blink. Suddenly, she shot up, a wave of dark hair flipping back, and caught his expression before he could recover.

Elena Voss.

Breathless, he spun to his table. Marilyn had scurried off. The other participants so far were a few tables down, some on the other side of the tree. He and Elena were as good as alone together. He wanted to crawl under his card table, hide behind the starched white tablecloth. Was there any chance she hadn't recognized him? Any chance she didn't realize he had been checking her out, his eyes cartoon-character huge, his pupils heart shaped? Drool running down his chin? He swiped his hand over his face. No, he hadn't actually drooled.

His stomach clenched. Embarrassment worse than the time his pants ripped in middle school clutched him.

"Mr. Higgins, how delightful to see you again," said a cool voice.

He swallowed his discomfort, turned back to her. Elena's poise stood in stark contrast to his flustered shame. All her hair had landed perfectly, draping over her right shoulder in soft, touchable waves. She extended a hand—nails painted the same purple as her snuggly dress. Snuggly, low-cut dress. *Keep your eyes on her face.* Almost numb with humiliation, he barely felt her hand in his. Did she mean to play nice today, or was this some kind of trick?

How sweaty is my hand? Elena had already let go. He snatched up his cocoa to have something to do with his hand as he said hello in a pinched voice. A few drops of cocoa splashed the front of his shirt.

"Careful there. It's hot." Her berry-colored lips quivered. Ripe, asking to be tasted. Merriment twinkled in her eyes, cheerful as the tree lights. When she wasn't threatening to ruin his life, her undeniable beauty shone even brighter.

Which Elena was he getting today? The sensitive one from the town hall, the mean one from the street, or this brand-new one, with a smile that unexpectedly stopped his heart? He'd certainly found her attractive from across the room at town hall and on the darkened street, but seeing her in full light, up close, was a whole new level.

No matter her motives, he'd better be polite, since potential customers were filling up the room as they spoke. Customers she wanted and he desperately needed. He couldn't risk acting like a jerk and making everyone think they'd get the same treatment if they visited Sweet L's.

Say something. Anything. "Your cookies look nice."

She smirked.

That came across weird. Sounded like something a gross guy in a dive bar would use as a pickup line, not a line to show the competition he could be cordial and businesslike too. If only she didn't make him so damn nervous.

His hand went to his collar; he undid another button. A vast gray expanse filled his mind as he searched for a single appropriate, interesting comment. Anything to get off on a better foot than the one they'd started on. If he had to spend all afternoon next to the gorgeous troublemaker, he had to find some composure. She looked stunning in that dress, but he couldn't let her know how stunning. She'd think she was winning. *Keep calm, prove what a competent business owner you are. People are watching.*

"Your cookies are nice too," Elena said. "They have a quaint little homemade look."

He caught himself before he could answer her backhanded compliment with some attitude of his own. He'd give her a little small-town, gentlemanly charm instead. "Thank you. That's exactly what I was aiming for."

Elena's lips dipped into a quick frown. Ha! She didn't know what to do when he didn't take her bait. She began to arrange immaculate purple boxes, a few shades lighter than her dress, on her table. Silver ribbon formed a bow on each box, and each ribbon had a little card with a holiday scene painted in shades of purple threaded through it. Beautiful to behold. He couldn't make another remark about cookies, though.

It seemed they'd be stuck with each other for the next few hours. Could he keep knocking her for a loop? He certainly didn't want to spend all afternoon lobbing insults back and forth, especially since she seemed better at put-downs. What would happen if instead he tried to draw her out, change the subject? Would that shift the energy between them and make for an easier day? But how to manage it?

A quirky option came to him, and he blurted it out before he could second-guess himself. "This place is nice, right? Makes me feel like I'm at the Independence Inn."

Elena paused, hand frozen over a cookie box, then slowly angled her face toward him. "As in Stars Hallow? As in Chef Sookie might come by and set up a cookie swap table?"

A grin broke across his face. She knew the *Gilmore Girls*. "Exactly. Just don't burn the place down, okay? We don't need to recreate that episode."

"Who me? I would never." Did he detect the hint of a smile on those glossy lips? "I work in an office; you work in a kitchen. You're the one who likes playing with fire."

At first, he thought she meant extending the olive branch to someone set on ruining his business. "Hey, I've never set a kitchen on fire in my entire career."

Elena set out a stack of business cards. He should get business cards. No matter how much trouble her professionalism caused him, he had to admit it impressed him.

She crossed her arms and appraised him. By the windows on the south wall, a violinist and cellist began to play "Baby, It's Cold Outside." "I bet you've set lots of fires," Elena said.

This time, her words didn't have an insulting undertone. Rather, her fire-starting comment felt almost suggestive. He gave her a long look to gauge whether she meant to discombobulate him with her remark. He might not be as quick with words, but looking at her was the easiest thing in the world. For half a heartbeat her eyes lowered before darting back to meet his. *That's right, eyes on me, Elena. Mine are on you.* Slowly, a fraction at a time, color rose up her neck to flush her cheeks.

Equal heat spiked in him to match hers, but before he could respond, Marilyn introduced an editor from *Home Baker's Quarterly*. A midthirties woman in a navy skirt suit, the editor thanked Marilyn, then took the microphone. She explained the rules of the swap again, said there were free magazines for everyone. More bakers filtered in, and soon both Lawrence and Elena were too busy exchanging cookies to say a word to each other. The whole time his brain buzzed, eager for another chance to impress her, to make her smile.

CHAPTER TEN

She made Lawrence blush. Blush multiple times like a nervous kid asking out his first crush. Sure, he'd made her blush too with that appraising, inscrutable, enticing blue stare, but he probably hadn't noticed, since the editor had made the announcement at the same time.

On the outside, she busied herself handing out samples and making friends at the swap. On the inside, she pumped her fist in triumph. Last night, she'd called her dad to ask him for some tips on handling adversaries with dignity. She didn't want to be caught crying a second time. Dad had explained the importance of exploiting your opponent's known weaknesses. Elena had intended to continue flexing her marketing skills to intimidate Lawrence if she ran into him at the swap.

She hadn't expected to catch him checking her out. And his priceless, befuddled horror when he recognized her made it even better. Of course, she hadn't worn her sexiest sweaterdress for him—she never dressed for a man—but she couldn't help loving the effect it had on him. She told herself she enjoyed his consternation only because it gave her an edge in their cookie war, not because she cared if Lawrence found her attractive. Though she'd have to be made of ice not to feel a little flattered—a little heated—when he looked at her like that.

A mother and daughter duo quizzed her on Sparkle Cookie baking procedures. Without having to think about it, she rattled off the facts, throwing in a compliment for the iced sugar cookies they'd traded her. Her attention slipped over to Lawrence's table as the women savored their Sparkle samples.

Lawrence appeared to be hitting his stride, shaking hands, joking with people he must know, and even introducing himself to strangers. He didn't have any logos or branding on his boxes, but telling people his bakery was on Main in New Hope near the gazebo resonated. People said they'd be sure to stop by before some ceremony everyone kept mentioning. Many women returned to his table to chat him up—grandmas mentioning pretty granddaughters, moms elbowing their grown daughters to step forward to talk to the handsome baker.

Elena doubted anyone would need a business card to remember Lawrence. She hadn't, after all.

Not that she watched him continually, but she hadn't seen anyone else make his face turn a festive red.

"Be sure to visit the New Hope location when we open on Christmas Eve," Elena told her guests before they stepped away. "We have loads of delicious flavors."

The women looked over their shoulders at Lawrence. "We'll be sure to visit you too, L," said the daughter, a cute blonde in an ivory boatneck sweater. He nodded, his expression neutral, to Elena's delight.

Elena's muscles clenched as she forced a smile. The blonde's aggressive flirting rubbed her the wrong way. This was a professional occasion, after all, not an excuse to seduce a baker.

A lull in the exchange hit. People drifted to the cocoa bar or over to the windows to gaze at the snow-covered pines. The string duet played the opening bars of the "Dance of the Sugar Plum Fairy." Elena swayed to the music.

"You like this one?" Lawrence asked.

"Almost as much as I like the *Gilmore Girls*." She had to push him a bit on the subject, had to know more. Had he been trying to trip her up by being friendly? Or had the comment been as genuine as it seemed? "I must say, you're the first guy I ever met who watches that show."

A part of her wanted to ask if he watched with his girlfriend, but she reminded herself she was here on business, unlike that blonde woman, who kept looking over at Lawrence from across the room like she wanted him to invite her back to his bakery this instant.

"I started out like any other little brother, forced to watch my sister Lonnie's favorite shows after school every day. Joke is on her, though, because that show is funny as hell. You better believe I'd use it to my advantage sometimes. Never let her know how much I liked it. Insisted I got to pick the movie Fridays if she made me watch too many reruns. Or made her get up for the snacks—that was the best perk."

"I don't think my brothers watched a single episode with me." Elena didn't intend to sound like a pitiful sad sack, but Lawrence furrowed his brow. True, she had spent many afternoons alone in her room drawing while her brothers played in the back yard or dominated the TV selections in the family room. Old loneliness crept in. She ran her hand through her hair. "Anyway, you're right. It's a great show."

An awkward silence started to stretch out between them.

"You were right too," he said.

"Huh?"

"About drawing new customers. Not relying on my regulars."

"Did I say that?" She didn't mean it as a challenge, but she saw color creep up his neck once again. Watching his skin react to her had an addictive quality; the more it happened, the more she wanted to be the cause.

"Maybe not those exact words." His voice hitched. "You inspired me to put the bakery out there more."

"Glad I did some good." The way she remembered it, she'd been condescending to cover her own hurt feelings the last time they talked. Did Lawrence hold grudges? Or would he give her a second chance to be . . . to be what? Friends? Friendly?

She'd promised to squash this man like a bug. In her defense, she hadn't expected him to be wearing a clingy Henley, showing off the strong lines of that perfect torso without any regard for her feelings. She certainly hadn't expected him to throw out a *Gilmore Girls* reference. Rather than squash him, she wanted to squish against him. Feel that powerful body press into hers.

Better be careful, or she'd be the flustered one.

She could put out a small feeler. To be nice. "I know they're not your cup of tea, but do you think we should swap cookies? To get a good read on the competition, I mean."

He sidled over to her table. He smelled like the fresh air outside the inn. Blue eyes looked into hers. He offered a half smile. "For research purposes."

Biting her lip, she pushed a lavender box toward him. His fingers grazed hers as he took it. As one, they snatched their hands back, avoiding further eye contact. She watched his hands as he untied the ribbon, inspected the card.

"Is this hand-painted?" Now his attention darted back to her. "This looks like the New Hope gazebo. Did you make this?"

She managed a nod. A dismissive chuckle. "Yeah, sometimes I paint."

"Impressive." Carefully, he set the miniature picture to the side. Then he unwrapped the cookie, took a decisive bite. "Huh. You guys don't use real butter, do you?"

"What? How could you tell that from one bite?'

"I wasn't one hundred percent sure, but thanks for confirming." He winked. If she didn't check herself, he might gain the upper hand despite all her preparation. Her traitor eyelashes tried to flutter back until she suppressed them at the last possible second. "It's the aftertaste. Margarine coats the tongue, overpowers the cocoa."

"Mr. Higgins, that is our best-selling cookie you're talking about," she said, voice full of mock outrage.

"You don't really have to keep up the Mr. Higgins thing. I was kind of a bastard when I said that the other night." Aha! He admitted it.

"You sure about that, Mr. Higgins?"

"Well, when you say it like that, I never want you to stop."

Without warning, an image of him with his lips on her neck slammed into her. Her voice breathy in his ear, saying, *Like that, Mr. Higgins.* The blush tried to come back, heat all over. *Don't let him get the advantage.* She took a steadying breath. "I'll keep that in mind."

Lawrence finished the cookie, held his chin in his hand, tapped his cheek over the shadow of stubble. The exact place she longed to run her fingers across in spite of herself. She did her best not to admire his forearms, the sleeves of his Henley pushed up almost to his elbows. "I've had worse. It's fine. The best thing about your samples is the painting."

She could thank him, be genuine, or keep up the banter. Keep him at a distance. "I'm not much of a cookie girl anyway. Crème brûlée is more my jam."

"Oh! Bougie lady. I've got bad news: I suck at crème brûlée. Always end up overcooking it."

"Seems I'll have to look elsewhere for a good dessert."

That response stumped him. She saw him chew on the inside of his cheek. The pause gave her a moment to consider her behavior. Had the innkeeper Marilyn spiked the hot chocolate? Because Elena was flirting, which was not part of the plan. The opposite of the plan, in fact. It might be okay to turn on the charm to disarm him, but she found herself too thrilled by his responses, electricity zapping and building in her. And not because it put her at a business advantage. Ever since she'd caught him checking her out with those bright eyes, her motives had started to shift. A rockslide, outside her control.

Back off, while you still have the ability.

The magazine editor tapped the microphone, saving Elena from further missteps with Lawrence.

"On behalf of myself and everyone at *Home Baker's Quarterly*, I would like to thank you all for participating in today's holiday cookie swap. I hope you gathered lots of yummy goodies and made some new friends." The editor smoothed the front of her navy jacket. "Thanks to Marylin and the Snowcap Inn for hosting this year's swap. You have a beautiful place here, Marylin."

Marilyn, cocoa carafe in hand, took a modest bow.

"One final bit of business before we go. I'm pleased to announce *Home Baker's Quarterly* will be hosting a cookie competition for the best original recipe that emulates the spirit of Christmas. I know we have bunches of talented bakers here, and one of you could win our grand prize of ten thousand dollars!"

The room burst into claps and excited chatter. Beside Elena, Lawrence let out a low whistle. A ten-thousand-dollar budget increase would make him a more powerful competitor, make it harder for her to reach Derick's opening-day sales goal. *Keep your eye on the ball, Elena. Vosses are bosses.*

In the clamor following the announcement, Elena packed up her table and slipped out of the party without saying goodbye to Lawrence.

CHAPTER ELEVEN

Ten thousand dollars. Enough money to cover his rent increase for months. Enough time to build his business. A lifeline. The day had started out on a horrible note thanks to his landlord's brutal letter. He wouldn't have dared to hope a solution would present itself a few hours later. What's more, he wouldn't have guessed he'd get to spend the day chatting up Elena Voss, or that she would be more fun than he'd originally thought. Knees weak with relief, he scanned the crowd to see where Elena had gotten to.

At some point he'd left his table to get closer to the front of the room while the editor provided more details on the contest. He wound through small clusters of women, everyone shorter than him, but he still couldn't see Elena. A little blonde grabbed his elbow, said she had a question about the bakery.

"One moment, please, I'm looking for my—" *For my what?* His eyes fell on Elena's table. Everything was gone, neatly packed away and carried off. It made sense she wouldn't need to stay. She'd given out all her samples, and as a representative of a national chain, she wouldn't be eligible to compete for the cookie prize.

Why, then, did it feel like a gut punch that she hadn't stopped to say goodbye? Adrenaline swelled, quickening his pulse as he wondered if he should run out to the parking lot, see if she was still around. No. No, he better not. He had to remember she had come for work and her work was done. If she'd enjoyed spending the afternoon with him—her smiles and jokes appeared real—it was over now.

And what the hell was he thinking? He wouldn't need ten thousand dollars if she weren't here doing her utmost to make Sparkle Cookie succeed. What was the end game? Start dating her, only to have to break up when Sparkle ran him into bankruptcy and he had to move into Nana's basement? He couldn't imagine a woman that put together and well-spoken would want to date a guy who couldn't keep his bakery open.

He did his best to give the blonde a polite response to her question. Then he circulated the room, saying quick goodbyes. Marilyn gave him a hug.

Cleaning up his table, he began to feel like he'd been up for a hundred hours. The floor was a magnet, pulling him down. Too much socializing, too much straining to come up with clever remarks to make Elena smile. On the second smile, he'd noticed she had dimples. Despite everything looking up from this morning, he was drained. Good or bad, spending the whole day out among people instead of in the bakery kitchen took its toll.

Half an hour later, he shuffled into the bakery on heavy feet.

"Hey, boss, you look like you've been through it," Carmen said the moment he walked past her. Sugar followed in his wake, her head also low. His whole body shook as a yawn coursed through him. Carmen yawned in automatic response. "Don't start that, Lawrence, or we'll both fall asleep."

"I'm sure I'm not as tired as you," he said.

"Can you believe those kids had me up at four in the morning? It doesn't make sense from an evolutionary standpoint that the young try to kill their caretakers with exhaustion. But don't worry about me. I kept the place running."

Open hours had ended before Lawrence returned. While Carm wiped crumbs off the bakery case shelves, Lawrence took out the broom to sweep under the wrought-iron café tables peppered around the front of the house. "I don't suppose those locusts left us any coffee?"

"You know they didn't. But I made a half pot for us."

"What would I do without you, Carm?" He meant it as a sign of appreciation for her hard work. He also literally wondered if this place would still stand when Carmen retired.

"Don't worry about that for now, mijo. I've got some life left." She filled two Styrofoam cups, stirred in sugar from the old tea tin they used as a canister. "Unlike you. Your nana told me you grilled her about making small talk with strangers and how to appear confident when you feel like . . . how did she say you described it?"

"Like a nervous bowl of jelly on the inside and a perspiring freak on the outside." He dumped the sweepings in the trash, then pulled out the bag and tied it off. He would haul it to the alley dumpster later. Right now, he needed to sit and drink that coffee. Carm brought their cups to the table beside his tree. "Nana said, 'Be yourself.' Turns out, a whole day of being myself is too much."

What would Nana think of his conversation with Elena, his camaraderie with the enemy? Nana always gave people the benefit of the doubt, and she would probably advise him to give Elena a chance. Elena, Elena, Elena. Enough of her for the day. He slapped his hand on the tabletop, surprising them both.

"I'm going to get an early start tomorrow, no matter how tired I am," he informed Carm.

Her brows knit, the line between them deepening. He told her about the rent increase, about the *Home Baker's Quarterly* contest. Sugar yipped when he mentioned the prize money, reacting to the charged air and Carm's sharp intake of breath.

"Incredible, boss! I know you can come up with something great." Carmen stood, snapped her towel at him. "Don't just sit there, get to work."

"Yes, ma'am." She might call him boss, but Lawrence knew he answered to her. If she said it was time to get to work, it was time to get to work. Without waiting for direction from him, Carmen went to the kitchen to put away the latest stock order.

When he got in the kitchen, he felt grounded and his energy began to build back up. He poured eight ounces of white sugar, followed by eight ounces of grainy brown sugar, into the stand mixer bowl. He used a metal bench scraper to soften butter, kneading it back and forth on the bench before adding it to the bowl. Was there anything more beautiful than sugar and butter creaming? Sugar crystals breaking into the butter, lightening it, the mixture fluffing before his eyes.

From the hooks by the mixer, he grabbed a clean spatula, then he scraped down the sides and sent the ingredients for a second spin. Back at his bench, he sifted flour into snowy mountains, measured the leavening. The aroma of ginger bit into the air as he grated it fresh from a knobbled root. This was his happy place; he would do anything to protect it. His stress began to float away and his tight shoulders loosened. The world seemed okay when he focused on his ingredients.

Moments later he had orange peel in pretty spirals simmering in simple syrup. He jotted down a note to source dried cranberries. Could he use this candied orange and ginger cookie recipe for his contest entry? The batch he'd tested earlier had a great kick from the ginger, but would it be too overwhelming for a holiday cookie? He might scale back on the ginger, although that could mean the cookie would be too sweet, overpowered by the sugar and candied peel.

He tapped his pen on the workbench. Carm's cell phone rang, and she stepped out to take the call. Besides salt, what else could he add to cut the sweetness? The acid from the orange peel wasn't doing it.

When Carmen returned to the kitchen, Lawrence could tell she needed to leave early, even if she didn't want to admit it. Carmen darted from shelf to shelf, rotating ingredients as she put them away so the freshest were in the back and those about to expire got used first. Without pause, she moved on to wipe down the stovetop.

Watching her frantic activity, Lawrence felt pity. "Does Dr. Garcia-Peters need an emergency babysitter?"

"I told her I have to work until six." Carm huffed, crossed her arms. "She's the on-call doctor."

He looked at the wall clock above the big flour bins. Dr. Garcia-Peters wouldn't miss helping a patient on his account. "It's almost five. You can skip out."

"I owe you one," Carm said, untying her apron without further argument. On her way out the back door, she said, "Don't forget to scoop the snickerdoodles. I'll bake them off first thing in the morning."

He would have to work twice as fast for the next hour to make up for Carmen's absence. No time for experimenting with his new recipe. He ticked off the never-ending list as he worked. Line up four-ounce snickerdoodle balls, then put them on the rolling cart in the walk-in cooler. Make a fresh bucket of sanitizing solution. Double-check the register. Check to make sure tomorrow's orders were boxed.

In ten minutes, sweat rose on his brow. A crick pinched his neck. He kept working, stopping long enough to blot his face on his apron before charging to the dishwasher to rinse his mixing bowl.

Yes, Lawrence would do anything to save his bakery. Even work two jobs. Even keep things with Elena Voss professional. If he dwelt on the dress, her mouth, how she thawed when he found common ground between them, he'd forget all about what was best for the bakery. He had to stay focused on work.

For the most part, he managed to keep his attention on the recipe, although memories of Elena tossing her hair over her shoulder still popped up when he least expected them. He lost count of how many times he had to shake his head to chase them away.

CHAPTER TWELVE

"And how does one become president of marketing? You've been vice president for, what, two years now? Almost three?" Elena's father asked. Her mother gave her a sympathetic nod. Mom looked lovely tonight in a black silk dress, her long, dark hair twisted in a chignon. Signature red lipstick, diamond drop earrings. Always perfect.

A waiter arrived at the table with a wine bottle, sparing Elena from responding. After inspecting the label and tasting the sample pour, Dad nodded to indicate his approval. The waiter wrapped the bottle in a white napkin, filled the ladies' glasses first, then the gentlemen's. To no one's surprise, Dad had selected a luxurious, formal restaurant.

The atmosphere made it difficult to relax, and Elena longed for the gift of more informal conversation. About twice a year her family made time to sit down to dinner together, and this was what Dad wanted to discuss?

Elena's brothers, Alexander and Oliver, stared her down as if they were interviewing her for the job themselves. No wonder

Alexander's wife came up with excuses to avoid these meals. Oliver's girlfriend, an elegant redhead, looked on the verge of crying from boredom. Elena didn't blame her. So far, they'd heard about Alexander's latest trial win and some spectacular contract Oliver had negotiated for an influential client. At one point, Mom had the decency to ask Oliver's girlfriend, Darcy, about renovations on their house, but then got steamrolled by Dad after a short exchange. Used to following Dad's lead at the Voss family firm, Mom didn't initiate another topic.

Elena nibbled on a stuffed mushroom to buy herself more time.

"I'd like to see you in that position in the first quarter of the new year," Dad said. Her brothers nodded in agreement.

A dinner at a trendy restaurant should have been a great way to pass the evening and put her in a good mood. Instead, irritation pricked at her. She wanted to trade the crystal glassware, gold-rimmed plates, and atmospheric low lights for her bed and a pizza. A night of streaming old Christmas movies. She needed a miracle on 34th Street to rescue her.

Elena took a long sip of the earthy red wine. She wished she could slug down the whole glass to make this conversation annoy her less. The worst part was how she hated the person she became around her family: a spoiled brat who couldn't appreciate all her family gave her. She paused, the wine dry on her tongue. She was truly grateful for their generosity, but she'd gladly trade the cash for a deeper emotional connection.

The conflict within her must be plain, because Darcy shot her a compassionate look. "I guess if my boss Derick got run over by a bakery truck, the position would open up," Elena said.

Darcy giggled; the rest of Elena's family didn't react. Unblinking, mouths shut. Like they believed she might be serious.

"That's statistically unlikely, Elena," Alexander said. "You need a more obtainable option."

"Accidents happen all the time," she said. Hey, if they weren't going to get the joke, she might as well continue having fun. Not that it was much fun to act like a cranky kid to get her family to back off. A healthy adult would say, *I'd like to discuss something else, please*, but her family had a knack for draining the healthy adult right out of her. "In fact, that's how I got the VP spot. The woman who had it before me got flattened. Good for me, too bad for her kids."

"Very amusing, Elena," Dad said. He straightened his charcoal-colored tie, then used silver tongs to place another mushroom on everyone's appetizer plates. Elena folded and unfolded the linen napkin in her lap while she waited for the rest of his verdict. "However, your brother is correct. It doesn't matter who has the job above you, there is always a legitimate way to get it from them."

"I did well today at a cookie swap near our new location in New Hope." The glow from the cookie party, from teasing Lawrence about burning down the inn, felt far away. Lawrence got her jokes, got her references. "The swap represented a crucial step in my sales plan."

"That's wonderful," Mom said. She had the most emotional intelligence of the Vosses. Elena gave her a grateful smile.

"Why would a cookie swap be necessary?" Oliver asked. Darcy elbowed him, a discreet but pointed nudge. "What? It doesn't sound very high-stakes."

Elena deflated further, avoiding their gaze by studying her plate.

"Now, Oliver, it matters to your sister," Dad said. He meant to support her, but he didn't realize he still undermined her work with his phrasing. Important to *her*, not to the world.

"Anyway, I'm thinking of giving it all up to go live in this artists' commune in California I read about in the *New York Times*. I think the original leader got arrested for running a cult. Maybe that role is available."

Now no one knew what to do with her, and the table went quiet for a second time. Even Darcy couldn't guess the right reaction. With a slight shake of her head, Darcy pretended to search for something in her emerald velvet clutch. How did Elena's brothers still have the talent to make her into a sullen child?

Diners at nearby tables talked animatedly about holiday plans and ski vacations. Mellow jazz played softly on the overhead sound system. Meanwhile, at the Voss table, the light scrape of Alexander's steak knife on his plate felt too loud.

Elena's throat went thick. *Stop making this worse,* she chided herself. *Stop using sarcasm as a cover.* Maybe one day she would summon the courage to tell her family she didn't feel like talking about work and ask them to share something else with her instead.

"All right, ladies and gentlemen," Dad said in the stern voice he used to address juries, "Elena doesn't wish to discuss her work. She's made that clear."

More silence. Whatever would they talk about if work was off the table? Had anyone read a good book, or was there no time for that? Oliver shifted in his seat; Alexander shamelessly checked his email. Elena wanted to kick them both under the table like they used to do to each other when they were kids. Had either of her brothers done anything besides work since she'd last seen them at a cousin's wedding five months ago?

"I heard there's a trip to Barbados in the near future for you two," Darcy said, catching Mom's eye. Mom's face softened, and Dad nodded in encouragement. Elena tried to radiate appreciation to Darcy for daring to bring up something new.

"That's right," Oliver said, patting his girlfriend's slender arm. "Four days of fun in the sun for Mom and Dad. Trusting me and Alexander not to burn the firm down for ninety-six whole hours."

Here we go, right back to work. Elena fought not to roll her eyes.

"I'm sure I'll dip my toes in here and there," Dad said, offering the understatement of a lifetime. On every family vacation Elena could remember, Dad had put in a full day's work for a normal person. Reduced hours for a lawyer, to be fair. Mom had tended to work in the evenings after playing on the beach with Elena and her brothers. "And don't worry. We'll hand out Christmas checks tonight. Better early than late, since we'll be gone."

Her brothers gave Dad their biggest smiles. Elena did her best to smile too. Of course, she appreciated the money, which her parents dutifully handed out each Christmas, even if she would've preferred a less valuable but heartfelt gift. Thankfully, her job covered her bills, so after buying new art supplies and putting a little in savings, she usually ended up giving the rest away to a women's art initiative.

"Speaking of beautiful beaches and gifts, that reminds me," Dad said. Elena perked up, sitting straighter in her chair. "Thank you for the painting, Elena. It's superb, and I've hung it in my office."

"I'm happy you like it, Dad." A bit of warmth crept back into Elena. Dad might be aghast at the prospect of painting for a living, but he did admire her art. Nothing confused her about her family more than the fact that they weren't total ogres. They enjoyed her art, even if they couldn't recognize the work she put into her paintings.

"Good job, E. You'll have to make me one." Alexander held up his wineglass and clinked it against hers.

See, they aren't actually the worst. The topic soon circled back to trials, contracts, and briefs. No matter how much more she wanted from them, she tried to acknowledge that they did their best. With the possible exception of Oliver, who couldn't give a compliment if his life depended on it. He didn't know how lucky he was to have cheerful Darcy by his side.

Over aromatic, flavorful shrimp scampi, Elena observed Darcy and Oliver's interactions. Darcy tended to look at him with adoration and laugh at the dull stories he told. For his part, he did worry about her comfort, asking if her steak was done correctly and giving her his jacket without her having to ask when he saw her shiver. Darcy must see more good in him than Elena could. She hoped her brother would treat Darcy well.

Now that the conversational heat was off her, loneliness set in. A longing for someone to sit beside her, to share a knowing glance with her when her family drove her nuts. Watching Oliver and Darcy together triggered it. Mom and Dad held hands between courses, their fingers clasped on the tabletop, a sweet gesture that made Elena's sense of isolation increase. Sure, Alexander was alone tonight too, but not lonely. Her sister-in-law had avoided dinner, but Alexander placed a to-go order for a dessert to bring home to her. Dessert made Elena think of crème brûlée, of Lawrence's surprise when she said she'd have to look elsewhere for it. She thought she might prefer to try his, even if it wasn't perfect.

Perhaps next year there would be someone special beside her at dinner. Not someone with a work conflict—she could picture her father's horror if she brought a business rival. Such a man had to exist, right? A guy with no baggage, who didn't give her any reason to question her choices?

Her family failed to notice she didn't say another word during dinner.

With a quick toss of his credit card, not pausing to look at the charges, Dad paid the bill. Elena joined in the chorus of thank-yous. Then she gave hugs goodbye, the longest one for her mom. Right before leaving the restaurant, Dad passed her a gold envelope to open later in her apartment. Alone.

That's how she spent the remainder of the night. Alone. Half watching *The Grinch* in bed while scrolling Amazon for self-help books. She ended up using some of her Christmas money on a workbook about setting boundaries and a journal. Another merry Christmas indeed.

CHAPTER THIRTEEN

Lawrence reasoned that visiting the Sparkle Cookie storefront site might provide him with inspiration. It would remind him of everything at stake and might give him ideas to outmaneuver them. The odds of Elena happening to be at the unopened storefront at the exact time he stopped by were low. After hours spent mulling over the best course to take with the candied orange ginger cookies, getting out to clear his head was the ticket.

Plus he had to think of Sugar. She didn't want to spend all day in a stuffy bakery. The weather boasted a balmy twenty-six degrees. She'd love the chance to stretch her legs.

"Don't give me that face," he said to Sugar when they got out of his red truck. Sugar cast a cranky look in his direction. Dogs couldn't glare, could they? He must be imagining it. "You've got on the pink sweater Nana made you, and you refused the booties. Don't complain to me if you're chilly. What is all that fur good for anyway? Do you know how much of it I had to shake off my own sweater before we left? You'd have me running around looking like a yeti if you had your way. Don't deny it."

They walked from the parking lot in the newer section of town toward the strip mall that housed Sparkle Cookie. It sat between a dry cleaner and a liquor store. The liquor store window was protected by a metal gate.

"See, I told you they've got nothing on our place." Sugar trotted behind him. When they were closer, Lawrence saw the big *Opening Soon* sign. Another sign said *Try our world-famous flavors*. "Our flavors aren't world famous."

And they weren't minutes from the highway. He imagined hungry road trippers taking the nearby exit and falling for Sparkle's sparkle before they had a chance to get to the historic downtown for a real cookie.

Past the signs, he noticed the interior of the bakery was almost complete. A bakery case and an enormous Sparkle logo in lavender glitter adorned one wall. On the opposite wall, a backdrop made of the faux lavender roses made a picture-perfect spot. Over the roses hung a neon sign—it wasn't lit, but he could still read that it said *#iSparkle*. "That's how they spread like a virus, Sugar. They use these kitschy hashtags, and soon everyone is scrolling past their cookies."

"Sparkle Cookies *are* on everybody's feed," said a familiar voice behind him. "And did you call me sugar?"

Inch by inch, Lawrence turned toward the speaker. Yep. Elena Voss. She wore a purple button-down shirt under a black peacoat. A few buttons undone at the top of the shirt, a silver heart pendant dipping low, so low he didn't dare look. Her face twitched with a suppressed smile, eyebrow raised. Pleasure shot through him when their eyes met. Maybe, if he were honest with himself, he'd admit he felt happy to see her again.

Next to Elena stood another woman, shorter, with black hair to her collarbone and a gold nose ring. She looked at Lawrence like she was afraid of his answer.

"As a matter of fact, Elena," he said, doing his best to sound self-assured, "I was speaking to Sugar Higgins here. Sugar, Elena Voss. Elena, Sugar."

Elena dropped to her knees, held out her hand, and Sugar danced about, sniffing the air. Sugar must not have sensed a threat—silly dog—and she nuzzled into Elena's palm.

"And I'm Priya," the other woman said.

Lawrence quickly stuck out his hand to shake Priya's, abashed he'd been too entranced by Elena to remember his manners.

"This is Lawrence Higgins," Elena said, scratching Sugar's back.

"The baker you keep talking about?" Priya asked.

His ears perked up at that comment. Elena had been talking to her coworker about him? She thought about him outside of work, like he thought about her?

"I don't keep talking about him. I remember mentioning his reservations about the new site at Monday's meeting." She wasn't a smooth liar—he could tell by the way she didn't look up when she spoke, keeping her focus on Sugar. After a few more scratches, she stood. "What do you say, Mr. Higgins, should we take a look inside? Or did you want to continue to wander the streets talking to yourself?"

"I was talking to Sugar. She's a great conversationalist."

"Whatever helps you sleep at night."

I'd never sleep if you were in my bed. The idea came out of nowhere, biology faster than good sense. Elena's hands on him. His body wishing for things his mind wasn't ready to confess it wanted. Funny how his resolve to keep things professional melted like butter in a hot pan the instant he saw Elena.

"You can only come in the customer-facing front," Priya said, all business. "There are proprietary elements in the kitchen."

"Priya's right," Elena said. "Pinkie-swear it."

The first time they touched had been when his hand bumped into hers at the cookie exchange. An accident. This time she held out her hand, pinkie extended in offering. She wore the glove he'd returned to her the night they met. His own hand was in a mitten Nana had knitted, which he ripped off without hesitation.

Hand to hand. Pinkie to pinkie, to be fair. Still, progress. Their fingers twinned around each other, separated by that damn glove. He tightened his finger a smidge to give hers a small squeeze.

"Repeat after me," she instructed. Priya rolled her eyes, then started texting on her phone in its Hello Kitty case to avoid watching them act like idiots. "I, Larry Hopkins."

He tugged gently on her pinkie; she stepped a hair closer. "Not this again."

"I, Lawrence Higgins. Wait, what's your middle name?"

"Benjamin."

"I, Lawrence Bartholomew Higgins—"

"I'm not saying that," he countered. This time she squeezed his finger. In truth, he would say anything she desired, but he had to at least put up a tough front. As if she didn't literally have him wrapped around her little finger. "I, Lawrence Benjamin Higgins, being of sound mind, unlike Elena . . . Hang on. What's your middle name, Ms. Voss?"

"Rachel."

"Unlike Elena Rachel Voss. See what I did there? You thought I was gonna give you a hard time like you gave me, but I'm a nice guy. I used your actual name."

Pure trouble snapped in her dark eyes. An impulse struck him to put his other arm around her, pull her close, kiss that smirk away.

"Can we go inside? It's freezing." Priya stomped her booted foot, and Lawrence couldn't blame her. Elena let go at once, then unlocked the door. Priya eyed Sugar. "I guess we can make an exception on the no-dogs rule, since we're not open."

They all stepped into the strong smell of fresh paint and sawdust. Priya made an excuse to visit the forbidden kitchen, no doubt to avoid any more pinkie swears. Meanwhile, Sugar got to work checking the perimeter, sniffing each and every corner. Now that Lawrence and Elena were alone together, the spark between them dwindled, awkwardness taking its place.

Making a slow circle, he took in the room while Elena rooted through her tote. The walls had a light-purple shimmer to them, he noticed. Gold veins twinkled in the granite countertop. Elena turned on the hashtag sign, which, sure enough, was a neon purple.

"Is it always so dazzling in here?" Lawrence asked to break the silence, blinking as his eyes began to water from all the glowing.

"It is if I have my way," she said. She took out her phone and snapped a picture of the logo on the south wall. Elena Rachel Voss probably got her way all the time. Look how she had him doing the opposite of what he should be doing because he hoped she wanted to talk for a few more minutes. "Priya and I are here to photograph the progress for our social media. Customers love to see behind the scenes."

"About ready to open, I'd say."

"Yes. As planned since the business license application was in order." She stopped taking pictures to catch his eye. "I'm sorry about that. I know I'm the villain here, but I don't have any real control in this situation. I can't stop us from opening in New Hope. Nothing can stop Sparkle."

A week ago he'd believed he could stop them. Now here it was, almost ready for a line of customers out the door. No, he couldn't stop the opening any more than she could. The only course left was to be sure to draw as many customers as he could away from Sparkle to Sweet L's.

"Unless," Elena said, "you were casing the place, planning to throw a brick through the window. That would delay us, at least." Her tone was light, teasing, but her eyes were soft, sympathetic. Gorgeous dark eyes, dramatic lashes like the kind you saw in a cosmetics commercial. "I could always be extra picky about the glass to replace it. Buy you a little time."

Would she do that? Did she feel bad about the unstoppable force of the Sparkle Cookie corporation? The possibility flickered in him.

Not the right moment to confirm it. The last thing he wanted was a repeat of their town hall argument. Too heavy, and the opposite direction he intended to head. "Nah. I've been waiting outside for the last two days, hoping you'd show up. Thank goodness you did, because Sugar and I were turning to ice."

"We can't have that."

She took more pictures, looking over her shoulder at him between each click. That knockout smile of hers had disappeared, and her attention flew to random objects—stacked boxes, a table with chairs propped on top—anytime she caught him looking at her. He remembered her rushing from the swap after two hours of banter. He thought of his own personal promise to choose the bakery over getting to know her.

Did she think they could put the rival bakery situation aside? He mulled over her admission that she didn't have control over the New Hope Sparkle location opening. Did separating Elena from her job mean he didn't have to choose her or the bakery? The possibility he could end up with the best of both worlds tempted him. He could explore his increasing attraction to her. Dangerous to even hope for, but deeply desirable when she smiled at him as she had today.

Then a horrible thought occurred to him: did she have a boyfriend? A woman that pretty must have her pick. The possibility he'd mistaken her joking manner for flirting made him press his lips into a disappointed line.

Hmm. No smooth way to ask that question either. Much as he loved to slip into his shell and avoid social awkwardness, it might be better to be bold and lay his cards on the table. He could always sell the bakery, change his name, and move to Canada if he humiliated himself.

He paused.

Now. If I'm going to take this chance, it has to be now. Before I second-guess myself or blow it more out of proportion than I already have.

"Elena?"

She had her back to him and went still at the sound of her name. She didn't face him immediately; she waited long enough for a knot of fear to form inside him. Then she turned.

Eyes dark, yet bright with expectation. "Yes?"

"I can't make crème brûlée, but I do know a great place that can. If you'll go with me."

CHAPTER FOURTEEN

"I can't believe you subjected me to watching you make goo-goo eyes at the baker," Priya said when they got back in the car.

"Forgive me? Pretty, pretty please?" Elena clasped her hands, fluttered her lashes. In Priya's defense, it must have been awkward to witness that exchange. Elena didn't know what had come over her out there. In the balance between professional and shameless, the scales had tipped. Priya rolled her eyes again as she started the car. Turn signal chiming, Priya went left in the direction of the highway. An air freshener printed with the Sparkle logo swayed on the rearview mirror, waving around its plastic cookie scent.

"What happened to all your *I can't get involved with a rival business owner* stuff, huh? You told me you kept it strictly professional at the cookie swap. I have my doubts about that after what I saw today, young lady." Priya squeezed the wheel, exasperated. "And every time we go out and guys approach us, you can never find a single one worth talking to. Now the only guy you'll take a chance on is the worst possible one for your career."

"I'm sorry I was an insolent flirt, and on company time, no less." Elena gritted her teeth, gave Priya an exaggerated, regretful grimace. Priya sighed, shook her head. "I promise when I write in my self-improvement journal tonight, I'll explore my bad behavior."

Priya snorted. Yesterday on lunch break, Elena had shown Priya her new journal and the daily affirmations she'd written inside. At first the idea had seemed silly, like something that would make Dad roll his eyes. Surprisingly, she'd found the affirmations helped process her complicated feelings about her family and job.

"Okay, it wasn't that serious. I don't care at all about the company time; I want to be sure you're thinking clearly. You made such a big deal about how this guy is trouble and he's a roadblock to achieving your goals. You were lofty, inspiring. Looking out for yourself. Where did that girl go?"

They sped up the on-ramp, joined the crush of cars and semis commuting toward the city. True, Elena had made a convincing case for not getting personal with Lawrence. She'd managed to persuade herself for several days that she didn't want anything more—even though she'd found herself smiling at random moments, thinking about their conversation at the cookie exchange. When he stood there looking like an absolute snack, however, her strength had dissipated like paint in water. "But did you see him?"

Priya's tough facade cracked, a goofy smile taking over. One hand on the wheel, the other crept up to fiddle with her gold earring, a sure tell she wasn't actually upset. "He is super hot, I will give you that. Not my type, but an undeniable smoke show."

"He's not my type either." Maybe some hormone-induced primal instinct had taken over here. If she indulged it, it might go away. "My type is usually skinny, paint-spattered artists with a grudge against the world. Oh, Priya, I thought I could be strong. I believed I *wanted* to be strong. But there's something about him. You know, like when you're not even hungry but then you see a tasty cookie just sitting there. You know you don't need extra sweets in your diet, but there are chunks of chocolate, and macadamia nuts—which do have their health benefits—so you grab it and gobble it up without thinking."

Priya chuckled at Elena's dramatic description before her expression went back to serious.

"This is going to end up like me and Arjun," Priya warned, summoning the name of her most toxic ex. "It was all hot and heavy, but we never saw eye to eye, and then it was all cold and angry. You remember those days."

All too well. Last year, for a month straight, Priya had shown up at work each day looking like she'd spent the night before crying her eyes out. Puffy lids, dark circles. More than once, Elena had needed to discreetly comfort her in the copy room while Priya did her best not to sob.

Arjun was a nice guy apart from Priya, but something about them together made them both insane. They'd fight—sometimes in public, sometimes with Elena there, trying to disappear into a barstool—then a dozen roses would arrive at Sparkle headquarters and Priya would forgive him.

How many times had Elena witnessed them tussle over Priya's career focus? Arguments about Priya's investment in her job, which often involved business trips that separated them week after week. Arjun wanted to put down roots, get married, plan for a family. In those days, Elena itched to give them both a good shake while bellowing, *You don't make sense together; cut each other loose.* She'd sit there, staring into an espresso martini, thinking she had all the answers.

"What if I vow that I'll keep it casual?" Elena asked. Bumper-to-bumper traffic gave Priya the opportunity to look at her square in the eyes. "I've agreed to one date. It might be awful, and we can both move on."

"First of all, please don't bring up promises to me. I do not want to relive the trauma of that pinkie promise I witnessed. I thought you were going to jump on that man and maul him like a mountain lion."

"I am a lady!"

"A lady who admitted she wants to devour him like a dessert until there is not a crumb left."

Elena balled her hands into fists, pressed them against her temples with a groan. "You're right! I'm losing control, I'm about to binge. I can feel it."

"Again, I find myself wanting to say *kids these days*." Priya might be straightforward, which had always thrown Arjun, but Elena knew her friend only wanted the best. "I had to learn the hard way, and now you won't listen to my wise words. I have to let you fly free, little bird."

Elena peeked out from behind her hands. "Will you help me shop for a new outfit? I haven't been on a date in two months, and all my nice clothes are cursed. Bad vibes from bad dates."

"But I want this date to go poorly so you don't completely lose your focus at work."

"We could both go to that new boutique you keep telling me about."

"Ugh, Elena. How dare you use my love of retail therapy against me? Of course I'll go shopping with you. I can't even believe you have to ask."

They high-fived. Visions of a slinky dress in any color but lavender danced before Elena's eyes. She tapped the app for her salon, booked a blowout before all the Saturday afternoon spots got snagged.

"As long as you understand I am not endorsing your actions." Priya waggled her index finger in admonishment.

"Yes, yes. I understand."

They spent the rest of the drive dissecting every word Lawrence had spoken, each gesture he'd made, for clues about his intentions. Was he looking for a casual fling like Elena insisted she wanted?

Did he hope for something more, a relationship? Excitement bounced inside her, pressing down any remaining reservations that tried to nag at her. It was one date. Getting to know him couldn't hurt, right? It wasn't like she would slip up and give him corporate secrets over dinner.

Soaring on the high of her flirtation, Elena didn't even feel the usual dread set in when they returned to the office. She waved at the receptionist, who looked startled to be acknowledged.

"Shopping tomorrow after work?" Priya asked while they waited for the elevator.

Elena was about to answer when the elevator dinged and the door slid open, revealing their coworker Alan clutching a cardboard box. A box filled with the items from his desk. A plant, a framed picture of his wife and new baby. To Elena's horror, Alan had tears in his eyes.

"What's wrong?" both women asked as one.

Alan stepped out of the elevator. His eyes darted around, and he held so tightly to the box that his knuckles had gone white. Panic balled up in Elena's chest as she waited for him to answer. Alan had a family; his wife was on maternity leave from a part-time job. "The Michigan stores posted a two percent loss," he said after a steadying breath. "Derick let me go. Didn't even give me a chance to see how this month's initiatives would turn out. I know numbers were about to improve, but he didn't want to hear it."

"Over two percent?" Priya whispered. "That's insane."

"How could he?" Elena said, scanning around to ensure no one was eavesdropping. Even the walls had ears here, and any information had a way of making it to the C-suites.

"Because he's a heartless animal." Alan's tears dissipated, fury taking their place, anger denting the space between his brows and twisting his lips. "I don't know what I'm supposed to tell my wife. She's already stressed from no sleep. I hate him, I hate him."

Alan spun on his heel, headed toward the exit.

"Wait," Elena called after him. "Hold on a second; we'll help you figure something out."

"No offense, but I can't get out of this nightmare fast enough," Alan said. "I wish you both luck. You'll need it with that sociopath."

Without further comment, he retreated down the hallway and out of view. Priya put her hand on Elena's arm, told her they would check in on Alan later when he'd had a chance to process. Priya pulled Elena onto the elevator. "Act natural, Elena. And don't utter a single syllable about the date in this building."

Elena's ears buzzed; her heart thundered. The margin of error at Sparkle Cookie corporate had never been thinner. Razor thin. Priya's hand felt clammy against her skin, and she knew her friend felt equally afraid. By the time they reached the second level, Elena had forced her features into a calm mask even as her emotions rioted inside. Who knew who Derick would set his sights on next?

CHAPTER FIFTEEN

Elena wouldn't stand him up or change her mind, would she? This distressing thought popped into Lawrence's head without preamble, intrusive, elbowing its way in. His lips dropped into a frown, regret suffusing him. Regret for giving her several days between accepting his offer and making good on it. A delay gave her more opportunities to mull over the compelling reasons they didn't make sense. The professional rivalry. The fact that she was out-of-his-league pretty.

No matter what other people said about his appearance, he knew he was the reacher in this situation. Beautiful and an accomplished woman to boot. Those paintings she made looked as good as anything he'd seen in a museum, and she had a job with a killer title—VP of marketing at a major corporation. Fancy business cards and all. Not that he'd looked at the one she'd included in the sample she gave him multiple times a day. He figured she was in her midtwenties, a few years younger than him. Sure, he owned his own business, but he didn't exactly run the tightest ship.

He disliked working for other chefs because they expected him to do things on their schedules. Elena struck him as someone with a packed schedule that she stuck to. Probably got more done in a day than he could ever dream of. She'd be producing dazzling works of art while he played Xbox in his flannel pj bottoms, hair mussed, Sugar chewing a bone beside him.

"Lawrence?" Nana adjusted her big glasses and looked him over. "Pumpkin, you haven't touched your cookie, and you've spoken all of two words since you got here. Are you okay?"

"Yeah," he managed. He shifted in Nana's fussy mauve armchair—the one all the cousins fought not to get on holidays—and took a cookie off a floral china saucer. He bit into the cookie, registering its tart yet creamy taste from a distance, his cluttered thoughts keeping him from enjoying it.

"Is lemon cheesecake too outrageous for a cookie?" Nana asked.

"Everything you make is good, Nana." His thoughts drifted back to his last relationship and how much his laid-back attitude had infuriated her. His ex-girlfriend was a garde-manger chef at an elegant hotel restaurant. She'd had a schedule and stuck to it. No puppies hiding in her kitchen or extra time off for coworkers. Would career-driven Elena get similarly annoyed with him? Why wouldn't his mind give him a break from these awful thoughts?

"Listen up, kid, I'm planning to take these to the Junior Women's League luncheon tomorrow; you have to be honest with me."

Nana's direct tone shook him out of his fog. He took another bite, rolled it around his tongue. "Cut back on the lemon."

"I knew it." Nana snapped her fingers, scratched out a line on the recipe card lying on the mahogany tilt-top tea table. "No zest. A touch of juice will be enough."

Nana's recliner whirred as the motor inside raised the footrest, leaned the chair back. With an *oof* and a quiet complaint about old bones, Nana settled into the worn fabric, an eye-popping paisley velour. He chewed the inside of his cheek while Nana took her embroidery hoop off her lap and started embroidering a flower onto a tea towel.

He decided he would do his best to impress Elena with his date-planning skills, start off on the right foot. No trying to play it cool or casual. But maybe it was too late to start off on the right foot, considering he'd made her cry within minutes of meeting her. Okay, *get* on the right foot, make sure she forgot all about their unlucky beginning. Make sure he got the fun, flirty Elena, not the serious, business-focused Elena.

He planned to take her to Francesco's for dinner and dessert, but that was pretty standard as far as first dates went. True to his word, Francesco's did have amazing crème brûlée on the menu, and the candles in empty bottles of Chianti were romantic. Would it be exciting enough? Why couldn't he come up with something more original? A creative woman like Elena would have high expectations; he needed to rise to her level.

"If you don't exhale soon, pumpkin, you're going to pass out, and I can't lift a big guy like you off the floor without upsetting my knees." Nana didn't look up. She sewed away, then said in a casual voice, "Are we going to talk about what's bothering you, Lawrence?"

How to put his myriad fears into words? "Am I a hot mess, Nana?"

Nana paused midstitch. "A what, dear?"

"A hot mess. Like, do I seem like I don't have my sh . . ." He caught himself in time, remembered he was talking to Nana, not Trey. "Does it seem like I don't have my life together?"

"You own a marvelous bakery, and you run it almost single-handedly."

"But you had to give me the investment money, and I haven't been able to pay you back. It's been two years."

"I don't think that's unusual. Businesses take time to be profitable. Besides, I told you, that money was a gift."

"I know, Nana." No matter what Nana said, he intended to give her the money back. Not because she needed it but to show her he'd made good. To show himself he could do it on his own.

"Let's not forget, I had to give Charlie a gift too, and we all know that divorce was his own fault." Nana loved all of her grand-kids, but she also loved dropping nuggets of gossip about them to other family members. First, he'd heard that his cousin Charlie was to blame for the end of the marriage. Juicy. Nana had a trove of secrets, he was sure. He wondered if she had any dirt on Lonnie he could use to torment his sister. He did owe Lonnie one, though, since she'd introduced him to *Gilmore Girls*. "Do you need more money? Let me get my checkbook."

"What? No. Absolutely not." He didn't need money. True, some months he couldn't afford to pay himself, and the rent increase loomed like a knife-wielding, deranged boogeyman. Still, he'd sell a kidney before he took more of Nana's money. She was comfortable living off her teacher's pension, but expenses added up. "When I got here, I noticed those boards in your front steps are getting pretty rotten, Nana. You need to replace them. Use your money for repairs."

Nana's house, right near the heart of town, was a beauty, but it was an old beauty, built in 1923. All the charming elements, like wainscoting, solid wood doors, and a spacious porch, outweighed the fact that the house needed near constant renovations to meet modern code standards. Lawrence wished he had the time to repair the steps himself. He made a mental note to tell his dad to come take a look at them ASAP.

"Never mind about that. I know which spots to avoid. Anyway, I think a few hundred dollars to support my favorite local business would be all right." Nana pressed the button, and the recliner began to return to its upright position.

"Don't you dare, Nana. I will rip up that check."

"You wouldn't. My checks have kittens printed on them. Inno-cent kittens."

"I didn't say it would be easy, but you'd give me no choice."

"Oh, you're no fun. I'm going to waste it all on bingo, then."

That got a laugh out of him. Sugar wagged her tail from her spot by the fire that he'd built in Nana's fireplace, figuring they must be happy about something significant. "I worry I don't have much to offer," he admitted.

"Who are you worrying about offering to, young man?" Nana said, peering over the top of her glasses. Shrewd, Nana, very shrewd. He hadn't intended to hint at feeling inadequate socially, just professionally.

"No one. I . . . I don't know. Someday in the future, I might want to impress someone."

"If you attempt to impress this nonexistent person anywhere within the borders of New Hope, I will hear about it before you try to kiss her good night, so fess up!" Nana pointed the needle with a long trail of red thread in his direction.

"I cannot believe you think I would give up a kiss on the first date." He held his fingers to his throat in a mock pearl-clutching gesture. "I have my standards."

"Back in my day we didn't consider it a successful date if there was no smooching."

"Nana Banana, you shock me."

"Please. With that attitude, you'll be lucky to get a second date." Nana tossed a bobbin of thread at him; he ducked, laughing again. Sugar's tail beat against the stone hearth. "In all seriousness, you have seemed anxious about making a good impression lately. All those questions you had about conversational skills before the cookie swap. Was that because of her?"

"I didn't know Elena Voss would be at the swap. That was because I spend too much time in my comfort zone here in New Hope."

"So, her name is Elena Voss? I will use my Google skills to look her up. Is she pretty? What am I saying? Of course she is. Why would my handsome grandson have a date with some ugly stepsister?"

"Nana, I taught you those Google skills, and now you're going to use them against me?"

"What I do with the knowledge you impart is my own business." Nana separated a few stands of gold thread from the floss and threaded the needle.

When she finished, he said, "If you Google her, you'll probably find out she works for Sparkle Cookie."

"That dreadful chain that wants to steal your customers? Oh dear, Lawrence. How star-crossed." Nana clucked.

"Do you think she only agreed to the date because she wants to weaken me so she can ruin Sweet L's from the inside?" A new fear he hadn't come up with before. His stomach twisted; his breath caught again. What if Elena didn't see their upcoming date as anything but an opportunity to get a leg up on the competition?

"Do you really think that's her intention?"

He ran his fingers over his jaw. Was that what he thought? Deep inside, in the place far away from all his eccentric worries, he trusted her. At least enough to risk getting to know her better. "I'm not sure, Nana. I think she's legit. Legitimate, I mean."

"Then trust that instinct, sweetie. Take her at face value unless she gives you a reason not to. I think any young lady would be excited to spend an evening with you, for you. You have a lot to offer."

"Do I?" He didn't mean to be self-pitying, but he did wonder what would attract Elena to him. Was she like all the people who only saw him as a buff ideal, not a human? Maybe he should be content his height and muscles had piqued her interest and not expect anything deeper.

"I don't know too many other grandsons in their twenties who make time to visit their grandmas." Nana gave him her best, sweetest smile, which warmed him through. Made him feel more confident, more sure of himself.

"That's easy, Nana. I love you."

"I love you too, pumpkin." Nana set down the embroidery hoop, beckoned Sugar over for a pat.

"And I love spending time with you. You're awesome."

"Now that is one hundred percent true. Some grandmas complain about bunions and medications. I like more interesting topics. Did you know Gladys Martin got pulled over on Spring Street for going fifty-five in a twenty-five?"

Lawrence rubbed his palms together, eager to hear all the local dirt straight from Nana, the best of all sources. If Nana said Elena was interested in him for himself, it must be true. He must be worth it. He couldn't allow his social anxiety to get the best of him.

Nana gave him a break from ruminating as she spilled about Gladys Martin's wayward behavior ever since the octogenarian had purchased an all-wheel-drive SUV. After, Lawrence went to the kitchen to make them tea. While he waited for the kettle to boil, he looked out the window with its white lace curtains, mulled over Nana's points. He also considered his own tendency to let his shyness come across as aloof, uninterested. A great way to protect himself from disappointment, to put the ball in the other person's court.

His gut told him he should be willing to take a small risk for Elena, to show her outright how much she intrigued him. Before he could talk himself out of it, he sent her a text. Not to give her the details of the date—he'd already done that—but simply to say Looking forward to seeing you.

CHAPTER SIXTEEN

After Alan's firing, the atmosphere at Sparkle Cookie headquarters went from frosty to downright glacial. Derick expected daily sales reports from his team to ensure marketing strategies were effective. Every night Elena painted to relieve stress, and every morning she arrived at work more tired and burnt out than the day before. Derick shifted half of Alan's work to Elena and the other half to Priya with no mention of a pay increase.

"Any luck?" Priya asked in a low voice, stopping by Elena's desk.

"It's tight out there. Nothing yet. How about you?" Neither woman would say aloud why they needed luck while inside the Sparkle Cookie building. Both had confessed their intentions to find a new job last night via text.

"Nothing within a hundred-mile radius and nothing in a city I can afford, even if I relocate."

"He's on his way up, look busy," Sarah, Derick's assistant, yelped, running past the cubicle, a streak of lavender. Poor Sarah had taken to watching for Derick's car to arrive each morning to give everyone a chance to hide. Priya sprinted back to her desk, nearly spilling her coffee in her haste, and Elena opened yet another spreadsheet. Percentages and pie charts swam before her eyes.

She swore a chill wind blew from the elevator as Derick got off. Unwilling to risk getting caught slacking, she ignored the vibration from her phone alerting her to a text message. At the last possible moment, she noticed flecks of paint on her sweater and began picking them off in earnest. Bits of yellow ochre crumbled to the floor.

"Daily reports in my in-box in ten minutes or less," Derick told the whole room, not bothering with a hello. Sarah followed behind him, caught his overcoat as he tossed it back.

A sour taste rose in Elena's mouth; she washed it away with a sip of coffee. Despite getting up early to get ready, she must've looked extra pitiful this morning, because Mel the barista had broken the law to give her ten espresso shots.

At the moment, the numbers in Elena's region looked acceptable. Not fantastic, but nothing bad enough to draw Derick's wrath either. Crossing her fingers Derick wouldn't scream at her from his office, she sent the report. The original description for her job classified her role as being responsible for crafting campaigns and social media posts. At best, that work—the inventive work she didn't loathe—represented a small fraction of her day. She spent most of her time trapped in spreadsheet hell.

How had she gotten so far from her original goals? Years ago, when she summoned all her courage to tell her dad she wouldn't be going to law school or seeking a position at the family firm, she'd thought she had escaped the worst of the grind. It turned out she'd jumped out of the frying pan and into the scorching fire. This job was meant to be the perfect compromise between her and Dad. What a joke.

Maybe I'd be better off at Voss, Voss & Voss, she thought. Dad could give her a job as a legal secretary for one of her brothers to make ends meet while she got more education. A paralegal certification loomed in her future, a specter of failed ambitions. Creativity in her workday would go from five percent to zero. On the plus side, at least her parents didn't treat her or their staff like dirt. Elena's throat tightened; the computer screen blurred as her eyes filled with tears. *Never let them see you cry. Vosses are bosses.*

A strident ring from her office phone made her jump. She grabbed a tissue, wiped her eyes. Derick's line. *Get it together.* "Good morning, Derick. How can I help you?"

"Come to my office." He hung up without explanation.

The same terror that had overwhelmed her when Alan told them he'd been fired hit her. Muscles quivering, she made her way to Derick's office. He sat like a cruel king at his desk, a thousand-dollar leather chair his throne.

She pushed her hands against her stomach, against the tight knot forming there.

"Voss, you're the only one I can count on to produce these days." Relief came on so strongly she almost gasped. Dad's training kicked in, and she steadied herself before Derick could realize how frightened she'd been a breath ago. On the wall behind his desk, she saw a Phillies pennant among framed district performance awards. *Human, he's only human. Picture him eating peanuts and watching baseball.*

"Yes, I have shown you consistent gains. As you can see, the survey results from my trip are favorable." *Don't let them see you afraid.* Dad had drilled it into Elena that women tended to upspeak at the end of their sentences, lowering their perceived credibility. She would not let her voice waver. "And I've met the goals from my annual review, with weeks to spare."

Always press an advantage, always highlight your contributions.

"As you should. I didn't call you in here to discuss your regular duties, though." Derick steepled his fingers, leveled his gaze at her. He didn't offer her a seat, and she wouldn't take one. She straightened her spine, willed her hands not to fidget. "Social media regarding the Sparkle Cookie New Hope location has improved, just as I instructed you it must. Several people left comments about the wonderful samples given out by a friendly young lady. Apparently, they even came with customized miniature painting of New Hope scenes."

Uh-oh. Had she violated some company policy by not getting all merchandising approved by Derick? She swallowed, folded her hands so they wouldn't tremble.

"Clever. Very clever, Elena. Beat them at their own game. Fight small-town mentalities with a taste of their own homemade medicine." A smile spread on Derick's face, highlighting his vampire-sharp canine teeth. She blinked, questioned her hearing. Had Derick stooped to admitting she had done something right? That one of her ideas worked? "I'm only going to offer this to you. Don't mention it to your coworkers. If you get those grand-opening numbers I want, I will authorize a fifty-five-hundred-dollar bonus."

Stunned, Elena took a step back. A bonus like that could help cover expenses while she looked for new work, even help her afford to move if she had to. Her endless hard work was paying off right when she had all but given up. But Dad would remind her not to gush to Derick, to act like a bonus was the least she deserved. "I'll look forward to that."

Derick raised his brows, his surprise at Elena's cool reserve obvious.

Ever her father's daughter, she added, "Give me the terms in writing, please."

"As you wish. Get back to work, Voss." Elena turned to leave. "And Voss, the next time you visit that dump, I want a full accounting of the strides you've made breaking into that market for us."

A shiver she couldn't hide shook through her. The next time she planned to be in New Hope was for her date with Lawrence tomorrow night. Derick couldn't elbow his way into that, couldn't drain the excitement from her. He could never know.

Because she would not sit across from Lawrence at dinner while secretly trying to ingratiate herself with his customers. No, no matter how personally advantageous, she could not do it. Something deep inside her recoiled from the mere suggestion, an animal retreating from a predator.

"Tell Patel I want to see her now. Her daily report is disappointing."

Elena assured Derick she'd send Priya in and went to warn her friend. Priya's soulful eyes filled with tears at the news of Derick's summons, and she trudged away to face the music.

Back in her cubicle, Elena put her head in her hands. Gave herself a minute to calm the emotions competing inside her. She could manage this; she could survive at work and explore her connection to Lawrence. Right? Down the hall she heard Derick roaring at Priya, not caring if he embarrassed his loyal employee over a small mistake. Had Priya even made a mistake? Sales fluctuated due to a multitude of factors. None of that mattered to Derick. This culture of shame, the fear of her dad finding out she'd failed at work, dominated Elena, made it impossible not to do her best.

Her phone screen lit up with a new notification. A text from Lawrence! She seized it and read his message. Looking forward to seeing you. She held the phone to her chest, joy leaping in her heart, chasing away the darker feelings. A text like that from a different guy might be nothing more than sweet talk, but from Lawrence, she knew it was genuine.

Same here, she typed in response.

If she was careful, she could protect this part of her life from Derick. She could have it all.

CHAPTER SEVENTEEN

Elena arrived in a heart-stealing red dress. Her glorious dark hair in loose curls, her lips glossy, inviting. "Wow. You are incredible," he said. They shared an awkward hug—too much space between them. She smelled like citrus, bright and clean. Her left cheek grazed his as they parted, skin soft against his for that brief touch. "And hello, by the way."

"You don't look so bad yourself," she said in her light, teasing way.

He didn't tell her his outfit—a slim button-down and flat-front pants—was entirely his sister's doing. Lonnie had made him hold up every item in his meagre wardrobe during a frantic FaceTime call. Before his sister's help, he'd gazed at his clothes in wide-eyed horror, unsure if he owned anything suitable. Lonnie had knocked it out of the park, because even he could see the sky-blue shirt highlighted his eyes. "Thank you. I rolled out of bed like this."

She rewarded him with one of her pretty, bemused smiles.

Lawrence held open the door to Francesco's, and they walked together into the cozy space. Succulent aromas from the classic

Italian kitchen greeted them. Simmering red sauces, fresh-baked bread, roasting meat. Besides an exceptional menu, Francesco's boasted romantic dark-wood paneling, numerous tables for two, and cream roses at every table. Next to him, Elena drew in a quick breath as a hostess in a black dress led them to the best table in the house. Had he chosen a good spot?

As soon as Elena agreed to the date, he had called in a favor from Francesco himself. A few months ago, a supply chain issue had left Francesco without flour to bread his cutlets, a specialty of the house. Francesco's twins had gone to school with Lawrence, so when he asked Lawrence for some flour to cover the shortfall, Lawrence agreed without conditions. The good karma came back when Lawrence called for help with the date. Francesco had promised him the L-shaped booth for two right by the stone fireplace.

Every single guy in New Hope knew that little booth almost guaranteed a cuddle at the end of the date, if everything went well. Francesco had gone the extra mile and adorned the table with half a dozen of his signature roses. *I can't be too out of practice if I pulled this off*, Lawrence assured himself.

"Do you like wine?" he asked Elena, peering at the list when they sat. Stupid question. "I mean, I'm sure you do."

An elegant woman like Elena probably knew all the best vintages. He wasn't a total fool when it came to wine because of his culinary education. He'd focused on pastries, but he had still completed coursework in cooking, menu building, and wine pairing.

"Do I look like a drinker?" Elena asked, raising a brow. He felt his face blanch, blood rushing away to his galloping heart. "I'm sorry, Lawrence, I shouldn't tease you. I do like wine, very much, thank you. Especially Pinot Noir. Is that okay for you?"

"Anything you want." His voice came out in a croak.

Elena reached past the flowers and candles, laid her hand over his. "I forget how sarcastic I can be. Do I make you nervous?"

He let out a breath he definitely knew he was holding, his chest burning. His eyes lingered on their joined hands. *Our first real touch.*

"That obvious, huh? Believe it or not, this is me doing my utmost to be relaxed." Her fingertips grazed over the back of his hand. If she meant it to be comforting, it was having the opposite effect, making him hyperaware of their bodies. Of the feel of her. "I wanted to come across aloof, like I do this all the time, but the truth is, you intimidate me a little."

"Really? I didn't think six-foot-five guys got intimidated by anyone."

"They probably don't. I'm only six three. So, there's the problem." He turned his hand over to make them palm to palm. He wanted to lean over and kiss her hand, but it seemed too sudden, or strange. Instead, he curled his fingers over hers. His hand enclosed hers entirely.

"I'm nobody to be worried about. I get nervous too," Elena said.

"That's hard to imagine. You project a lot of confidence."

"That's my dad talking."

He'd assumed the self-assurance was inborn. "Oh yeah? How so?"

"My dad is an amazing man, accomplished, brilliant, unable to understand anyone who isn't. Dad made a point to push me out of my comfort zone until I learned to be outspoken. I had no choice but to mimic what I saw modeled. Hard to tell if I really feel as confident as I act." Her little laugh when she stopped speaking suggested she wasn't bothered by her dad's personality; the way she looked away, out into the dining room, suggested otherwise.

The server, a skinny young guy Lawrence didn't recognize, interrupted this glimpse into Elena's life to take their order. Lawrence ordered a bottle of California Pinot Noir, and Elena suggested they share the caprese appetizer.

While they waited for their drinks, Elena told him more about her dad—a high-powered lawyer who expected his children to be equally poised. If the topic bothered her, she did an excellent job concealing it, this time keeping eye contact. "My brothers are both lawyers. They're naturals. It never came easy to me."

"You didn't want to be a lawyer, then?" Elena's willingness to share put him at ease, made him eager to hold up his end of the conversation.

"No way. I'm not the type to fight with people for a living. Not that marketing is my dream job either, but here I am."

Hold up, Elena didn't want to work for Sparkle Cookie? He wouldn't have dared to hope. He stopped his thoughts from racing away with the prospect of her ditching that job, making his life easier on every front. He didn't believe Sparkle would be half as successful without her. "What did you want to do?"

Their waiter set the caprese between them. They let go of each other's hands to make room for the oval platter of ripe tomatoes, mozzarella, and balsamic vinegar drizzle. Elena took a helping, and he tried not to get inky balsamic on the tablecloth as he transferred a tomato to his appetizer plate.

"I wanted to be an artist, but it's hard to make a living from painting. A lucky few manage, I guess. I even got accepted to a great art school on the strength of my portfolio. Except my dad wouldn't hear of it. Too worried I'd end up starving in some garret. No matter how I begged, he refused. Flat would not pay for it.

"He told me he loved my art but loved me having a stable future more. My high school friends told me to strike out on my own. By then my confidence was too shaken to risk taking out a massive student loan. We compromised on a degree in marketing with a minor in graphic design."

Didn't sound like much of a compromise to him. Lawrence searched for a thoughtful response, pressing away immediate comebacks like *your dad sucks.* "I saw some of your work. It's stunning.

We hung up your tiny painting of the gazebo on our bulletin board in Sweet L's. Customers keep asking about it."

Elena finished chewing her tomato. "Mmm, that is good. The perfect balance of the tomato's acidity and creaminess from the cheese."

He appreciated anyone who enjoyed fine food.

"Absolutely," Lawrence said, wondering why she didn't respond to his compliment about her painting.

"Am I right? I have no idea what I'm talking about. I looked up ten conversation starters to have with a chef. See, there's a hint for you from my dad: you can find self-confidence online. Just avoid the dating apps if you don't want to get dragged right back down. That's a tip from me."

"I hope to avoid them," he said, to gauge her reaction. If she smiled, it meant she didn't want him looking for other women to date.

"Solid plan," she said, her face unreadable.

The waiter returned to take the dinner orders, bouncing from foot to foot like he didn't have time to waste. The restaurant was full, since it was Saturday, but Francesco's had a slow pace. At least Lawrence didn't feel as on edge as the waiter. He pulled his shoulders from around his ears to make his body language match his calmer mood.

"Fettucine alfredo for me," Elena said. "I can't resist it."

"Wait till you see how they do it here," Lawrence told her once the waiter left.

"How?"

He didn't answer, to wind her up.

"How do they do it?"

"No way. I'm not spoiling the surprise."

"Ooo! I love surprises. Good ones, at least. I assume this one is good. They won't dump the noodles on my lap or anything like that, right?"

"I said I can't give anything away."

"This is a new dress, Lawrence Higgins. I warn you . . ."

She'd bought a dress for their date? Hell yeah. Biggest sign of interest she'd given so far. No woman would waste money on a dress for a first date if she didn't think the guy worthwhile. "I promise nothing will happen to your gorgeous dress."

"If that white sauce comes near me, I swear I'm tearing this dress off and eating dinner in my underwear, just watch me."

"Hey now! If that's your plan, I'll dump the fettucine on you myself." He might not be as quick with the verbal sparring as Elena, but that one was easy.

"You're lucky we're in such a nice place, or I'd fling this tomato right at you." She giggled, a high, happy sound. Lawrence had never been threatened with a food fight on a first date. He liked the way her mind worked. One minute telling him her history in a polished manner like a news anchor, the next making some absurd comment. "Then you'll have to take off your shirt. Give me an eyeful of whatever under there had all the ladies scoping you out at the cookie swap."

The waiter pulled up a silver cart beside their table, putting an end to their very promising discussion about stripping. Elena's dark eyes watched with rapt attention as the waiter scooped noodles from a bowl and into a large Parmesan wheel. Most of the Parmesan had been used for other recipes, leaving behind a pale-yellow bowl made of cheese held together with the black rind. Using a pair of tongs, the waiter swirled the steaming-hot sauced noodles around in the remaining cheese. Elena clapped when he pulled the noodles out, trails of now-melted cheese dripping. Absolute decadence.

"There you go, Elena, the freshest fettucine alfredo in all of New Hope," he said, the bliss in her expression infectious, making him smile. The waiter placed the shallow bowl in front of her. Without pause, she started wrapping a noodle around her fork with the help of a large spoon.

"It's the most beautiful thing in the whole world," she said reverently.

No, that's you. It was more than the sensual red dress hugging her in all the places he wanted to touch. More than the long hair he wanted to tangle his fingers in, his hand at the back of her head, holding her close for a kiss. It was also her willingness to share about her family, her enthusiasm for painting. The cute way she admitted to researching culinary conversation starters. The way his palm still felt more alive in the place where she'd touched it, irrespective of the fact that she'd long since removed her hand.

All he could do now was hope the rest of the date impressed her as much as the fettucine.

CHAPTER EIGHTEEN

The moment she had been waiting for arrived. Their jumpy waiter delivered a pristine crème brûlée in a scalloped dish. Caramelized sugar formed a glassy surface, and three of the most perfect raspberries along with bright-green mint leaves made a colorful garnish. Lawrence watched her hover her spoon over the dessert, taking it all in before she disrupted its beauty.

"Don't you want to crack it? That's the best part." Lawrence seemed more at ease than he had at the date's outset. Considering their other encounters, she suspected he had some degree of social anxiety. At the town hall meeting, he'd stumbled over his words, only hitting his stride as the argument got more heated. His intimating size made it easy to miss the vulnerability behind his bungling attempts at conversation. "The hallmark of a great crème brûlée—besides not curdling it, which most people, not me, can manage—is a strong crack when you break the sugar top. You need the right amount of sugar and then torch it until it's smooth as ice on a pond. The torching part is the only element I don't mess up."

"See, I knew you had pyromaniac tendencies." Elena never had an issue making chitchat, even if she often worried later she'd said too many ridiculous things, tried too hard to be funny. Her minor eccentricities shouldn't come as a surprise to Lawrence after they'd spent several hours together at the cookie swap.

"All chefs do, although bakers are the sanest," Lawrence said after a beat.

Lawrence held up his end of the back-and-forth, but she decided to take it easier on him. The temptation to keep him at arm's length with sarcasm was outweighed by her desire to be authentic. Since he'd made such an effort to plan a great date, she figured the least she could do was offer a real response.

"I'm actually waiting because I want to take a picture so I can paint it later." She looked down at the flawless dessert, a tendril of shyness gripping her now. "But I hate when people are on their phones at the table. So rude."

"I'll make you a deal," Lawrence said, "I won't deduct any points if you promise to show me the painting when it's done."

Elena never minded telling people she loved to paint. Showing them her work, on the other hand, made her timid. She did a better job of hiding her insecurities than Lawrence. She gave him a smile and coy nod before the phone's flash illuminated the table. Once she had the picture, she tapped her spoon in the center of the cara-melized sugar, broke it into shards.

"Music to my ears," Lawrence said.

The silken texture of the vanilla custard base and the complex, nutty flavor of the sugar melted into her tongue. "Mmm. Amazing. You weren't lying about this being the place to get a good crème brûlée."

"Glad I didn't disappoint." Pride made his handsome features all the more striking. She caught herself gazing at him too openly, assessing what a splendid portrait subject he would make. He ate a spoonful of his crème brûlée, his eyes rolled back. "Perfect. Even though I can never eat crème brûlée without reliving the nightmare of my custard practical exam in school."

"Do tell," she said, encouraging him to be vulnerable as she had about her family and painting.

"I forgot to put the ramekins in a water bath, threw them in the oven, and thirty minutes later had a mess that managed to be both burnt and raw. Chunky, watery disaster."

He shook his head, lips in a half smile. She decided to risk a playful jab. "Stop, please, you're ruining my dessert."

He shrugged, a lopsided smile on his face, and she sensed he appreciated her faux disgust.

After they finished dinner and he paid the bill, they both walked to the exit, quietly chewing on the peppermints that had come with the check. *Wait until Priya hears about this perfect date*, Elena thought as he helped her into her coat. Then she noticed Lawrence looking down at her feet several times, finally staring right at them once they were back on the sidewalk.

Please tell me he isn't going to ask for feet pics on a first date, Elena thought, dread building at a rapid pace. It would be just her luck to have a wonderful night only for it to end on an outlandish note. "Everything all right?" she prompted, an edge creeping in her voice.

"Uh, yeah, sorry. I do have a weird question, though."

Great, here we go, I knew this was too good to be true.

"Shoot." No stranger to bad dates, Elena found herself alarmed by the sinking dismay she felt as Lawrence hesitated.

"I wanted to surprise you with a visit to the New Hope village light show, but I'm worried about you walking on the icy paths in those shoes."

Ekk! An impulse to jump up and down, thrilled by his thoughtfulness, overpowered her, made her as bouncy as their waiter. "I have winter boots in my car. Take me, take me. I'd love to go."

"Okay, okay. Don't bounce around in those shoes. There could be black ice."

Impulsively, Elena grabbed his hand and led him back to her car. They wove their fingers together as if they'd held hands a thousand times.

"Here, take my bag." Elena thrust her handbag at him, letting go of his hand to perch on the passenger-side seat. She kicked off her gold pumps, then pulled on tan shearling boots. "Is it all outdoors?"

A shell-shocked Lawrence, clutching her bag like a giant with a toy, eyes huge, nodded yes. Was he thrown by her feral enthusiasm? She didn't have it in her to play it cool. Light displays were one of her favorite aspects of the holidays. Shoving aside her stuffed work tote and stacks of folders, she retrieved an oversized black sweatshirt from the back seat. Huge white paint splatters marred the sweatshirt, but beggars couldn't be choosers.

Back on her feet outside, she shimmied out of her peacoat and gave that to Lawrence as well. The sweatshirt hung to midthigh, an inch above the red dress's hem. She took back her coat and buttoned it up. "All set and don't laugh at my absurd getup. Let's do this."

"Yes, ma'am," Lawrence said. She couldn't tell if he was joking or if she'd startled the sense out of him.

"I do not mess around about light shows." Once again, she took his hand. "Lead the way."

"I'm sorry I didn't think to warn you to dress for the weather."

"Who cares? We're seeing lights!" Between the strict schedule at work and the fact that her family lacked a festive spirit, Elena didn't get to do many seasonal activities. Not counting the cookie swap where she'd been on duty for Sparkle, jolliness came primarily in gingerbread latte form. On Friday nights she put on TV Christmas movies, which didn't count because she watched them alone, her lonesome laugh echoing in the apartment. Still, the optimistic stories raised her spirits until fatigue pulled her into sleep without seeing the endings.

"Who's leading the way, me or you?" Lawrence asked, eyebrow raised at her comical charging ahead.

"Whoops, I forgot I have no idea where I'm going." Elena stopped in her tracks, surveyed the uneven rooftops of the historic buildings. To the north she saw a distinct glow cutting through the darkness. She pulled Lawrence in that direction. "Has to be this way. Am I right?"

He gave her a look of pure admiration, blue eyes shining down at her upturned face. In all her life to this moment, no one had ever looked at her with that particular expression. Everyone tended to look at her expecting something. Her parents wanted the latest achievement, her boss wanted better numbers. Fellow artists regarded her with envy, disdain, or disinterest. Never had she seen such straightforward kindness in another person's eyes.

Her breath came out in a sigh, clouding the cold air with its warmth. *Let this last forever.*

Lawrence looked away, breaking the spell. A bit of its magic remained, crackling in the narrow space between them as they left the restaurant parking lot hand in hand. Another novelty: holding hands on a first date. More obvious attempts at physical affection were the norm, while sweet gestures like this one were elusive.

Proceeding down Main, they came to the bookshop next door to Sweet L's Bakery. The window display called to Elena, and Lawrence followed along. "Look at that special edition of *Pride and Prejudice*." Elena pointed to the hardback book, an impressionistic rendition of the two main characters on the cover.

Lawrence leaned closer to peek in the window. "Can't say I ever read that one."

"You are missing out. It's the best story."

"I'm still recovering from the trauma of my sister making me watch the movie every Sunday night for weeks. During football season."

"Yikes. I can admit that's excessive. Have I done it? Yes, I have. Never subjected anyone else to my insanity, at least." She gave him a wicked grin. "Your sister does have great taste."

"And she knows it."

"Hi, Lawrence." A middle-aged man in a buffalo check flannel shirt popped his head out of the bookshop door. "Oh hello," he said to Elena. "I'm Ramon Martinez. This pile of bricks is my bookstore."

"I love it," she said. Lawrence introduced her, and then they moved on.

A biting wind blew down the street, hurling flurries. Lawrence drew her closer, put an arm around her to shield her from the blast. They huddled in the alcove by the bakery door until the wind calmed. She felt the rise and fall of his chest where her cheek pressed against it, the strength of his arm. She had a sudden desire to kiss him. She turned her face up to his, but he was craning his neck to see the street. Too soon the flurries settled and he stepped out of the alcove.

"Aren't you going to offer me a tour of the bakery?" she asked, hoping to prolong the intimacy. She told herself the undeniable attraction pulled her closer to him. Not the safety she felt in his arms as he protected her from the cold, chose to take the brunt of it while offering her the warmth of his body.

Lawrence brushed his hair out of his face with his gloved hand, looking from the alcove to the street with confusion. She suspected he didn't know what to make of her offering to delay the light show after her rabid hurry a few minutes prior. "Um, okay. Wait. Tell you what, let's go to the light show before they run out of hot chocolate. Then, if you're not sick of me, we'll stop back here."

She put a hand on his forearm—to be closer to him, and to calm him. "How did you know hot chocolate is my weakness?"

He bit his lip. "I saw you with that crème brûlée. Almost made me jealous."

"I have got to work on my poker face."

This time he reached for her hand, and together they went toward the light show, Elena wondering as they walked how two hours with him had chipped away at her resolve to keep this casual.

Each time he was attentive as she spoke, especially about her family, a piece of her resolve crumbled. She felt safe confessing that her dad's expectations dominated her choices, a truth she'd only recently realized herself.

She hadn't accounted for any of those factors when she calculated her ability to keep her feelings in check.

These thoughts had no time to linger, however, because she could see the lights in more detail now, and the wonder of it drew her, a moth to flame. Unafraid of getting burned.

CHAPTER NINETEEN

I think she wants to see the lights more than the bakery. I hope I'm reading her right. He reminded himself to trust his instincts—Nana said fake it till you make it. Elena's ping-ponging interests both delighted him and freaked him out in equal measure. It was exciting to be with someone full of feeling, but he wished trying to understand her confused him less. Right when he thought he had the situation well in hand, she said something that made him doubt himself, skin heating, pulse quickening.

Had he been oblivious to a hinted kiss back in the alcove? He'd been dying to kiss her, to feel her lips on his while she pushed her body against him, melting the cold. Then he'd worried she'd think the middle of a date was a weird time for him to make a move. Then again, she'd asked to see the bakery, which would have meant time alone. Kicking himself for potentially missing a signal, he snuck a furtive glance at Elena. He couldn't remember a time he'd been this consumed with a date's success.

Elena squealed when they stepped under the light show entrance arch. Hundreds of red and white lights twisted around the arch in a candy cane pattern, casting a red glow on the surrounding snow. She swept his hand to meet both of hers, held it to her heart as she exclaimed, and he knew she was still having fun. The relative darkness of the street felt far away as they strolled the winding cobblestoned lanes lined with displays. All around them other people in puffy coats, scarves, and hats chattered, oohed and aahed. For Lawrence, no one else existed. He couldn't take his eyes off Elena as she experienced the magic for the first time.

She'd never seen the village public works assembling the huge wire frames, Santa in multiple pieces, the gingerbread house's four sides in a pile waiting to be bolted together. Seeing it through her eyes recalled how he'd viewed it as a child, almost believing no human effort had been required. That a North Pole made all of light had appeared in New Hope overnight while the town slept.

He couldn't help watching her, drinking in her expressions and reactions. Elena looked different tonight compared to her normal, polished appearance. The stained sweatshirt over the dress, the tights and snow boots. Cheeks pink, hair windblown. Elena Voss was the furthest thing from the corporate drone of his fears. Her eyes danced from display to display. The more he got to know her, the more he wondered how she managed to sit still in a cubicle all day.

"The mice," she exclaimed, pointing at a display of rodents sitting down to a Christmas feast at a long, low table. He knew this display well, one of his childhood favorites. No more than a foot tall but full of intricate details—a Christmas ham, a figgy pudding—the mice were a perennial hit with first-time visitors. "And why does the air smell like cinnamon?"

"Does it?" He knew cinnamon pinecones were scattered throughout. He'd heard the ground crew arguing about who had to rake them last week when he walked by on his way to work, but he preferred to let Elena assume it was natural. He took a deep breath. "Wow, it does. You're right."

"This is amazing. You must be able to see the lights from the highway."

"You can. That's how we lure all the unsuspecting tourists."

"How many do you have locked in your basement?"

"How many what?"

"Tourists."

He laughed. "I cleared them all out. They were too needy. 'Feed us. Give us water. We thought this place would be nice.'"

"I wish someone would trap me here so I didn't have to go back to work on Monday."

He wished he could be the one to keep her. It felt too vulnerable to say, like she might misunderstand or think he was rushing things. Or worst of all, think he meant to keep her an *actual* prisoner. He pictured her running in the opposite direction, screaming, *Get away, freak.*

If he didn't get out of his head, he'd drive himself insane.

Elena caught sight of the drink stand and sped up to join the line outside the shack styled like a Swiss chalet. While they waited, she marveled at how precious everything was in New Hope while he nodded along, enjoying the way she saw the town.

New Hope was a great place—he loved his hometown—but he knew the reality wasn't always picture-perfect. Rising rents, neighbors who fought over petty stuff like tree trimming, kids in school who made fun of boys who baked. Some of those creeps still lived in town, like Tommy Jankowski, who managed to put Lawrence down to this day whenever their paths crossed. Too bad Tommy wasn't around tonight to see the absolute stunner on Lawrence's arm.

"I'm getting the Mexican hot chocolate," Elena said, checking out the chalked A-frame menu board. The queue crept forward. "But the eggnog sounds good too. What's best?"

"I always get the wassail."

Elena pressed her lips together, stunned. "That's a drink? I always figured it meant dancing or something."

"Wassail is a spiced ale. Delicious."

"So the lyrics should be *here we come a-boozing*?"

"I mean, they sing about moldy cheese in that one, so why not?"

"Hi, kiddo," Pamela said when they reached the split-log counter. The florist must have taken tonight's volunteer shift. He introduced her to Elena, and Pamela gave him a significant stare when she recognized his date from the contentious town hall meeting. Sometimes it was beneficial to know everyone in town, sometimes it meant you got the best seats in restaurants; other times it meant everyone knew your business. He could imagine the phone calls he'd get from Mom and Nana come morning.

If Elena wanted a festive drink, he would face any small-town scrutiny to get one for her. All the proceeds from the drink stand went to a conservation fund for New Hope's historic buildings, and all the townies took turns manning the stand. All except Lawrence and Trey. A previous mayor had enacted a lifetime ban against them volunteering ever since that unfortunate night when they were both twenty-one. That cold night they'd sampled more spiked drinks than they'd served. They'd wanted to avoid frostbite; it seemed like the most sensible way. One of the most entertaining nights of his life, even if no one would let them live it down all these years later.

Besides, the fire department had rescued the Santa light figure from the clock tower. He and Trey hadn't tied it too tightly with garland. No harm done.

One day, if things between him and Elena went well, he would tell her the story.

"One wassail for you, I'm sure," Pamela said. She pulled a marker from behind her ear, wrote his name on a cup. "And for you, Elena?"

"I want to try something I've never had before. I'll take a hot toddy, please," Elena said with conviction. When they stepped out of line to wait for their drinks, she whispered, "What even is a hot toddy?"

"You crack me up. What happened to the hot chocolate or eggnog?"

"I feel like expanding my horizons tonight."

"Well, for your information, it's hot whiskey, lemon, and honey."

Elena scrunched her nose. "Hot whiskey sounds weird. I have to try it, though. I can't be boring and stick to the same old thing."

Hard to picture Elena choosing the boring option under any circumstances.

"Good for you, get out of that comfort zone," he said, as much to himself as to her.

Pamela set their drinks on the counter and called out, "Kiddo," not bothering with his real name. He could smell the whiskey in Elena's drink as he gave it to her.

"Look at this little cinnamon stick. How darling." She stirred her drink with enough speed to hand-whip a meringue. A lemon slice studded with star anise swirled on the surface. "Here goes nothing."

She tapped her Styrofoam cup against his, then took a sip. He waited for her to cough or splutter. Instead, she smiled. "Ahh, that is smooth. Turns out hot whiskey is amazing."

He wondered how many of his friends and neighbors would be ribbing him tomorrow for walking around the light display grinning like a sappy maniac at Elena. Probably the town's entire population.

They wove around another couple taking a selfie in front of the mistletoe display. The guy almost elbowed Elena while trying to get a better angle. Lawrence steered Elena away, glaring at the dude, whose eyes widened when he saw Lawrence.

All around them, harassed moms wrangled shrieking children, attempted to get usable photos for Christmas cards. Here in the center of the village, a band played rock versions of carols on a temporary stage. "Jingle Bells" at earsplitting decibels, reverb from the amplifiers. Sound vibrated all around them, trembled in his chest. He checked Elena—still happy and dazzled. Meanwhile, his brain began to frizz out from the excessive stimulation, a sensation like electric zaps in his temples.

"Let's go over here," he said, and drew her to a clearing a few paces back in the trees. Not everyone knew there were pockets of calm hidden throughout. He and Elena sat on a wrought-iron bench tucked between towering Fraser firs. Here the only illumination came from delicate white lights strung in the branches. A sharp breeze shook the branches, the lights twinkled. Beneath their feet lay a soft covering of pine needles. His mind slowed.

Elena looked up at him again, the way she had in the alcove. He touched her face, wished he'd taken off his glove so he could feel her soft skin. This was the moment. *I should ask first. That's the right thing to do. That's what people do, right?* How had he forgotten first-date etiquette? It hadn't been *that* long. The drowning feeling from a few minutes back returned. He felt like a hand was compressing his heart, cutting off his breath. *Say it, say it, ask already.*

"Kiss me?" she asked. He should've known Elena wouldn't be uncertain. He leaned in, held her pretty face in his hands. Cold forehead to cold forehead, and then he kissed her. Hot like whiskey, sweet like honey. Intoxicating.

She parted her lips, and all his worries slipped away.

CHAPTER TWENTY

Midnight approached, the moon luminous, as they returned to the bakery, tipsy from the drinks, the kiss, each other. Elena hummed "Here We Come a-Wassailing," and Lawrence fumbled with the keys. A perfect night. Yes, she'd all but abandoned her intention to avoid emotional investment. Who could blame her? Delicious dinner, delicious drinks, delicious Lawrence. Why pretend she wasn't impressed, that she wasn't a bit captivated?

What a contrast to her normal mood during a date. No wonder, considering the unromantic dating trends. Men on the dating apps had started asking her to come straight to their apartments, not offering the bare minimum of a drink or coffee first. No pretext of wanting to get to know her as a person. The mere fact that Lawrence had made a dinner reservation put him in a class unto himself.

In this enchanted town, with this unicorn of a man, she'd have to be made of steel to resist. She didn't care what Mel or Priya or sensible Elena thought; she wanted a second date. And a third. This itch got worse the more she scratched it. *A little more and I'll be satisfied.*

Lawrence shoved the door. Jingle bells rung as it swung open.

He held out a hand to prevent her from entering. "Do I have to make you pinkie-swear to not spy on *my* proprietary baking secrets before the tour?"

For the most part, they'd avoided talking about either of their jobs. Elena intended to keep it that way. Derick's ultimatums didn't exist here. She wouldn't tell her boss another word about New Hope, even if he resorted to physical torture instead of sticking to psychological. "That's the last thing you have to worry about."

"Then you may proceed." He made a gallant sweep of his arm and let her walk in before him.

The aroma of fresh-baked cookies was all around her, which made perfect sense but wowed her nonetheless. Nothing like the antiseptic odor in the Sparkle test kitchen. More like walking into a life-size gingerbread house. Like finding a home where someone put cookies in the oven for the kids to eat after school. A home she'd imagined many times growing up. Vanilla, chocolate, sugar as much a part of the building as the beams and exposed ducts above her. A few weeks ago, she'd thought he was crazy to proclaim his cookies could be that much better than Sparkle's. Now she could smell their superiority all around her.

The tree in the window provided gentle light, and she felt the instant relief warmth brought after an hour outside. Her ice-cold fingers and the tip of her nose came back to life. She took in the worn pine floors, mismatched café tables—thrift finds, perhaps—an old bookcase repurposed to hold bags of day-old cookies at half price. A simple black letter board with white letters spelled out the cookie names and prices. In her mind's eye, she saw the lovely people she'd met tonight, Pamela and Mr. Martinez and others, clustered at the tables, laughing, talking, and eating.

"It's marvelous," she told him on a breath.

"Well, thank you." He dipped his head, looked away. "I won't lie, I was a tad nervous about bringing you in here. We focused on baking technique in culinary school, only did one class on business and marketing. I know there is a lot I could do better."

True, her marketing experience noted things that could be improved. Sell branded mugs alongside the cookies to drive up profits, add some chair pads or love seats to encourage people to linger, to buy more. Small changes. She didn't mention them to Lawrence, too ashamed of how hard she'd hit him with the bakery's flaws the night of the town hall.

When she'd used her dad's training to protect herself, to lash out in response to their tense exchange at the meeting, to prove her superiority.

She faced the empty bakery case, hands on hips. "For starters, I'd suggest making cookies to sell, since your sign claims you do."

"Ow. You appall me," he said, shaking his head in mock disgust. "I wouldn't let my babies sit out overnight, exposed to the air, getting all crusty and dry. Break a customer's tooth, get sued. No, my dear, here at Sweet L's we bake fresh every day. As you can see, we wrap leftovers well and don't charge full price for anything short of perfect."

"Well, they never told me that in Sparkle Cookie school." Whenever Elena and the marketing team made a visit to a store, the cases were fully stocked. Guidelines dictated a minimum of five per flavor at all times, no excuses. Granted, the rule applied to open hours. It never occurred to her the cookies couldn't stay in the case.

"Tsk, tsk. How much you have to learn."

"Is that right, chef?"

Lawrence put a hand to his heart, then he wrapped his arms around her, lifting her off the ground. She yelped in elation as he spun her in a circle, kissing her neck. A trail of heat, the mesmerizing sensation of his mouth on her skin, the friction from the stubble on his chin. A charge raced down her spine. "If you call me that, you'll drive me wild," he said.

What happened to the shy guy who took half an hour over dinner to come out of his shell?

"What? Why?" she asked. What was it about that little word?

"Well, that's some culinary culture right there. It's a very hier-archical world. In a professional kitchen, the chef makes a request, and everyone automatically agrees. They say, *Yes, chef.*" He brushed his thumb over her lip. Gentle pressure on a soft spot. "When I hear it from this pretty mouth, years of conditioning make me think, ask to kiss her again and she'll say—"

"Yes, chef," she murmured in a low voice, moving her lips to his ear.

He slowed the spin, let her slide down his body to stand. He kissed her again, the tentative wariness from the clearing gone. Evaporated. Any sliver of control she thought she retained went up in flames as he pressed one hand to the small of her back, the other at the nape of her neck. The way he fit their bodies together.

The clothing layers she'd added earlier became too hot all at once, coldness a thing of the distant past. She broke away, unbut-toning her coat with quick fingers. *Come to your senses*, a little voice said. *Shut up*, she countered. When she'd told Priya she wanted to gobble Lawrence like dessert, she'd been kidding. Or exaggerating. Now a real sort of frenzy, a bottomless hunger, took her over. She pulled the paint-splattered sweatshirt off, tossed it onto the chair that already held her coat. Lawrence held his hands out to her, and she flew back into his arms.

Get a hold of yourself. She was tall, but he was taller, and she rose to her tiptoes, clung to his neck to keep him close. His tongue grazed hers. Her fingertips dug into his shoulders, into the strongest muscles she'd ever felt, the power of them weakening her.

He's worth more than a meaningless hookup or a few dates. He's boyfriend material. This unwanted realization came crashing at her, a cold splash of water right to the face.

She backed away without warning. Broke from the circle of his arms. She combed her fingers through her hair to smooth the places where his fingers had tangled it. Wasn't casual all she wanted? She could have the hookup now, but would she be able to keep her feelings under control?

A sentiment she'd never experienced flooded her, bigger than logical thought and hard to name. Surging, wanting. For an encounter that she had meant to be primarily physical, touching him stirred up a storm of emotion instead.

"I'm sorry," he said. He held up his hands, palms out. "I don't know what came over me, I didn't mean to . . ."

She felt his absence everywhere, her arms without him, the emptiest they'd ever been. A hollowness in her chest. Yes, he'd been chipping away at her defenses, but now she was acting ready to tear down her own walls from the inside.

A terrifying feeling, a new feeling. The flint of desire striking something deeper into flame inside.

"No, no, it's not you." Ordinarily, this would be where she'd employ a flip remark to disguise her true feelings. Nothing came to her, Lawrence's alarm increased, and he took a step away. "I've had the most incredible night. I'm scared to . . ."

Not only didn't she have a coy comment, she didn't have anything. Her mind was blank, grasping in fog for an answer just out of reach. What was happening? How had years of being taught to think a step ahead brought her to this pass? *Always have an answer. Always make a strong impression. Be articulate.*

"I'm scared—not of you." Of course not of him, though she needed to repeat it to erase the concern etched across his face. She would never admit to being interested in a relationship on a first date. It scared her to even consider it. Especially not with someone she'd sworn to Priya and herself was only a hookup. She couldn't say *I'm afraid of how much you've charmed me tonight.* If she gave those words voice, she couldn't take them back. Too great a risk. "I don't know what's scaring me. I want to slow down."

Again, he reached out his hands, not saying anything but somehow knowing what to do. He gave her a gentle embrace, kissed the top of her head. She heard his heart racing to match her own, slowed her breath to slow his. This hesitant contact might give her a chance to remember her own motives. To ground herself and decide if she still wanted to push ahead, closer to him.

He caught her chin in his hand, tipped her face up to look at him. His eyes compassionate, his tone soft, he said, "Come with me. I'll show you around."

Together they went through a swinging door into a small kitchen, a single overhead light on above the oven. Enough light to see by; hopefully not enough for him to notice the shame coloring her face.

"Every Sweet L's cookie begins with the best ingredients I can source." His tone soothed her and he stayed close, touched her hand lightly as he showed her around the kitchen. He pulled a large square canister from a wire shelving unit. With a practiced flip he popped off the lid. "Pure cane sugar."

White crystals shimmered, shifted as he tipped the canister. He grabbed a plastic spoon from an adjacent shelf, dug out a small scoop. He held the spoon to her lips, eyes on hers. She opened her mouth, then the crystals lay on her tongue, gritty and impossibly sweet.

Sweet as you.

"This is grand cru chocolate from France." He opened a second canister heaping with shiny chocolate disks. He shook out a disk for her, slipped it into her mouth. "Bitter and dark, the ideal contrast to a sweet base dough."

The chocolate melted, coated her tongue with its complex, almost smoky flavor. The unrest roiling inside her began to calm. She focused her attention on his easy movements, on the way he seemed relaxed and fully in his element.

Her exhilarated but too-fast heartbeat began to slow as she followed him to a stainless-steel refrigerator, double the size of an ordinary household one. With a woosh, he pulled the door open. Bricks of butter formed a tower on the top shelf.

"Eighty-two-percent-fat butter. I won't ask you to taste it, but get a look at that color." He peeled back the corner of the inner paper wrapper on one of the blocks. A yellow she'd never seen on store-bought butter. A yellow she knew she wanted to remember for the next time she mixed her paints. All her senses thrummed; true calmness spread over her for the first time in ages.

"What you have here is very special," she said.

He smiled, touched her cheek. He didn't try to press home any old argument about how his bakery was better than hers. Instead, he seemed proud to show it off for itself, for the pleasure of its details, for the slow, wonderful sensation of beautiful things. For a kind of art she had never considered.

"I knew I'd get you with the chocolate."

You've got me.

"There's something I want to show you. Will you come with me?"

CHAPTER TWENTY-ONE

Elena had thrown him off-balance with her sudden passion, followed by the equally sudden shutdown in the middle of their kiss. At first, he feared he'd crossed some boundary or made some other stupid mistake. She'd promised it wasn't his fault, and she said she didn't want to move too fast. Maybe she didn't want to give too much.

Then her reactions to the kitchen tour encouraged him, and he figured giving her the opportunity to flex her creative skills might be a good way to slow things down without ending the night outright.

He opened the door to the second cooler and pulled out a small, two-layer chocolate cake. It was pretty rough, since it only had a crumb coat of icing so far. The thin layer of Italian buttercream he'd applied this morning caught crumbs from the cake and trapped them once it set. Additional decorative coats of icing would remain pristine thanks to the crumb coat.

"I thought you only made cookies here. What's this?" Elena asked.

"You are right, I only sell cookies, but I make cakes on the down-low for a select few. My buddy Trey ordered this for his fiancée, Iris. It's her birthday tomorrow."

"It's . . . interesting." Elena gave the cake a suspicious once-over.

"It's not done yet, and that's why I need your help. Do you think your artistic skills would transfer to cake decorations?"

Elena assessed the cake, clicking her tongue as she considered it. "I can try, provided your friend won't be heartbroken if it's not perfect."

"He's getting the best-friend discount—which means free—so he can't be too picky. Also, I'm pretty good at laying down the base layers, but piping work isn't my forte. Usually, my assistant Carmen gives me a hand. She's had to leave early the last few days and didn't have time to decorate for a pro bono job."

"Okay. I'll give it a try. It always looks fun on TV." Her willingness to experience new things charmed him, made him wish he were easygoing in unfamiliar situations.

"Now, no one touches anything in this kitchen without washing their hands, not even you."

"Wouldn't dream of it." She pulled an elastic band out of her dress pocket.

"You're practically ready to run the place," he said as she secured her hair in a tight bun. The different hairstyle showed off her long neck and defined cheekbones. She caught him looking.

Laughing, she went to the handwash station, and they took turns soaping up at the small designated sink. When the health inspector came by, one of the first things he did was check that the soap at the handwash sink was stocked and the water ran hot. Clean hands were the foundation of a clean kitchen. Lawrence balled up their damp paper towels and tossed them in the open trash can near the workbench.

"Ready for a world-class education in cake decorating?" he asked her, balancing the cake on one hand.

"Whoa, aren't you scared to drop it?" Elena stepped forward as if she might have to catch the cake.

"It's pretty stable on its cake round here, see?" He held the cake aloft, high over her head, to show her the cardboard base.

"Don't you dare drop it on me, mister." She ducked. His spine straightened, proud he'd gotten her to relax and joke again. "Although that would be pretty funny. Make for a great story."

"Cake making is serious business; I won't be pulling any pranks. You, however, I'm not sure about."

"I promise to be good."

"That remains to be seen. And I have my doubts. Okay, we put this little guy right here." He placed the cake on a turn-top stand and let Elena give it a whirl. He adored the way her eyes shone over the things he took for granted. "Now, tools and icing."

Elena leaned against the workbench while he laid out an offset metal icing spatula, premade plastic icing bags filled with various colors, and a rose nail. He'd gotten used to giving cooking demos in school but never for someone as gorgeous as Elena and his nerves kicked up a notch as she watched his every move. *It's okay, take it easy, she hasn't dipped out yet, even after that reaction in the front of the house.*

He let Elena peel back the plastic wrap from the surface of a bowl of pale-pink icing, then he took big blobs of the frosting with his spatula. He slapped them on the sides and top of the cake.

"Man, I thought you were being modest when you said decorating isn't your strong suit, but this looks awful," Elena teased, hip checking him. At least she wasn't planning to never touch him again.

"Voilà." He spun the cake, holding the edge of the spatula against it as the frosting transformed to a smooth surface in a matter of seconds.

Elena clapped. "Oh my, is that how you do it? You should see me trying to frost a cake. I always use a butter knife."

"That's a shocking fact to spring on me, Elena. Warn a guy before you drop that bomb." She hip-checked him again, then rested her head against his arm for a second. Okay, heading in a better direction. "Your canvas is ready."

He handed her an icing bag fitted with a rosette tip and filled with dark-pink icing. She stared at it, her tongue sneaking out of the corner of her mouth. "I have no idea where to start."

"May I?" he asked, reaching for her hand. She nodded, and he felt grateful for the excuse to touch her, be close to her again. "Balance the metal tip on your left forefinger, and hold back here with your right hand to put pressure. Uh-oh, hold on a sec—"

A vision of her squeezing the frosting all over her hand from the top of the bag by mistake stopped the lesson in its tracks. He retrieved a rubber band from a nearby drawer and tied off the top. "Just to be safe."

"I appreciate that. I assume you've seen the paint stains on my hands and realize what a mess I can be."

"I like your multicolored hands." She snuggled in closer as he put his arms around her to demonstrate the technique. Her hair smelled incredible, like flowers. He didn't know enough about flowers to guess which ones. Maybe the type that bloomed wild on a sultry summer night. "Now, a little pressure here. Good, good. Lift it away."

"We made a rosette," she exclaimed, as enthusiastic as if she'd piped a complex masterpiece fit for a royal wedding cake. This was his favorite part of baking, the fun of discovering the magic you could make.

"And what a perfect one too. Are you hustling me, Elena Rachel Voss? Have you secretly won *The Great British Bake Off*?"

"I wish. That show is the best. Relaxes me like no other. And they call cookies biscuits. How cute is that?"

His eyes ran over her sweet, cheerful face. "Not as cute as you. But cute."

"You're kinda cute yourself." She arched an eyebrow. His whole body yearned to close any gap between them, to kiss her again. She brushed against him when she moved. Afraid to upset her, he stood still as she piped a second rosette on her own. "This is fun. What's next?"

He showed her ruffles, dots, even buttercream roses with light-green leaves. The roses were much more advanced than rosettes, and she couldn't quite master them. He basked in her look of admiration as she watched him pipe them on the rose nail at super speed and transfer them to the cake using the spatula.

"Who's the hustler now, Mr. Higgins? Those roses are perfect," she said when he added the final one to the cake top. "I'm going to practice, and next time I'm going to beat you at your rose game."

"So, there will be a next time? You promise?" he asked, without giving himself a chance to fret or hold back. He couldn't forgive himself if he didn't try.

The kitchen felt unnaturally hot, even with the ovens off, in the pause before her response. She turned away from the workbench, placed a hesitant hand on his chest. *Breathe like a normal human*, he ordered himself, so she wouldn't feel his apprehension. He watched her take her own deep breath, sensed she was debating her answer.

"I absolutely do." Her fingers traced up to the place where his shoulder met his neck. She bit her lip and again gave him the impression she wasn't sure about the next step. "One last kiss before the night is over?"

He touched her cheek with the back of his fingers. She leaned against his hand, looked up at him with deep, dark eyes.

He kissed her, or she kissed him, he couldn't tell who moved first, just that he had her against him again. And how much he needed it to stay that way.

CHAPTER TWENTY-TWO

"To keep a long story short, hands down the best date of my life." Saying those words felt daring. A big admission, but one she couldn't hold inside. Not here in her own apartment with Priya. Besides, how dangerous could it be to admit she'd enjoyed herself? "We've been texting too. I can't tell you how relieved I am he's not one of those guys who blows you off after a date, acts like he forgot you existed for a week, then slides into your DMs at two AM on a Sunday. You know the type.

"Anyway, Lawrence has this cookie recipe he's working on for a big competition, and he's been asking my opinions on it. He's coming here tomorrow night to bake a practice batch with me. I've been telling him a bit about how toxic things are at work, and he said baking helps him unwind and maybe it will help me too. This is all to say, I don't think he was too bothered by me backing off while we were—"

Priya put up a hand to silence Elena. "Nothing about this story has been short. I am very happy for you; no one deserves it more. But wasn't the whole plan to have a hot hookup and move on?"

Without warning, Elena's thoughts flashed back to the rioting emotions and desires that had swelled up in her as they kissed. "I can still do that."

"Yeah, right. You don't even sound like you believe yourself anymore. I'm not sure I ever believed you. Listen, are we going to work on our résumés or not? I skipped the gym for this."

"You skipped the gym because I have queso."

"Fair." Priya dipped a blue corn chip into the bowl of spicy cheese on the coffee table. She looked adorable and workout ready in a sage-green leggings and crop top set, her hair in a perky high ponytail.

"My bad for gushing. Let's get started." Elena cracked open cans of mango hard seltzer for each of them, then turned on her laptop. Priya sat cross-legged on Elena's sofa, a plush, seafoam-green piece she'd found at an estate sale. Kitty-corner to the sofa, Elena sat with her feet tucked under her on a scallop-back blush-pink upholstered chair.

"I wish we could be real in these things," Priya said, twirling a gold-and-ruby ring around her thumb, a habit Elena noticed whenever Priya felt annoyed.

"Something like *managed to be productive while suffering from the high-control efforts of a megalomanic named Derick*," Elena suggested.

"Exactly. That's the kind of information an employer should know up front. And they need to be honest about their messy work cultures in the job posting. This position requires you to be available every day of your life and to answer your supervisor's emails in the middle of the night."

"How does Derick send so many emails? Or does he make Sarah do it?"

"Probably Sarah. That poor thing is one more rough day away from a complete nervous breakdown. I found her shaking head to toe by the vending machines because they were out of peanut butter cups, and you know how hangry Derick gets."

Elena didn't know how much longer she could stand Sparkle without having her own mental collapse. HR was notoriously incompetent, often making conflicts worse, and the corporate culture rewarded anyone who stepped on others to get good numbers. Elena stared at the half-finished canvases—abstract florals—leaned against the wall by her cluttered bookshelf. A thin line of smoke curled up from the flame of the eucalyptus candle on her TV stand.

She scratched black acrylic paint off her thumbnail, pondering her next move. There had to be a way to earn her fifty-five-hundred-dollar bonus ethically. She'd saved all of her Christmas money this year but would feel more secure with a larger cushion while on the hunt for a new job. Asking her parents for help was an absolute worst-case scenario. Such a request would only fuel Dad's deep-seated fears that Elena would end up broke.

Furthermore, and more importantly, she had to do it without exploiting her connection to Lawrence. The mere thought made her stomach turn. Of course she hadn't breathed a word to Derick about her night in New Hope, even though she'd met multiple local business owners. Could she post great opening numbers without poaching Lawrence's business? If he won the *Home Baker Quarterly* cash prize, she could give him some affordable marketing ideas that would set him apart from Sparkle. Surely the two bakeries could coexist.

Elena munched salty chips, and Priya typed away on her own laptop. Granted, Elena knew from extensive market research that Sparkle locations tended to drive out local bakeries. Not across the board, but it happened more often than not. Instead of opening her résumé document, she opened a blank page and began brainstorming ideas to help both bakeries—Sparkle and Sweet L's—survive.

Seeing her ideas in black and white made them feel more achievable. Except for this to work, she would have to be honest with Lawrence that she needed her location to do well. And she'd need to convince him she wanted to protect his bakery at the same time. The base of her skull began to throb. There were so many ways this could go wrong. Hopefully, he would be receptive, willing to trust her. And she'd have to overcome her dad's perennial advice to keep her cards close to the chest, step outside her comfort zone to be up front with Lawrence.

Was she ready for this step? Could she admit she no longer thought a simple hookup was possible or even desirable?

Sunday morning she had free-journaled for twenty minutes, trying to untangle her uncertainty. To determine if she could take a leap toward something more than a fling.

She'd made such a big deal to Priya about how she couldn't get serious with a rival business owner. That she'd have one night and move on. Because how could she introduce him to her parents? Dad would flip when he found out Lawrence owned a competing business. Her proud, logical (okay, stubborn) side wanted to stick with her original plan.

The part that had enjoyed the best date of her life had other ideas.

In the end, she scratched half of it out, then wrote, *Give it a chance.*

This is the chance. Take it, she told herself. She typed a note in her document that she would explain the situation to Lawrence tomorrow night during their baking date. There, that made it official. She would give emotional honesty a shot.

A notification ping made her heart skip, and she seized her phone. Lawrence?

"Sorry. It was me," Priya said. "Can you believe Kiaan deigned to text me? He failed his chem test. All I said was *u ok*, and look what this punk kid sent back."

Priya held out the phone, and Elena saw rows of middle-finger emojis taking over Priya's screen.

"Failing tests isn't like him. I'm sorry, Priya."

Priya huffed, blowing a strand of hair off her face. "I hate that I can't help him. My mom made him an appointment with a therapist. He better go."

Priya's forehead creased with worry, tugging at Elena's heart-strings. Between work garbage and her brother, Priya also seemed poised for a breakdown. No one would be sane come the new year. "I hope he realizes soon how lucky he is to have you for a sister."

Priya dropped her phone back on the sofa. "He should. Brat."

Another text message alert sounded, this time for Elena. Hoping again for a text from Lawrence made the fact that it came from Derick twice as bad as usual. Her stomach twisted.

Nice work. Debrief tomorrow. Beneath his remark Derick had sent a screenshot of the New Hope village page, in which Elena could clearly be seen wandering the light show, hand in hand with Lawrence.

She shrieked an expletive. Priya looked at her with startled eyes. Why hadn't she thought to check social media this morning? Lawrence might have been able to get this taken down. She knew Derick had been monitoring anything to do with that town. Stupid, stupid mistake. Priya stood, then pried the phone from Elena's tight grip.

"Shh, don't cry." She patted Elena's shaking shoulder while reading the message. "He cannot do this. You were off duty. This is wrong."

"He doesn't care," Elena said, voice thick.

"You have to show this to your dad. He'll know what to do."

"I can't! Then my dad will know I'm having problems at work. And that I've been swanning about town with a dashing baker."

"He doesn't have to know the extent. Give him the highlights."

"Priya, this is a man who butchers witnesses on cross-examination. He'll get the truth out of me before I speak."

Priya gave Elena's shoulder a little shake. "Elena, Derick is pure evil. You cannot allow him to do this to you. You had a great time on Saturday; you want to see Lawrence again. He's been thoughtful and respectful. You cannot and will not let Derick back you into a corner."

Considering how Derick terrified Priya, Elena found the speech all the more stirring. She sucked in a breath, her thoughts zigzagging around possible adverse outcomes. If she kept her communication with Dad to text, she would have a better chance of not revealing information she wanted to keep to herself. She snuffled; Priya handed her a tissue from the box on the end table.

"Go on. Put on your big-girl pants and do it."

"I don't wanna. I wanna hide in my bed and watch *A Christmas Story* on repeat until I fuse to my sheets."

"I will steal your TV without a second thought. I don't care your dad is a powerful lawyer. I will commit a crime to get you to do what we both know is right." Priya thrust the phone at her.

"Maybe I should paint first. Gather my thoughts."

"Elena! Don't make me slap some sense in you."

"I can't burn any bridges at work." As soon as she said the words, she recognized how senseless they sounded. Derick had crossed a line. Even if it made her uncomfortable, she could keep her job while advocating for herself. Dad would give her actionable advice. She opened her hand and accepted the phone. Felt the weight of it in her palm.

Priya looked over her shoulder while Elena wrote Dad a succinct text explaining the situation in basic terms.

She squinted her eyes. "Press send for me; I can't do it."

Without hesitation, Priya stamped the send arrow and the message swooshed away.

"And now we wait," Elena said.

"Wait for the seeds of Derick's destruction to grow. Hope for a bountiful harvest." Priya sat back on the sofa, pointed to Elena's laptop. "Get back to work. We need new jobs now more than ever."

The next morning Elena was wishing she already had a new job. She hovered outside Derick's door before rolling her eyes at her cowardice and knocking.

"You're not on my calendar, Voss," he said as she entered, sparing her a quick glance before looking back to his computer screen.

"I'm here about your message last night."

"Ah, yes. Nice work. Give me the details."

You don't owe him an explanation. Be direct. "No."

He turned his attention away from the screen, looked at her, lips slightly parted. He blinked. "What?"

"No." She clasped her hands, squeezed them to release some tension in her body. "I was there on a personal matter. I have no intention of reporting back every time I leave the city."

"I thought you were a team player." His voice dropped an octave to his scariest, most intimidating register.

She hesitated; the words lodged in her throat. Her answer, she realized, would mean choosing Lawrence over the job. In a small way, perhaps, but nonetheless significant. *Don't make excuses; your word is final*, Dad had said last night.

She looked Derick dead in the eye. "We are never discussing my personal life. Do not ask again."

She waited, but he didn't respond. She turned her back on him and walked away. Once outside his door she let herself breathe, depleted but proud of her choice. Of the stand she'd taken. For herself.

CHAPTER TWENTY-THREE

The instant Elena opened her apartment door, she wrapped her arms around Lawrence and gave him a long kiss. He held a canvas bag filled with ingredients in one hand and used the other to caress her cheek. Had they only seen each other a few days ago? It felt like forever. He'd found himself missing her while he worked, and especially when he went home at night to the two-bedroom, two-story old house he shared with Sugar. Yesterday, Elena had hinted she had problems at work, and he'd spent the afternoon worrying about her well-being. Her kiss suggested she'd missed him too, and his lips curved in a smile against hers.

"How is everything?" he asked as soon as they parted. Elena seemed muted, less chipper and less chatty than normal.

"Ugh. C'mon in." She held open the door so he could enter. "It's a long story. Let's get settled in first."

She took the grocery bag and walked into the kitchen while he slipped off his shoes at the front door. Elena's artistic side was on full display in her apartment, not a trace of her corporate self anywhere. In the living room he saw her art hanging, gigantic canvases

144

on the walls. Smaller canvases leaned in piles against the walls and feminine furniture. By the window, an easel held a work in progress, waves breaking a blue sea. The splendor of the image held him transfixed until he broke away to scope out the rest of the room. Pretty, full of color. The place smelled nice thanks to some lit candles on the coffee table, and beneath that he detected turpentine.

"I don't know how to make wassail. Will a glass of wine do?" she called from the kitchen.

"Sure, sounds great." He noticed a record player and wondered if he should offer to put on music in case there were any awkward silences he needed to cover. Uncertain, he perched first on an armchair, then popped up to switch to the sofa as Elena walked out with stemless wineglasses.

Sitting on the sofa gave her an opportunity to sit next to him. The wineglasses were mismatched, which surprised him; he'd expected her to have everything curated, perfect. Tonight marked the first time he'd seen her in casual clothing—soft ruby sweatpants and a cropped sweatshirt that showed off her superb midsection. He opened and closed his hand, longing to touch her bare skin. Cautious about rushing things after her reaction the other night, he opted to put his hand on her knee instead. She wore her hair in a long braid draped over her shoulder.

He rested his arm against the sofa back, an apprehensive invitation. Elena curled against him. Her hair smelled like vanilla extract. Good thing he'd had the sense to ditch the armchair. No way they would've both fit.

"What's going on, sweetie?" He gauged her reaction to his first serious attempt at an endearment. She nestled closer.

"I had the most anxiety-inducing confrontation of my career," she confessed. He rubbed her arm, waited for her to continue. He was used to vivacious Elena who conversed easily. Who could have made her so upset, and why did he feel his hands tightening into fists? He continued stroking her arm to comfort her and calm his angry reaction to this mystery offender. "My boss really oversteps, and I finally had enough. Even went to my dad for help, which I usually avoid like the plague. I ended up confronting my boss for the first time ever."

"What did you say?"

"Exactly what my dad told me to, which was that when I'm not working, how I spend my time is none of his business."

"Sounds fair. You deserve a life."

"I know. But it was still awful having to talk to him. And do you know what he said back? 'I thought you were a team player.' He knows he can't force me to be on duty twenty-four/seven, but he still tries to make me. I cannot stand him. Bosses are the worst."

"Why do you think I work for myself?"

She gave a low chuckle. "Do you ever make yourself mad?"

"All the time. Especially when I procrastinate."

She held out her hand, measured it against his. Her fingers reached about two-thirds of the way up his. "Don't suppose you'd be willing to hang out by the Sparkle headquarters waiting for a lanky guy in a suit with slicked-back hair so you can tell him to treat me better?"

"You're not going to believe this, but intimidating random dudes is my party trick. Sometimes I do it to make them laugh, other times I do it to put them in their place. Like the time in high school a guy kept waiting around the ice cream shop for my sister's shift to end. Creeped her out. He was a senior like her and I was a sophomore, but I still had four inches on this guy. One day I waited too, stared at him for a good ten minutes. When Lonnie clocked out and he realized I was her brother, he never bothered her again."

"I love that story."

"Didn't your brothers look out for you?"

"I went to an all-girls private school. No need."

"Very classy."

"Yeah, I guess."

"It's gross when guys can't respect people. I figure I'll get some good karma reminding them there's always someone bigger and scarier." He kissed her hand, glad the moment felt right this time. "Still, it's messed up I have to be the one to make them play nice."

"Is that so?" She looked up at him with her captivating brown eyes. Captivating indeed, for they imprisoned him. "Don't be too good, though."

He kissed her again, this time sliding his hands over the smooth, warm skin of her abdomen. When she arched into his touch, he gripped her waist, held her there for another kiss. He pulled back. "All right, you, settle down. Trying to use me for my body. You could at least offer to taste-test the cookies first like you promised."

He cherished the frustration that crossed her face. "Is that all you think I'm after?"

"You just admitted you plan to deploy me to scare your boss."

She walked her fingertips up his chest, made him regret being the one to slow things down. "Fine. I'll prove I'm after more than your body. Let's go."

She stood up, but seemed to think better of it before she leaned over. The end of her braid brushed against him as she placed her hands on his shoulders. Her tongue crept out to lick the corner of her mouth. "Now you've awoken my competitive side, and I'm out to show I can resist you longer than you can resist me."

"What if I admit defeat right now?"

"That's no fun." She wiggled free and made for the kitchen, tossing him a look over her shoulder that made him leap up to follow.

In the kitchen she started setting out his premeasured ingredients. He forced his heartbeat to slow, his blood to redisperse while he opened a container of the candied orange ginger cookies. Elena washed her hands, then plucked out a cookie. He watched as she chewed it pensively.

Nothing worse than waiting for reviews.

"I like it, it's sophisticated." She broke open a second cookie, sniffed it. "But I get what you were saying about it being on the strong side flavor-wise. If it were for a fancy holiday tea, it would be perfect. However, our audience is home bakers who want something to share with their families."

"Uh-oh, is marketing Elena coming out?"

"You summoned her. Tell me, what inspired you to make this cookie in the first place? What was the message you wanted to send?"

"I . . . uh. Hmm. I never thought about it that way. I kinda started mixing things together to see what would taste good."

"I understand. My paintings begin like that too. Not to taste, obviously—that would be a terrible idea. But I like to play with colors until I find what feels right. Not to bring up Sparkle again, but I do a lot of the content for our newsletter, and I always try to tell a story about each cookie."

"I'll have to check it out."

"Anyway, think about it for a minute. What is your ultimate goal?"

He crossed his arms, looked out the window above her sink. The weather forecast had called for a clear night, yet snow was descending in sizable flakes to the street below. When he pondered it, he realized he must have a goal for his cookies, an emotion or experience he wanted to evoke. Nostalgia or surprise. "I guess . . . I guess I want to make a twist on a standard gingerbread cookie. Show what else the ingredients can do."

"Good. That gives me something to work with." She opened his mason jar of flour and the small container of fresh ginger. Her eyes traveled around her kitchen, landed on a canister next to the coffee machine. She gasped so loudly it startled him. "What if we ditched the candied orange and did coffee instead? Coffee is my favorite thing in the entire world, and Sparkle's caramel macchiato cookie is a best seller. People love that flavor."

Ideas began skipping through his mind. Possibilities. "Something like a gingerbread latte, maybe? Coffee would balance out the sweetness in the base that's been worrying me. And it could make for an interesting substitute for the orange peel."

"Build on your base idea."

"This is promising."

She handed him a mixing bowl, a vintage pink Pyrex. Inspiration made his movements quick. He started shifting flour into the Pyrex, asked her for another bowl for the wet ingredients.

"I'll make the coffee. We can even drink some," she said excitedly.

"Elena, it's nine at night."

"So?" She opened the bag of grounds, held it out for his approval. She had good taste in coffee—multifaceted, with a hint of chocolate.

"What a good sous-chef you are," he said.

"Want to make me the second-in-command, huh? Maybe I want to be head chef."

"Nice try, shorty."

She spluttered laughter.

"I'm five foot ten. That's gigantically tall for a woman." She straightened her posture to underscore her point, gestured to her long legs as if he hadn't already been drinking them in.

He reached for her with both hands, found exposed skin at her waist again. His fingertips glided down to hold her hips. With a smooth motion he pulled her into him, fitted the top of her head under his chin.

"Which makes me five inches taller, which is almost half a foot. See? Like I said, nice try, shorty."

He felt the yielding sweetness of her body as he pressed her even closer. He cocked his head toward the window. "You know, you could talk me into almost anything. I might even walk barefoot through the snow out there if you asked right, but let's get one thing

149

straight from the jump." Here he dipped low so his lips brushed her cheek. He whispered, "In the kitchen, I am, and always will be, the one and only chef."

To his ecstatic gratification, he felt her pulse quicken as his lips moved to her neck. He could kiss her all night. But he wouldn't let her win too easily after she'd left him desperate on the sofa. He took a small step back and watched her sag, shoulders dropping, disappointed by the space between them.

Her dark eyes narrowed before she regained her cool.

"Is that how it is?" She cracked an egg into the second bowl. "Since you're the professional, I'll defer. For now. So, yes, chef."

What had he gotten himself into? It was his own fault. Her eyebrow rose in challenge. His knees weakened. "What have I done? You know how I love the sound of that on your lips."

She scooted closer. "I know all too well. And now you get to hear me say it the entire time we work. Don't forget, I'm a novice baker. Making this recipe is going to take a while, and I need to concentrate. Which means you can't distract me no matter what I say."

CHAPTER TWENTY-FOUR

Tormenting Lawrence was Elena's new favorite game. The perfect balm after a wretched day at work. Too bad she was also in agony thanks to the distance between them as they worked.

Lawrence baking made for quite the eye-popping performance. They'd prepared two batches of the cookies, Lawrence making adjustments like a chemist as they went. Physical pain set in as he hand-mixed the dough with a wooden spoon, his awe-inspiring arms flexing. The way he bent over the bowl, the line of his back. That miniscule clench in his jaw she spotted when he concentrated. How a shimmer of sweat formed in the dip of his collarbone. The all-consuming urge to tear that clingy long-sleeve T-shirt right off him.

"You okay, sous-chef?" he asked, flipping over a baked cookie on the pan to inspect the bottom. "You can't be tired after all that coffee."

Her throat went dry. "Tired is the last thing I am, chef."

"Say it again."

The more she said it, the more she liked how the word felt in her mouth, the more she pictured saying it in . . . other circumstances.

She began to wonder which one of them truly suffered when she said it. A chance to relinquish control, to not be the boss she always had to be. Let someone else plan, drive, decide. "It's hot in here, right? I'm going to open this window."

"If you think it will help."

She kept her eyes on the window as she cranked it open, not daring to look at him as he leaned a hip against the counter. "Yikes, it's sleeting out there." Her mind finally gave her a break from the Lawrence channel. Concern took its place. "I wouldn't have asked you to drive all this way if I knew the weather would turn."

"It can't be that bad, can it?" He joined her at the window. Globs of snow pelted the screen. The air smelled wet. On the street below, the snow had accumulated, looked to be inches high already. A car going about twelve miles an hour crept down the street, then skidded when the driver attempted to stop at the light. Elena seized Lawrence's arm as the car fishtailed, her knuckles white. "Sheesh. Okay. He's okay," he said. "If it's like this here, the country roads are going to be a disaster."

"Won't they plow?" she asked, still holding his arm as if he meant to drive off in that old truck as they spoke.

"You sweet city child. They might get around to it in a few days."

"How long is it supposed to last?"

He fished his phone out of his back pocket. On the weather app they saw a ninety percent chance of snow through the night and into the morning hours, looked into each other's eyes, silently wondering what to do. He tapped on a news app next, tipped the phone toward her so they could both read the headline about unsafe driving conditions. The highway was already backed up with multiple accidents.

"You can't leave in this. It's not safe."

"Don't worry. I'll be okay."

She detected uncertainty as he said it, his eyes flying back to the window. No more playing around; she had to convince him. Not a worrier at heart, she was surprised she couldn't shake the fear he'd end up spinning off the road and getting injured. She turned him toward her, held both of his arms while she looked up at him. "Please?"

His eyes flicked to the microwave clock. "I can't leave Sugar all night."

Elena let go of him and wrung her hands uselessly by her side. Poor Sugar. Any dog would go crazy alone for so many hours. Lawrence went to the sliding glass door to her balcony and pulled back the drapes. It was even worse without the streetlights. A total whiteout. He wouldn't be able to see two feet in front of him out there.

"Um." He tapped on his phone screen again. "Let me see if Trey can walk down and get her. He's a couple houses from me."

The grip on her stomach loosened. Lawrence sent the text. If he got in an accident, she'd never forgive herself for letting him leave.

They stood in silence, waiting for a response from his friend. The beep of the timer blared, jolting her. She pulled the cookies from the oven, set the sheet on the stovetop to cool. At the phone's chime, she spun back to face Lawrence.

"He says it started coming down there a few minutes ago. He'll go right now."

She held her hands to her chest. "That's a relief. You can stay. At least until we see if things improve."

The phone chimed again.

"He says . . . wait. Never mind." Lawrence's face reddened. Elena averted her glance to spare him the embarrassment. What *would* they do all night? Her sofa was cute, but it was miserable to sleep on. No support. And Lawrence's legs would hang off the end. As would hers, for that matter.

"I'll be right back," she said, and hurried to her room. She stuffed discarded clothes into the hamper in her closet, straightened out the pillows on her queen bed. In an effort to keep herself honest, she hadn't tidied up the room, incentive to keep him out of it. She spritzed sandalwood pillow mist on the duvet.

In the adjoining bathroom she changed out the hand towel, then dug in the medicine cabinet for a spare toothbrush. She found a hot-pink one printed with her dentist's address. Lawrence didn't seem like the toxically masculine type, and he didn't have much choice.

Thinking of teeth, she brushed her own, gargled with the mouthwash that kept her breath sweet through the morning. In case they woke up with their heads close together. Yes, that was why she freshened up. From a tray on the vanity, she took a perfume roller, glided the ball over the skin at her throat. Surely it would be okay to leave on light makeup for one night. She didn't want to scare him into the storm if it was still snowing in the morning.

Back in her room, she heard a tap on the partially closed door. "Come in."

Why did she sound like a chirping bird? You'd think a man had never crossed the threshold.

Lawrence poked in his head. "Everything all right? I'd rather die—literally—than stay here if it makes you uncomfortable."

She sat on the edge of the bed with a graceless plop. "Don't be silly."

"Sugar's safe." He held up the phone to show her a picture of the downy pooch licking his best friend's face. "I can chill on the sofa, if you—"

"No, no. This is fine." Did he want to leave? Maybe he was trying to let her down easy? Her own face felt as hot as his had looked a few minutes ago. *Be nonchalant. Stop acting like this is freshman year and you have five minutes before your roommate returns.*

She made herself lie back against the pillows propped against the upholstered headboard, another estate sale find. In the past, she'd prided herself on the boudoir vibe she had going; now she wondered if the plush bedcover and tasseled pillows came across as stuffy. The half-burnt-down incense on her dresser, a dusting of ash beside it. Fairy lights above the bed.

"Do you mind if I sit?" Lawrence asked, still hovering in the doorway.

"Of course not." There was that poised, polished voice she relied on. Then she patted the empty space beside her with a too-enthusiastic thwack.

Lawrence stretched out beside her, an inch or two between them. It was getting late and she had to work in the morning. Sleep. Yes. They would sleep, and everything would be less awkward when they woke up. She clicked off the bedside lamp, leaving only the fairy lights.

"Sorry, are you ready to sleep?" she asked, eyes on the wood-beaded chandelier. "We turned off the oven, right?"

"Sure. And, uh, yes. I turned it off."

"Do you need a glass of water or anything?"

"I do not. Thank you."

The antique gold clock on her nightstand ticked in the silence. Her heart beat in her ears. She sensed there would be no going back after tonight, no more pretense that she wasn't getting invested in him. Body and heart.

"My grandma said situations are only as uncomfortable as we make them," Lawrence finally said.

She chuckled. "Your grandma sounds like a smart lady."

"She is." The bed frame creaked and the mattress jiggled as he rolled to his side. He brushed an escaped strand of hair off her forehead, tucked it behind her ear. "Except now we're in bed together talking about my nana, which is not the mood I was going for."

She laughed; he touched the tip of her nose. In the low light the blue of his eyes looked deeper, less like water, more like late-evening sky.

"You told me the other day you didn't want to rush things. Personally, I think it would be impossible for us to rush anything, because I feel like I've been waiting for you a long time. Long before we met." He kissed her, slowly, in a way that made her realize she didn't need to worry. His kiss proved him more confident than he gave himself credit for. "But I also made that big speech about being respectful. So, I'm in a bind here. How far is too far?"

"We should go ninety percent, like the chance of continued snow," she said, almost tripping over the words in her haste. "If you're comfortable with that."

"I mean, I could go to one hundred percent if you wanted."

"One hundred percent, then."

He slid a hand over her stomach, up her rib cage. Her breath stopped, then so did his hand. He groaned, exasperation clouding his handsome features. "Only problem is, I didn't trust myself to have self-control earlier, so . . . um . . . I didn't bring anything with . . ."

She balled up her fist and hit the empty space next to her, shot a glance at her nightstand. "I have this thing about trying to balance the reproductive health burden placed on women by never purchasing condoms myself. I'm regretting my high ideals."

She covered her face with her hand to hide her growing mortification. *Situations are only as uncomfortable as we make them.*

Finger by finger, he pried her hand away. Another kiss, the tempting pressure of his lips, the taste of him increasing her remorse. He moved on top of her, balanced on his forearms as she reveled in the weight of his body. "We're agreed on ninety percent, then?"

She hooked her leg around his. "Absolutely, chef."

It was all over from there. Well, ninety percent over.

CHAPTER TWENTY-FIVE

Elena had a talent for making ninety percent feel like one hundred and ten percent. She slept with her head rested on his chest, arms and legs tangled with his. Morning light, veiled by sheer curtains, showed off the contours of Elena's body. Accustomed to waking early for the bakery, he didn't think he could fall back to sleep at this point. It was fine by him if they lay here all day, because the longer they did, the longer he could suspend time, pretend the outside world didn't exist. Who cared about rent or competitors when Elena's breath tickled his skin, when she let him hold her all night? The cold outside might as well be a thousand miles away, this place their hot, hidden refuge.

He lifted his free arm, turned it until he found the red marks where her nails had pressed. He smiled, the memory of her touch electric. She stirred, sighing, and he craved another kiss, a fresh chance to touch her, to watch her eyelids flutter and her lips part. His hand dove under the sheet to touch her.

Then he stopped himself an inch away.

What if, instead, he did something for her, to show her how much he . . . what, cared for her? Could take care of her?

He couldn't identify why he hesitated. A half-buried suspicion it would be hard to leave this bed not just now, but ever, added to his sudden confusion. Then a reluctance to admit that as much as he enjoyed her body, he also enjoyed her concern, how she'd worried about his safety in the blizzard. Hinted he mattered to her on a deeper level.

He shut his eyes to quiet his mind.

A plan formed, but what would she make of it? What if she thought he was overstepping, or got annoyed, or felt differently than she had in last night's dizzy passion? On the other hand, what if he ignored those persistent uncertainties and did what he wanted? What he hoped was right?

Moving as gently as possible, he unwound their bodies. Elena mumbled his name; he kissed her cheek to reassure her. "I'll be back, darling," he promised quietly. "You rest."

She pulled the sheet around herself, nestled into her pillow as he stood. He located his jeans on the floor, next to her red sweatpants. Pulled them on, the belt buckle rattling.

He slipped through the bathroom door and found an unopened toothbrush. Brushed his teeth and washed his face, hoped he didn't look too scruffy with his stubble. Walking back through the bedroom, he saw one of her long legs escape the sheet as she rolled to her side. All the sensations from the night before returned at once, sent his blood racing, warmed his cheeks. Getting back in bed would be the easy way to show her affection, but he was determined to level up and show her in other ways too.

In the kitchen, he took stock of her refrigerator's and cabinets' contents. Ramen, a half-eaten bag of granola, baby carrots. Not an egg in sight, and they'd used all his last night. The cookies still sat on the baking pans. He clicked one against the aluminum. Yep, it could substitute for a hockey puck. Back at the cabinets he found a major chocolate stash but nothing else valuable. Maybe he should take her grocery shopping.

Behind an oak milk—ew—carton, he found a few vanilla yogurts. Unexpired by one day. Promising. He thought the freezer might be even worse until he uncovered frozen mixed berries under several sad microwave entrees.

This task would require all his culinary creativity. From these ashes would rise a respectable breakfast.

Start with coffee. She loves coffee.

He shook grounds into the filter—she had plenty—and pressed the brew button. While he pondered the food situation, he texted Carm to tell her Sweet L's would be closed today. Most of Main Street would do the same, he'd bet.

Although Elena's ingredients left much to be desired, she had decent cookware. He cleared off the cookies, washed the tray, then spread it with granola. He mixed some of the pasty-smelling oat milk with the ground cinnamon he'd brought, poured it over the granola. Once that was toasting in the oven, he heated the frozen berries in a pot, used some of his leftover flour to thicken the juices. Of course Elena didn't have cornstarch, but the flour would do.

From the bedroom he heard an alarm's strident beeps. Elena groaned, knocked something off her nightstand that landed with a crack, and then swore with remarkable creativity. He took two footed bowls from the drying rack, put down a layer of berry compote, then a layer of yogurt, alternating the two until the bowls were full.

Another alarm, another shocking expletive that made him laugh under his breath. The sound of feet retreating to the bathroom.

He grabbed the granola from the oven, sprinkled it on the parfaits.

"Why does it smell heavenly in here?" Elena asked, coming into the room. She wore a dark-green satin robe that stole his ability to respond. "And you made coffee! Oh, I hope it snows all day so I can keep you."

"You don't mind I made myself at home in your kitchen?"

Elena narrowed her eyes. "You didn't look in the cabinet above the stove, did you?"

"Sorry? Um, no, I don't think so." This had been a bad idea; he should've asked first. He knew this would happen.

"Whew. What a relief. I wouldn't want to lose your good opinion."

"Huh?"

"People—well, not people, but men—get disturbed by what's in there."

She held a serious expression long enough his nerves started jumping, and then she smiled. He swung open the cabinet door. Two cracker boxes, a bag of chips, and some paper plates.

"I had you going, didn't I?" she asked, rocking back and forth from her heels to the balls of her feet.

"Man, you start early with your shenanigans."

"You make it so appealing when you stare at me with those startled eyes." Unblinking, she widened her own in imitation.

He took hold of her robe tie and yanked her to him, kissed her to stop her giggling. "You play nice."

"Or what?"

"I won't share my parfaits."

"Fine, then I'll be good." She ran her hands over his shoulders and down his chest. Not putting on a shirt had seemed like the right idea; now, as she looked him over, he wondered what flaws she found. Without comment, she walked away, taking her parfait to a table with the sides folded down to make it fit in the small space. She ate a bite, took a spiral notebook from a stack on the floor. "Sit down. And bring the coffee, please."

At the table he sat straight, then made himself lean back in the chair while holding his abs tight, hyperaware of his body. His appearance had always helped his confidence, but being vulnerable enough to let beautiful Elena stare at him unfiltered had him repositioning himself, hoping she'd still like what she saw.

She shook a pencil jar, searched until she found the one she required. "There's oat milk for the coffee if you want some."

"I'd rather add dish soap."

"A discerning gentleman." She turned the book to a fresh page, tipped it toward her so he couldn't see. The pencil scratched. She studied the page, then looked back at him. "The parfait is delectable. Thank you."

He nodded, but her attention was back on the notebook. She dropped the pencil on the table, rooted through the cup for another. He sipped his coffee self-consciously, aware of every movement he made. This morning light was pretty harsh. He shifted, knocked his elbow on the wall.

Not looking up, she said, "Are you okay?"

"Yeah." He wanted to ask her what she was doing but didn't want to interrupt. Her forehead crinkled, she tipped her head this way and that. Concentration like the kind he needed when baking.

"You're hard to draw," she said.

"Really? Sorry."

"It's a compliment." She used her forefinger to blend the lead, unbothered by the stain it left on her. Finger dancing and dragging. "Very symmetrical, classically attractive people can be harder because they come out looking too perfect. It's more challenging to capture their essence because they lack the irregularities that make depicting character easier."

"Well, thank you. I'm sure I have plenty of . . . irregularities."

"No. You look like someone a Renaissance master would paint." Her pencil raced over the paper, quick as his heart.

"I don't know about that."

"Defined musculature, beautiful bones. A face close to the golden ratio."

"Does that mean you can't do a self-portrait? You're perfect."

"Nah. My eyes are too big, one eyebrow is a fraction higher than the other." She used the pencil tip to point out this small abnormality. "My cheeks are on the full side. I could go on."

All those traits made her flawless in his opinion.

She tapped her pencil on the table, regarded him. "I know the secret to make this sketch look like you. It's in the eyes. They don't have the haughtiness you'd expect to find in someone so attractive. They're sympathetic."

After a few more strokes, she turned the notebook around and there he was, looking more like himself than in any photo he'd ever seen. Leaning in the chair, strong, definitely a flattering angle but with his eyes a little downcast, looking to the side. Awe expanded in his chest with his inhalation. How could she already see to the core of him? Not only see it but replicate it.

"Elena, you are beyond talented. This is incredible."

"No." She set the notebook down, took his hand. "*You* are incredible. I just managed to show you."

And there it was, the reason why he'd wanted to make her breakfast, to feed her and see her happy when she smelled the coffee. Or one of the many reasons. Because she saw him. The real him. Not the towering guy everyone made assumptions about or the shy kid who got teased for baking, but the real him. How those things about him combined and competed inside him.

And because behind the sarcasm and the jokes, the poise and corporate polish, he could see the real her too.

CHAPTER TWENTY-SIX

Elena cleaned up the dishes, which seemed fair, since he'd made breakfast out of nothing. He might be impressed with her drawing, but she was downright amazed at his ability to assemble a satisfying meal from odds and ends.

She set the last dripping dish into the rack, dried her hands on a tea towel, then joined Lawrence on the sofa with a second mug of coffee. "I have the worst Sunday scaries, and it's not even a Sunday. Usually, every Sunday night I have to paint until I pass out to cope with the Monday morning stress at Sparkle."

Lawrence put an arm around her, and she settled against him. "And here I thought cookies made people happy."

"They used to make me happy. Yours still do. I know you're going to win the magazine contest."

"I think *we're* going to win." He rubbed her thigh. "You had the latte idea."

"It's nice of you to give me partial credit. That's something Derick would never do."

"He sounds . . . horrible."

"Oh, he is." She checked the time on her phone. "And I have to be ready to see him in less than thirty minutes. Looking forward to surviving his regular difficult behavior plus the fallout from confronting him, and my own fury that he's tearing me away from you."

"First he treats you badly, and now he's going to steal you away? I don't like him much either. Are you gonna be okay out there? The snow stopped, but when I checked outside, it doesn't look like the plows could keep up. Any chance you could work remotely?"

A tempting prospect. A whole day with Lawrence. Not that the Sparkle culture encouraged work from home—they'd hate for someone not to be fully miserable—but guidelines allowed for it. "Let me check my email. See if any of the team is skipping out today. I'm sure Derick is immune to cold and is already at work, dreaming up new abuses."

Priya lived two blocks from HQ and would be going in, Elena guessed. It would be hard to argue she couldn't make it if her coworkers did. A shock of surprise went through her when she saw an email from Derick with the subject line *Snow Day*.

"Ahhh! Listen to this." She gripped Lawrence's hand. "It says, *Team, due to unsafe conditions, legal advises we work from home. Email hourly with updates. Be advised I will have intermittent access to my email, as I will be assisting my mother during her power outage.* Can you believe it?"

"He should keep his team safe."

"No, I mean the part about him having a human mother! I would've sworn he spontaneously generated. Grew like a fungus. In all the years I've worked there, I never thought he had a mom he cares about. This is the first tangible evidence of humanity I've seen from him."

A minute later Priya texted in all caps: HE'S A MAMA'S BOY?!?!

Do you think he'll lend her his blazer to keep warm?! Elena answered. Or does he own regular clothes?! Does he wear . . . FESTIVE SWEATERS?

Lawrence cleared his throat. "I should be heading out soon."

Elena's shoulders fell; she dropped her phone. A day spent working and kissing, kissing and working, disappeared as Lawrence stood. She'd gotten ahead of herself, assuming he wanted to stay here. They'd already been together for twelve hours. "Oh, sure. You have to open the bakery."

"Nah. We'll stay closed today. Folks will understand." He took her chin in his hand. "What's with the lip?"

"What about it?"

"It's sticking out."

She sucked in her bottom lip. For an instant she was back on that cold street the night they met. The prickly poise came back to protect her. "I wouldn't want to keep you."

He scrutinized her face, and she tried to make her features impassive. "Hey, if you don't mind if I stay, I'd be happier here."

"Really?" she asked, her turncoat voice hopeful.

"Spend the day with a beautiful woman or brave frozen streets to go sit home alone? Tough choice."

"Won't you have to get Sugar?"

"Sugar likes Trey better than me. I can't stand to disappoint her and bring her home already."

A swoop of anxiety. Fear like standing at a cliff's edge. Being up front was harder to do in reality than when she journaled about it. She tolerated being transparent in a business setting, but expressing her personal desires made her nervous. "Then stay."

He sat back down, and she crawled onto his lap. He held her hips, and she felt his warmth where their skin met. Despite his innate reserve, his expressive eyes held hers, unwilling to look away. She loved the sensation of his hand in her hair, then his lips against hers.

He pulled on the robe tie.

Her phone rang. Derick's cell.

"Get on the chat channel." In true Derick form, he hung up without further ado. She should give her resignation effective immediately.

"I have to start work," she told Lawrence, peeling her body away. She booted up her laptop, and he asked for the Wi-Fi password so he could place stock orders and check customer emails.

Although Derick ruined the mood, she couldn't deny the rush Lawrence gave her, even when they weren't touching. She loved the contrast between his quiet reserve and his physical confidence. The simple pleasure of looking over at him while he scrolled his phone. His comforting presence. He reached out to stroke her leg, and her heart asked, *Why can't every morning be like this?*

It was too soon to wish forever and always. It was best to live in the moment, relish him as long as she could.

He used a notebook on her coffee table to write out the recipe for the gingerbread latte cookies, writing as quickly as she drew. Another artist at work.

"Lawrence, can I tell you something?" she asked after they'd been working side by side for over an hour, falling into an easy rhythm. He'd even refilled her coffee at some point. If she was going to be honest with him about her work situation, this was the time to do it. The pit in her stomach said otherwise.

"Sure thing, sweetie."

"Derick gave me an enormous goal. I have to post a phenomenal opening or he's going to rake me over the coals. He promised me a bonus if I do well, which means he's expecting a stellar performance. I'm not in a position to quit. As much as that place kills my soul, I still prefer it to admitting defeat to work for my dad.

"I'm in an awful spot, because I don't want to do anything to hurt Sweet L's, but my job is on the line. Do you think you could tell some of your New Hope friends that we're not pure evil, that it's all right to go to the grand opening? I'd be happy to give you any marketing advice you might need or want in exchange." She caught her breath. Caffeine buzzed in her veins, made her extra edgy as she waited for his reaction.

He didn't answer her as he got up from his seat to pace around the room. Probably looking for a way out. Her words hung in the air; she wanted to grab them and stuff them back in her mouth. To complicate matters, he still wasn't wearing a shirt. Gaping at him made it that much harder to remain collected.

"You want me to endorse the competition?"

"Forget I asked. I wanted to be up front with you. About what my job expects. About what I have to do." For better or worse, she didn't regret telling him the truth. Now. Before things went further.

"And you don't think Sparkle will tank Sweet L's?"

"I think we can come up with a way for Sweet L's to have a strong quarter as well. And your product is superior. That always helps."

"Aha! I knew I'd break you down, convince you my cookies are better."

"Plus there's the contest. That would be a nice cash infusion for your place." She piled on the positives, the way her dad had taught her to do in a negotiation. Was Lawrence actually willing to help? "It's not without risk, I want you to know that."

Dad would've said to never mention the negatives. She couldn't live with herself if she followed that advice.

Lawrence looked up, as if the ceiling might have the answer written across it.

Her shoulders tensed.

"This can't be an all-the-time thing, you understand that? I can tell people to give Sparkle a try, but I'm not going to be able to support them long-term."

"I understand. I wouldn't want you to." She opened her résumé file, showed him the laptop screen. "I have a plan to change jobs, but I need to go into interviews with a strong performance history. This is temporary."

He turned his back to her.

"Lawrence, I'm sorry. Please look at me."

"I can't." He heaved a sigh. "Not in that flimsy robe. I have to be able to think clearly. If I look at you, I'm going to give you the keys to Sweet L's."

She held her breath.

"I'll do it."

She leapt up, bounded to him. Then she threw her arms around him, and he took her into his. Her heart thundered; he must be able to feel it. "This is the kindest thing anyone has ever done for me."

"You deserve all the kindness in the world, Elena. I'm happy to give you whatever I can." He lifted her up, she wrapped her legs around him. He carried her toward the bedroom. Derick's hourly update could wait. The entire world could.

CHAPTER TWENTY-SEVEN

Lawrence stood at the front counter, switching a mostly empty tray of brownie cookies for a full tray of protein peanut butter cookies, fanned in two rows. Next, he checked the minifridge behind the counter, counted the eight-ounce milk cartons to be sure he had enough. In twenty minutes, chaos would strike when the after-school rush came crashing through the door. Snowy boots, hyper voices. Lines of wiggly children craving sugar, sleepy caregivers desperate for an afternoon coffee to sustain them to dinnertime.

Moms loved that Lawrence took it easy on the sugar for these cookies and added vanilla whey powder for extra protein. Kids thought they were getting a treat, and parents appreciated the healthy adjacent snack. Everyone would be in and out in about fifteen minutes, then Lawrence and Carm would spend another fifteen sweeping crumbs and wiping up milk spatters.

"Batten the hatches, Carm. T minus twenty," he called into the kitchen. Carm dashed out, clacking her serving tongs in anticipation. Sugar whined, ready for the influx of cuddles and dropped peanut butter cookie chunks.

The jingle bells on the door chimed, and Trey walked in. "You better not buy me out of house and home before the kids get here," Lawrence warned.

"I'm here to get my cookie before those little fiends come chomping through."

Carm wrapped a cookie with perfect crisp edges and a soft center in wax paper. The register beeped as Lawrence rang up the cookie with his best-friend discount. Trey opened the lid of his travel mug so Lawrence could refill it with half regular, half decaf. "I didn't think you were ever coming back from the city," Trey said, giving Lawrence a significant look.

"Believe me, I didn't want to. She is something else." Lawrence leapt at every chance he got to talk about Elena. Every family member from his sister to Nana had listened to an unusually loquacious Lawrence rhapsodizing about the new woman in his life. Even his poor quiet dad—who usually had about a four-word conversation with his son once per week—had to hear Lawrence go on and on.

Talking about Elena was almost as good as being with Elena. Thinking about her rounded out the trifecta. Reading the Sparkle e-newsletter—a publication he should have scorned on principal—was an opportunity to contemplate Elena. No such thing as too much Elena, and he would take her any way he could get her.

"Not this again," Carm said, shaking her head.

"That bad, huh?" Trey asked, holding his cookie over the wax paper as he took his first bite.

"Don't worry about crumbs, man. You know what's about to happen here," Lawrence said, looking over his shoulder to confirm the push broom was within arm's reach.

"I had to yell at him to get off his phone this morning, can you believe that, Trey?" Carm said. "Me, the employee. He was too busy texting Elena to rotate the cookies—burnt two pans full. It still smells like charred cookies back there."

"What are you smiling for, bro?" Trey asked. "Since when do you burn cookies? What happened to our Lawrence?"

"Look at him; he's turning red." Carm patted Lawrence on the back. "Oh mijo. I hope she deserves you."

"It's me who should worry about being worthy," Lawrence said.

"Nah, don't say that. She's a lucky girl," Trey said. He balled the wax paper, made a perfect shot to land it in the trash can. Lawrence cheered, but Trey didn't play along. "Never thought I'd live to see the day you'd be slacking off at work."

"Hey, I'm only human." Lawrence gave a casual shrug, or what he hoped was casual. He hadn't texted Elena in over an hour, although he kept his phone in his pocket, dying for an alert. Under normal circumstances, he never brought his phone into the front of the house. Customer service standards were slipping, and he didn't care.

"And what's the deal with her job? You were pretty worried about that. Getting into a public fight and whatnot."

"We've got that all worked out." Lawrence's face hurt from smiling.

"Don't get me started on this one," Carm said, shaking her head again. She took off her glasses, polished the lens on her shirt. "I already gave you my opinion on this little scheme you two have cooked up."

"What scheme?" Trey asked.

"Elena convinced—" Carm began.

"No, we decided," Lawrence interrupted, "since she needs stellar grand-opening sales to keep her job, that I should try to help. Put out the word that people should give Sparkle a try. By the way, do me a favor: take Iris to the grand opening. And your parents. Tell Iris to bring her sister."

Trey snapped his fingers in front of Lawrence's face. "Hello? What? Have you lost your whole mind?"

"It's one day of sales," Lawrence argued. "And she's been helping me with a side project."

"I bet she has." Trey's eyes narrowed in suspicion.

"What is going to happen when she needs more support that only you can give, at the expense of this place?" Carm asked, tapping her foot, looking ready to shake a finger at him like he was a naughty child.

"It's not going to happen. We have an agreement."

"You trust her that much, huh?" Trey asked, crossing his arms over his chest.

"She hasn't done anything to make me not trust her."

"Mijo, you don't know her well enough." Carm threw up her hands.

"Yeah, dude. She needs to understand this place comes first, at least for now. Until you guys have been together longer."

"Her grand opening is an urgent situation." Lawrence couldn't stomach arguments; they required him to think of fast responses, stand his ground, contradict people he cared for. Nine times out of ten, he chose to avoid conflict, stuff his feelings. Heat flushed over his skin; his teeth clenched. For once, he didn't want to put the bakery first, not at the expense of Elena; he didn't want to spend another Christmas alone. Even with his family around him, he felt the lack of a person just for him. It was easy for Trey to be cautious—he had Iris to kiss him on New Year's Eve. Last year Lawrence had stood in the pub, timing a swig of his beer with midnight to avoid watching all his friends make out.

"This damsel-in-distress thing—"

"That's not what it is," Lawrence growled. Trey snapped his mouth shut, his eyes widened.

"Take it easy," Trey said, palms out toward Lawrence. "I get it. You're sure about this."

"I am." He rocked on his heels, debated storming off to the kitchen.

Trey and Carm shared a look Lawrence pretended not to see. Carm put a hand on his arm. "As long as you're sure, that's all we need to know. Okay, boss?"

"Absolutely, dude." Trey held out his fist for Lawrence to bump. "We cool?"

"Yeah," Lawrence said, tapping his friend's knuckles with his own, already regretting snapping at his friend.

"When do I get to meet her?" Trey asked.

Lawrence huffed out a long breath. "She's coming by tonight."

"Why don't you bring her by the pub for a drink after dinner? Iris and I can meet up, get to know her. She sounds very special."

"She is." Lawrence nodded, thinking of Elena's dark eyes, how they looked up at him through her long lashes. Trey told him to text when they were headed over, and he left as a stream of children dragging overstuffed backpacks and parents holding bundled babies began pouring in.

Lawrence did his utmost to concentrate on the chattering children, loud as a flock of geese as they hemmed and hawed over their orders. He and Carm danced around each other, wrapping cookies, taking payments, filling paper cups with coffee. Smiling at the kids, commiserating with the tired parents. Carm asking how much longer until winter break dozens of times, the keyed-up kids hopping around as if it were already the last day of school.

"I swear that school is cloning children," Carm said, wiping her brow on her apron when the rush ended. Sugar lay on her back, all four legs in the air, too overwhelmed to right herself after the parade of tummy rubs. "There had to be at least thirty more than yesterday. And those middle schoolers can eat! Why don't you let me take care of this mess, though? I'm sure you have stuff to do in the back."

Lawrence shouldered through the swinging door with a stack of empty trays in hand, grateful Carm had given him a reason to be alone. He replayed the interaction with Carm and his best friend over and over in his head. Plunging a dishrag into a bucket of sanitizer, he began scrubbing the workbench with all his strength.

When was the last time he and Trey had a disagreement? High school? There had been some beef in junior year after they both got in major trouble for hosting a party in Lawrence's parents' home while they were out of town. Neither wanted to take responsibility, and they were mad at each other for several days. Then they forgot about it and hadn't had an argument since.

The whole world felt off-kilter. Kitchen lights too bright, industrial dishwasher too loud, the accompanying detergent-scented steam unbearably hot. Good thing Trey had backed off, because Lawrence felt he'd been on the verge of a shouting match. Feelings that intense left him frazzled, anxious about the near future. Maybe Trey would still be mad at him later tonight, maybe Lawrence would still be mad at Trey; maybe things would never be right again.

He went into the office, sat, then laid his head on the desk. Outside, Main Street remained busy with after-school traffic. He struggled to slow his breath. Nothing felt right, his body and mind in turmoil, a headache trying to get a foothold in his temples.

CHAPTER TWENTY-EIGHT

Elena detected tension between Lawrence and his friend Trey as they sat together with Trey's fiancée at a high-top table. Trey seemed to be doing his best to draw Lawrence out, and Lawrence acted stiff, uncertain. Trey's bubbly fiancée, Iris, kept Elena entertained with stories of growing up in New Hope while the guys' conversation started and stopped multiple times.

Under the table, Lawrence held her hand as if he were afraid to let go.

"I'm going to run to the bathroom. How about you, Elena?" Iris asked, doing the greatest act of kindness known in the girl world. No decent woman would leave a newcomer alone with two best friends, one of whom the newcomer had just begun dating. Especially not in this mysterious, awkward situation. Elena got up to follow, kissed Lawrence on the cheek to comfort him before she left the table.

"Is everything okay with them?" Elena asked as they moved through the modest crowd. The bar had that lived-in atmosphere Elena expected from an independent place in the middle of nowhere.

Slightly sticky wood floors, peanuts in red plastic baskets, most of the light coming from neon beer signs and haphazardly hung holiday lights. Locals everywhere in jeans and sweaters, relaxing after a long day. A pool table and a dart board. Next to the games lay a small dance floor where couples swayed in each other's arms.

"You didn't hear this from me," Iris said as they stepped into the ladies' room. They stood side by side, fixing their hair in a cracked mirror above hard-water-stained sinks. "They had a little dustup this afternoon."

"Uh-oh. Why?" Immediate concern gripped Elena. What did this fight tell her about Lawrence? She pressed for more information. "Do they fight often?"

Another woman burst in, tears running in mascara-blackened streaks down her face. "Not now, McKenzie. Go tell Rudy you're sorry," Iris commanded the interloper. The woman nodded, tore a paper towel off the roll, and blotted her face before leaving. "McKenzie and Rudy have been fighting with each other every night for four years. I don't have the patience for it."

Elena didn't want a relationship like that, especially not after she'd seen what Priya had gone through with her ex. Too many fights—with anyone—were a red flag.

"Do Lawrence and Trey fight a lot?" she asked again, worry knotting in her stomach.

"Ha-ha, no way. I've known them both since second grade, and they've only had one fight before." Iris took lip gloss with orange undertones from her bag and began to reapply.

"Then what could've happened?" Elena asked, more curious than before about the reason. Iris started at Elena in the mirror. Elena pointed at her own chest. "Me?"

"I'm only telling you this so that you understand how into you Lawrence is. He got all heated insisting he wanted to support your grand opening. Trey was worried about him because none of us know you. This is his livelihood, you know. Lawrence came to your defense in a big way. Or in a big way for him, at least. He's typically chill to a fault."

Embarrassment that her request had made Lawrence argue with his friend clashed with excitement at Lawrence's faith in her. Elena chewed the inside of her cheek, unsure what to say, heartbeat skipping. Iris patted her shoulder.

"I'm not trying to freak you out or make you feel bad. Those two will be fine. I do want to give you a heads-up, though. If you're not super interested in him, you might want to pump the brakes. I've never seen him like this over a woman."

Pure delight surged in Elena's racing heart. She hadn't been able to stop thinking about Lawrence since he stayed the night. Time had changed for her. Now hours spent with Lawrence went quicker than any others; work hours dragged worse than before. Tonight she'd driven as fast as she dared, resenting every mile that separated them. When he held her in his arms, it had felt like catching her breath after being stuck underwater.

"You look scared," Iris said, twisting the cap back on the gloss.

"Do I? I guess I never had anyone this interested in me."

"And you don't feel the same?"

Elena closed her eyes. "I do. That's why I look scared. I wasn't expecting this right now. Or ever. I didn't think it really happened. I certainly didn't know if he would feel the same."

"Not trying to get in your business—we just met—but you seem nice, genuine. Take it slow, let it build on itself. Be careful."

Elena held the door open for Iris. "How long have you and Trey been engaged?'

"He'll say since April when he proposed, but I say since we were seven when I told him we were getting married."

"That is a long time," Elena said with a laugh.

Back in the main room, a country singer crooned from the sound system about a fast car and an escape plan. The melody strummed inside her. She wanted to run headlong to Lawrence.

"Look at those two fools," Iris said, nudging Elena. Trey and Lawrence were taking turns trying to sink unshelled peanuts in each other's open mouth. "I told you they'd work it out."

Elena loved to see Lawrence laughing with his friend, rocking back on the barstool to catch a peanut. Their fists pumped the air in unison when he managed to get it. Open beer bottles rattled as they banged the tabletop next. Fluttery excitement made Elena move to the music when she got back to him. He slung his arm around her. "Like this song, honey?"

"I do," she said, gazing at him, at the angles of his handsome face. The hair she loved to twist her fingers into.

"It's a good one."

A peanut hit him square in the face. He blinked in surprise.

"Ask her to dance, dummy," Trey said. Iris giggled, took Trey's proffered hand. They walked toward the other couples. Trey looked back at Elena and Lawrence. "Coming or not?"

"What do you say?" Lawrence asked, eyeing Elena. "Will you dance with me? I'm not the worst at it."

"I'd dance with you even if you were the worst."

On the dance floor, he put his arm around her waist, pulled her against him in one fluid motion. His right hand pressed into the small of her back; his left held hers against his chest. A beat later she put her other hand on his shoulder, against the washed-soft flannel of his shirt. Even though he'd told her he could dance, she didn't expect the natural way he fell into the rhythm. How easily he led her along, laid his cheek against her temple.

The music was at its loudest here, next to the speakers. The song thumped into her, filled her ears. Lights above shone red and green. The guitar twanged, Lawrence spun her, her feet left the ground as he swept her up. His strength still astonished her, the way he lifted her, his arms not even trembling. How he felt like a safe place to be. The only place to be.

He dipped her, kissed her. A couple of people clapped, shouted his name. His friends, a whole place full of people who knew him, wanted the best for him. What a man to warrant so much goodwill. To have friends who fought to protect him.

She hooked her arms around his neck, drew his face closer so he could hear her. "You know you mean more to me than any grand opening, right?"

"Don't you worry about that, baby," he whispered back. She couldn't resist kissing him again, couldn't believe her luck to be with him here. The song ended, and they danced into the next one without missing a step. "I'm not worried."

She couldn't take her eyes from his, wanted to look into them forever. The world outside held disappointments, uncertainties, misunderstandings, but nothing could touch her in a moment like this. Because Lawrence's eyes reflected all the desire and acceptance she felt for him right back to her. Better than a mirror, he saw a deeper, worthier version of herself than she could recognize on her own.

"Let me take you home," he said.

She didn't have to speak for him to know what she wanted more than anything. He waved goodbye to Trey, she hugged Iris. Then they were outside in the slicing cold, running hand in hand to his truck, heedless of ice. They parted long enough to climb into the cab; a second later she was on his lap. The steering wheel dug into her back as he kissed her insistently. A wordless promise. Nothing else on earth tasted like him, felt as good.

His hand bunched her hair, then he tenderly tipped her head back to deepen their kiss. He swore, his voice thick when they broke apart so he could turn the key in the ignition. "Elena, I've been dying for this."

She slid off his lap, feeling like something had been stolen from her, and buckled her seat belt. A foot's distance from him was too much. They laced their fingers together, and he kissed her knuckles as he drove to his house. *Let me take you home. Home.* The bar was only three blocks from his house, yet the drive seemed interminable, both of them too breathless and preoccupied to speak.

Soon enough they were stumbling up the stairs to his bedroom, shedding clothes on the climb, almost tripping over their own feet. She laughed when she bumped into him. He lifted her again and carried her the rest of the way. With his elbow he nudged the half-open bedroom door and stepped inside. He laid her on his four-poster bed. On the sheets that smelled like him.

She lost herself to his rhythms, listened to his breath as it grew more urgent, his touch as he sought her satisfaction.

She fell into the mystery and marvel of giving and taking, the bliss of true intimacy in a life that could be lonely. And later, when she landed, almost asleep, on his chest, his arms holding her as close as possible, she felt home indeed.

CHAPTER TWENTY-NINE

There was no better way to start the day, in Lawrence's opinion, than waking up next to Elena. By the time the sun rose on his fifth morning beside her, he wondered how he'd ever faced the daily grind without her. Today he got to keep her, since it was Saturday. Nothing to force them apart. She didn't have to rush back to the city for work, and he hadn't needed to get up extra early to leave her place in time to open the bakery.

The weekends—especially right before the holidays—were hectic at Sweet L's, which meant he still had to go in. But she'd be coming with him to the bakery. Between his usual duties, they planned to practice the cookies for the magazine contest, which was about a week away. Her willingness to commit a Saturday to perfecting the recipe more than repaid him for supporting her upcoming opening. Even Trey had made a point of saying how wrong he'd been about her motives when he heard all she was doing for Sweet L's. In return, Lawrence was telling every New Hope resident who would listen to patronize Sparkle's grand opening on Christmas Eve.

"Hey, sweetie," he said, gently shaking her shoulder. Such a waste to wake his beautiful woman before sunrise to put her to work, but that was the baker's life. She grumbled something incomprehensible, flung her arm over him. Warm and cuddly, she burrowed into him. Her hair smelled of last night's firewood, from the evening they'd passed in his sparse little living room watching movies with the fireplace going. The way she'd danced around the room, insisted on making him hot cocoa, and told him no one ever wanted to watch holiday movies with her kind of broke his heart. Made him want to watch them with her year after year to make up for it.

She snaked one of her long legs around his, smooth and strong. *Focus, focus. You have a lot to do.* He regretted the fact that he had to click on the bedside lamp, felt an almost physical pain when he made himself do it against every instinct. Her face scrunched as she closed her eyes tighter against the light. Fighting every natural instinct in his body, he sat up, swung his legs over the side of the bed. Against her mumbled protests he pulled his navy-blue comforter off her. No one could dare doubt his devotion to making Sweet L's a success. Anyone who saw him now would know he had super strength. After all, she was wearing his faded high school senior T-shirt and nothing else.

"Forget it, let the place go bankrupt," he said, reaching for her. She opened one eye and swatted him away.

"Don't you start with me. We're going to bake." She dragged herself into a sitting position, hair a bit wild.

"Wanna get in the shower with me?" he asked. He took her hand, nibbled her wrist.

"No way, chef. I'm not having everyone in New Hope crying because their precious bakery didn't open on my account."

He groaned, stood up. "Why do you have to be responsible?"

"Why do you have to make me want the best for you?" she asked, and then scampered away before he could catch her. A second later the balled-up T-shirt came flying from the adjoining bathroom. He lurched for the door, but she clicked the lock in the nick of time, laughing as he moaned her name.

"Coffee!" she demanded. He heard the ancient pipes whine and the water splutter.

"Stupid old house with its solid wood doors," he shouted in to her.

"If you can break it open, chef . . ." She didn't finish the sentence, making his imagination pop off. Oh, she was a savage one. He considered the likelihood of a shoulder injury if he threw himself against the door before admitting defeat. Looked like he'd be taking an ice-cold solo shower in a few minutes.

Half an hour later, when they walked into the bakery kitchen, he saw with relief that Carm had preheated the ovens. His fingernails were still blue from that shower. Add to that the bitter predawn cold, and he'd been able to get himself in the right headspace for a busy shift.

"Hi, mija," Carm said to Elena. His assistant had more than warmed up to Elena as they got to know each other. Some days he thought Carm might prefer Elena to him. "Where's my Sugar?"

"Can you believe that baby would not get in the truck this morning? She stood at the back door looking at me like I was crazy. I'm worried I might have spoiled her."

"You think?" Carm asked with a wink. "Do you want some coffee, Elena? It just finished brewing."

"Yes, please," Elena said, following Carm.

"Elena Rachel Voss, you did not drink that pot of coffee I gave you already?" Lawrence said in disbelief. Elena gave him a sheepish grin. "You're worse than Lorelai and Rory put together."

"Guilty as charged," she said, though she didn't seem remorseful that she'd managed to outdrink the two most notorious caffeine addicts in television history. With a wild gleam in her eye, she held up her enormous travel mug for Carm to fill.

"How do you carry that thing around? It must be a gallon of liquid." He winked when Elena flexed her biceps in response. "Cute. Well, since you're so buff, you can start rolling out the sugar cookie dough. I have to make four hundred stars and stockings today."

While Carm got Elena situated at the workbench, Lawrence riffled through a bin filled with cookie cutters and stamps. He located Nana's candy cane stamp and another of a snowflake. In addition to the stars and stockings he would decorate with icing, he wanted to make cookies with embossed designs. He'd use a plain round cutter, chill the dough again, and then press in the intricate designs right before baking. These cookies required expert judgment on baking time—a minute too long and the delicate details would overbrown. It had taken him many holiday seasons to get it right. Sugar used to help him eat the rejects. Yes, perhaps he *had* spoiled her.

A sturdy knock came at the back door. They weren't expecting any deliveries on a Saturday. It better not be a pushy customer who thought they could bully him into picking up their order early. It happened sometimes.

"Nana?" he said, astonished to see her standing in the gray morning light.

"I have it on good authority there is a very special baker in there working on a very special recipe today." Nana held her crocheted purse in both hands, a matching hat pulled low to the top of her glasses. "I intend to get to meet both."

"Carmen Garcia, that chatterbox," Lawrence said, stepping back to let Nana in. Nana went straight to the office, jettisoned her coat, hat, and mittens, then powdered her nose before she let Lawrence lead her to the kitchen.

Elena's unbothered expression indicated she'd been expecting this visit. The three of them conspiring behind his back. "Nana, this is Elena Voss, who doesn't seem surprised at all to meet you."

"I told Carm I didn't want to ambush the poor thing." Carm and Nana gave each other a kiss on the cheeks.

"No one worried about ambushing me," Lawrence muttered.

"You'd have worked yourself into a tizzy if you had advance notice," Nana said, waving him off.

Fair; he'd last introduced a woman to his family over two years ago. He wouldn't have been able to sleep thinking about all the ways Elena and Nana might not hit it off.

Elena rounded the workbench and hugged Nana. "It's lovely to meet you, Mrs. Higgins."

The elegant demeanor he saw less of in Elena these days was out in full force now. Man, she could make a graceful impression when she put her mind to it. He noticed her composure didn't strike him as cold anymore, merely respectful.

"Aren't you the prettiest thing," Nana said, tipping her head back to get a better view of statuesque Elena. "It makes sense. My Lawrence has always been the cutest boy in New Hope."

"Nana, I'm twenty-eight years old, and it's a small town. I don't know that it's much of an accomplishment."

"Excuse me, the cutest man in all of Pennsylvania," Nana said, correcting herself.

"I've been lucky enough to travel, and I might go so far as to say he's the best I've ever seen anywhere," Elena said, somehow making it both better and worse. He would've been right to get himself all worked up about this encounter if he'd known about it. Embarrassment flamed in his face, and an introvert urge rose in him to hide in his office until they changed the subject.

"Oh, I know you don't like when we talk about you, pumpkin." Nana patted his hand, and Elena smirked at the nickname. The morning was shaping up to be one of extreme temperatures, because now he felt too hot. "Why don't you let me get a look at this recipe?"

Carm took over rolling the sugar cookie dough, allowing him to gather ingredients while Elena showed Nana a typed copy of the recipe. He'd lost his handwritten one, maybe forgotten it at Elena's, but luckily, he'd remembered the measurements.

"And here he is with our *mise en place*," Elena said, not only using the culinary-school-approved terminology for premeasured ingredients but saying it with a precise Parisian accent. She could've conversed with Lawrence's French-born decorative pastry instructor without missing a beat.

"She speaks French?" Nana asked, taking a butter block from Lawrence's hand. "I know he's a looker, darling, but you are quite the dish yourself. I might be tempted to say he did well for himself."

"I sure did," he said, putting an arm around Elena's waist, keeping a polite distance so he didn't shock Nana.

"I don't know about that," Elena said with a self-deprecating laugh. He couldn't be this fortunate; he couldn't have really scored a knockout who thought *he* was the prize. "Do you know he watched a Christmas movie from 1945 with me yesterday?"

"Which one?" Nana asked.

"*Christmas in Connecticut.*"

The black-and-white movie had been pretty funny even though it was as old as Nana.

"A classic," Nana exclaimed. She and Elena began chatting about the plot points, laughing about a baby the heroine had to borrow so she could impress her boss and her love interest with her maternal skills. Lawrence's discomfort ebbed as he listened to Nana and Elena move on to debating the best song in *White Christmas*.

"Hold up there, young man," Nana said when he went to grate a ginger root for the dough. "You're not going to like this, but I firmly believe you should use ground dried ginger in this recipe. No, no, don't give me your speech about fresh versus dried. You want a good balance with the espresso. You know they'll compete if you use the fresh. It just so happens I brought some in my bag."

Lawrence opened his mouth to protest, then paused. Nana had a point. Moreover, she'd never steered him wrong before. Nana had impeccable taste.

"Elena, dear, would you get the crocheted bag I left on his desk?"

"Sure thing, Mrs. Higgins."

They watched Elena walk away.

"Pumpkin, she is a keeper," Nana said quietly as Elena disappeared into the office.

"Right as always, Nana. On both counts." Seeing Elena with Nana confirmed Lawrence's growing belief that Elena belonged here, with him. The possibility that she would quit Sparkle made his hope shine starbright. Their relationship could not only work; it could last. Without Sparkle between them, it could even be easy.

CHAPTER THIRTY

Elena thought of Lawrence first thing in the morning. To be fair, Lawrence made regular appearances in her mind all day, every day. Getting her daily caffeine fix recalled the morning he first made her coffee. Watching TV reminded her of the night they saw multiple holiday movies, his arm around her the whole time.

At her desk Monday afternoon, a fresh reason to reflect on him appeared, unexpected and thus more enchanting. She discovered his handwritten recipe for the gingerbread latte cookies in the notebook she'd brought from home to the office. Funny how seeing a simple thing like his handwriting could conjure him completely, make her feel he was beside her. She ran her finger over the blocky letters, the closest she'd get to him today. Both had packed schedules and wouldn't be able to make the drive for a visit.

A few weeks ago, she would've thought nothing of waiting twenty-four hours to see someone. What's more, she would've found it improbable she'd fall into addiction to any human being so readily. Sure, she'd had infatuations over the years, relationships she hoped would turn serious, but nothing compared.

One tablespoon of cinnamon.
Combine dry ingredients
Bake at 350 degrees.
Poetry.

"Elena, are you nuts? The meeting is about to start," Priya hissed over the cubicle wall.

Elena bolted toward the conference room, arriving a millisecond before Derick. Sarah skittered after him, carrying printouts, lips set in a grim line.

"No one who's been paying attention to the daily reports will be surprised, but there will not be any holiday party this year. The numbers don't justify a celebration. Elena, you're close, but Priya, you haven't been able to turn Alan's B region around yet." He pointed accusingly at Priya.

Priya didn't flinch; she glowered. "You *just* assigned it to me."

Derick balked, hands falling to his sides. Priya never talked back in meetings—no one did. When Elena confronted him over his text about her night in New Hope, she'd done it behind closed doors, too chicken to put him on the spot publicly. Elena suspected Priya's upcoming interview at a different company had emboldened her. A hint of a smile quivered on Sarah's lips. Had Priya chipped a faint crack in Derick's mighty facade? Elena longed to high-five her.

"Immaterial," Derick spluttered. "We needed to do better as a team. This comes from upstairs, not from me."

For the first time, it occurred to Elena that Derick's aggressive style trickled down from a higher source. Derick panicking about bad numbers because he didn't want to get chewed out by anyone in the C-suites gave her a cheap thrill. Maybe underneath it all, Derick wasn't very good at his job. Maybe he didn't have any more job security than the rest of them.

Rather than making her sympathetic, this prospect made her resent him more, because he didn't use his relative power to try to improve anything. Treating his team with respect would make them want to do a good job to protect him. If they worked harder to help him succeed, he wouldn't be in trouble with upstairs. Instead, he relied on fear and shame to cover for his own ineptitude.

"What is your justification for the numbers, Patel?"

"I already told you," Priya's voice wavered, but her posture remained upright and she didn't look down. Even Elena's dad would have been amazed by Priya's bravery. "The region you assigned me in the beginning of the year is on target. I can't be responsible for numbers I had no control over until recently."

"Regardless—"

"Also, I don't celebrate Christmas. Your holiday party didn't serve as much of an incentive. You missed Diwali this year by two months."

Elena almost sprang from her chair to hug Priya. "That's a great point," Elena said, trying to be bold to support her friend. "Incentives should be based on something the entire team can enjoy. Thank you for sharing, Priya."

She saw Priya fold her shaking hands in her lap. Elena put a hand on her shoulder to steady her, astounded by Priya's heroism. Derick screwed his face into a disgruntled frown, but even he knew better than to reprimand Priya for her valid point. Too bad. Elena would've loved for him to make a mistake that left him vulnerable to a lawsuit or termination.

"Moving on," he said. "Sarah, give me good news from the test kitchen. They need to give us a special, exclusive flavor for the New Hope grand opening."

Sarah jumped at the sound of her name, shuffled through her papers. "They plan on pistachio white chocolate."

"Disgusting. I hate pistachios. The clock is ticking. Get down there and talk some sense into them."

Sarah rolled her eyes, right to his face. What was happening? Were the tides turning? Had Priya's protest shown Derick to be an ineffectual straw man? "I can convey your request, if you wish, although this doesn't give them much time to pivot."

"Never mind," Derick roared. "I'll handle it. Dismissed."

Bubbles of excitement rose in Elena. Her limbs felt light.

"Not you, Voss." Derick held up a hand to stop her. This time his anger didn't make her heart sink and she didn't have to try as hard to access her dad's training.

"Yes?"

He waited until the other team members left the room. "Sarah is going to spend her life as an assistant. I don't know what Patel is thinking. But you and I, we're different. We have what it takes to be successful. I know we had our disagreements about New Hope, but you've done well there. You're on track to hit the bonus. Sparkle will dominate that place."

Her stomach turned, a bitter aftertaste from her morning coffee on her tongue. She would've preferred him sticking to his bullying persona. It was sickening to hear him think she would use his same unethical methods. "You and I aren't alike, Derick. I'm not so thirsty for success that I'll destroy everyone in my path. I'll do my job in New Hope, but I'm not trying to leave behind scorched earth. There are valuable established businesses there I have no interest in running out of town. You're not afraid of a little competition, are you?"

Derick scowled, and she half expected lasers to shoot from his eyes. She looked to the door, mentally planning her retreat, but forced herself to stand her ground. Rooting her feet to the floor, she made her body remain still. "Do not disappoint me," he said, then marched away.

Elena collapsed against the wall, sucked in a wobbly breath. She'd poked the bear, first when she'd told him not to intrude on her personal life and just now when she'd joined in the growing insurrection. If she was wrong about his tenuous position here, he could destroy her reputation with Sparkle top brass, even make it hard for her to get another job by making sure no one at Sparkle would give her a reference.

Yet she couldn't regret standing up to him. For herself, for her coworkers, and most of all, for Lawrence. *Nothing I do in defense of Lawrence can be wrong.*

She smoothed her skirt, arranged her hair, then used a tissue to dry her sweaty palms. Hovering by the door to collect herself, she closed her eyes. She pictured Lawrence with her, imagined him breathing and that she could feel the steady rhythm. The way he breathed when she lay in his arms as they fell asleep. Her frantic thoughts grew slower. With a final deep inhalation, she left the conference room, head held high.

Why was Derick loitering by her cubicle? He caught sight of her, a slow smile spread on his face. He looked at his phone screen, looked up to smile at her again. Was he planning to complain about her to upper management? Queasy, she took a step in his direction, refusing to let him see her unease. He nodded, then turned his back to her and returned to his corner office. He slammed the door, the angry thud reverberating through the quiet.

CHAPTER THIRTY-ONE

"Where is she?" Lawrence shouted, charging into New Hope Hospital's undersized emergency department. His truck idled at the curb outside the automatic doors, exhaust puffing into the surrounding air. He'd need to move it, but not until he saw Nana with his own eyes. His focus jumped from minor details to terror about Nana and back again in circles.

"Over here, Lawrence." Carm's daughter, Dr. Isabel Garcia-Peters, beckoned him from an alcove.

"She's going to be okay, son," his dad said, joining Lawrence as he followed Isabel through a maze of nursing stations and patient rooms. Dad had claimed the same thing when he called Lawrence seven minutes ago to tell him Nana had fallen. That she'd been transported to the hospital by ambulance. How could Nana be okay if she needed an ambulance and an ER?

A nurse in pink scrubs swiped back the geometric-patterned curtain around Nana's bed. Tears sprang up when he saw her lying there, an oxygen mask over her face. Frail and small under a sheet. Lawrence's mom stood by the bed, holding Nana's hand.

"Nana," he said, rushing over. Nana didn't move or open her eyes.

"She's not really with it right now, honey," Mom said. "They had to give her something for the pain."

"Did she hit her head?" Sweat formed above his lip; he licked it away. If she'd hit her head, then when would she wake up? He needed answers. Now.

"No. It's her arm," Dad said.

"We're going to take her to x-ray," Isabel said in a soothing tone, idly gripping the ends of the stethoscope around her neck as if the world weren't ending. She nodded to the nurse, who began to ready the bed to be wheeled away.

Lawrence made an automatic move for the door.

"You'll wait here," Isabel said. "Don't worry. I'll go with her."

With a click, the nurse pushed down the brakes. A soft groan came from Nana when the bed rolled forward.

"Be careful," Lawrence exclaimed. He felt his dad's hand on his shoulder, pulling him out of the way to let Nana and the medical team pass. "She's on blood pressure medication."

"They know all that, honey. Sit down, okay?" His mom took one green plastic chair, patted another beside her. Lawrence dropped onto it, put his head in his hands. His shoulders shook.

"What happened?" he asked. "Who called the ambulance?"

"Pamela saw Nana fall from across the street," Mom explained, rubbing his back as she spoke. "She rushed right over and stayed with her until the paramedics arrived. She wasn't lying there in the cold. Don't worry."

Everyone kept saying not to worry. If this wasn't a reason to worry, then what was?

"She was outside?" he asked. She could've gotten hypothermia.

"Yes," Dad said. "She went out to scatter some birdseed, and it seems one of the boards on the stoop was bad. It cracked, and she took a big tumble."

Lawrence's head flew up, his eyes flashed at his father. "I told you to fix that, Dad!"

His dad's brows knit. "No, you didn't."

"I noticed it the other day. I told you to-" He stopped midsentence. Had he told his father about the faulty step? He remembered he'd meant to. So much had been going on. Dad stared at him with blue eyes the same shade as his own. "This is all my fault, Dad. Nana's going to die."

"She is not going to die, Lawrence," Dad said firmly. Dad shared Lawrence's imposing stature; in fact, he stood one inch taller. His authority made itself known.

Machines chirped from other rooms; the whole place smelled like chemicals. Lawrence's stomach flipped. "It's all my fault," he said again, this time louder.

"It's not your fault," Mom insisted.

"I forgot to tell Dad about the board. And I didn't take the time to fix it myself."

"She's going to be okay, son."

She's going to be okay. Was that all Dad could say? He could be wrong, after all. Didn't he know falls were the worst thing for old people, even if they didn't hit their heads? She could need surgery. Die under anesthesia. She could develop pneumonia. Die from that. And what about her blood pressure? Tears slid down Lawrence's cheeks, dripped from his chin, landing on his jeans in dark drops.

"I have to try to get a hold of Lonnie and my brother again," Dad said, stepping to the door. He nodded at Lawrence, then told Mom, "Keep an eye on that one."

"Lawrence, try to calm down. We don't have much information yet." Mom pulled tissues from a box by the sink, handed them to him. Cheap and scratchy, they barely dried his face. "I don't want you getting all carried away how you do. You're going to make yourself sick. Here, I have water in my bag."

Mom cracked open a plastic bottle. He took it but gazed at the floor, forgetting to drink. "I got so wrapped up in all the stuff at the bakery. And my . . . my . . ."

How to describe Elena? He hadn't called Elena his girlfriend before, didn't know if she'd agree with the label. Now that it had occurred to him, he hoped she would. Thinking of her made him feel a touch better. She would stay composed, know the right things to say and the right questions to ask.

"And my . . . Elena."

"Nana told me your Elena is really sweet. When do I get to meet her?"

"Soon, I hope." He looked at his mom, who gave him a weak smile. She brushed his hair, damp with nervous sweat, off his forehead. She had to stretch her arm to reach, since he got his height from his dad. The fragrance from the rose soap she always used offered solace, a momentary belief that everything might turn out all right, as Dad insisted.

"Do you want to take a minute to call her?" Mom asked.

"She'll be at work. Her job is pretty important—she's a VP of marketing for a big company."

Mom didn't let on whether she knew which company Elena worked for, although she must be aware. Even though his parents hadn't been at the notorious town hall, their friends had, and Lawrence knew gossip that juicy would've reached their ears in no time. Yet Mom never took advantage of town chatter to push Lawrence into talking about anything he wasn't read to share.

"Leave her a message, then, if she doesn't pick up." Without waiting for him to protest, Mom left the room. Outside the door, he heard her speaking in murmurs to a nurse. More than anything, he wanted to hear Elena's voice. He hadn't ever interrupted her during the workday, and it felt like a big step somehow. Like acknowledging that things were serious enough to justify calling her with a midday emergency.

He held the phone to his ear, willed her to answer as the dial tone sounded once, twice, three times.

If she answered, it signaled a willingness to be there for him, even when it wasn't convenient.

Four, five, six rings.

I'm overstepping.

He should hang up. Send a text later.

"Lawrence? Are you there? I had to run to the stairwell so Derick wouldn't catch me on my phone."

"Hi there, baby," he said, sounding strangled, hoarse. His throat prickled. Finally remembering the water, he took a sip.

"What's wrong?" she asked, and he felt her alarm, her compassion, close. Her response exactly what he'd wished for, needed.

"My grandma fell; she's in the hospital. I'm here waiting for some real information."

"No, not Nana! You're not alone, are you?" The apprehension in her words echoed in the stairwell. Was she sitting on a step? Leaning against a railing? He ached to see her, to take hold of her hip, pull her to him.

"My parents are here."

"Good. Good. I can't stand to think of you facing this by yourself. You must be terrified. Your poor, sweet grandma. Do you want me to come? Tomorrow is the end-of-quarter meeting and Derick is on a rampage, but I'll take a half day. I could be there in about two hours?"

She'd risked her boss's displeasure already by answering his call, and he didn't want to get her in trouble. A selfish desire to have her near needled him regardless.

Mom and Dr. Garcia-Peters stepped into the room.

"Hold on a sec, can you, baby?" He put his hand over the phone's speaker.

"Nana's going upstairs to a room," Mom said.

Lawrence's face dropped; the anxiety spiked.

"I'm being cautious, Lawrence. I want to get her blood pressure regulated, see if we can get her more alert by backing off on the pain medication. Hang tight here for a few more minutes. Give me a chance to see which room they're sending her to," Isabel said. "And Lawrence, I called my mom. She'll be happy to stay late today. Don't worry about closing up."

Mom turned to him. "I'm going to find Dad. I think he went to park your truck."

The truck! He'd completely forgotten about the truck. "Elena, are you still there? Sorry. They had a quick update. They're going to admit her, but the doctor, Carm's daughter, she says it's just to be careful."

"Of course I'm still here."

Of course she was. He leaned his head against the door frame, visualized her hand on his face. "I ran out of the bakery without even telling Carm what was going on when my mom called. I've never been so afraid."

It felt awkward to admit his weakness, vulnerable to expose his fear, impossible not to be real with her.

"I hate that I'm not there to help." When she said it, he knew he'd made the right choice disclosing his fear, knew she wanted to comfort him as much as he wanted to be comforted.

"You don't have to leave work early. She's stable; we'll know more in a while. I . . ." He stopped himself, swallowed hard. "I needed to tell you."

"I'm glad you did. You can tell me anything. Let me come over tonight."

"But don't you have a big meeting tomorrow?"

"I can handle it." She paused. "What I can't handle is not being there with you."

He croaked out an agreement to see her in a few hours. The paranoia of what she would think or how she would react washed away. They said goodbye, and then he stood, phone in hand, hardly comprehending the force of emotion that flooded into its place. The sudden faith that Nana would recover; that Elena, true to her word, would be there for him. That together they could find their way past any impediment.

CHAPTER THIRTY-TWO

Elena sat alone in Lawrence's winter-sun-soaked kitchen, coffee in a chipped mug, her journal open on the round table. When she arrived last night, she'd found him slouched on his sofa, dazed. He'd buried his face into her midsection. She'd stood before him, fingers in his thick hair, desperate to help him, unsure how. In the end, she sensed he just needed her by his side, quiet and present.

All night he tossed in the bed like a fish out of water, reaching for her time and again to reassure himself he wasn't alone. Then, before dawn, his phone bleated, woke her with a racing heart. Neither of them had gotten more than a few hours' broken sleep. A tiredness she didn't know herself capable of settled into her bones. She yawned, her whole body quaking with the force of it.

The doctors had scheduled Nana for surgery this morning to repair her broken wrist, but her blood pressure had spiked, made her short of breath and panicky. She might have fallen again if not for the nurse by her side. Lawrence raced to the hospital at five, promising to update Elena as she shoved a granola bar and cup of instant coffee at him on his way out. A lousy breakfast but better than nothing.

"Do you think someone will give him something real to eat soon?" she asked Sugar, who lay at her bowl, munching kibble with conviction. "His mom is there; we don't have to worry. And Trey will come for you in a while. I'd stay, but I have the quarterly meeting today."

Sugar's tail swished across the linoleum floor at the sound of Trey's name, then stopped when Elena mentioned the meeting. Even the dog understood what a rough day lay before Elena. Thankfully, she'd had the presence of mind last night to pack well despite her antsy fervor to be with Lawrence as soon as possible, spilling her duffel bag twice as she hurried around her apartment. Hair dryer, curling iron, makeup, and best suit in a garment bag. Somehow, everything she needed had made it to his house. Derick and the CEO would have no clue she'd barely slept.

Pencil in hand, she closed her journal, impressed with herself for sticking to her new practice despite a hectic twelve hours. She'd decided to write out one complicated feeling toward her family per day in an effort to be less sarcastic and more honest the next time she saw them. With minutes to spare before her commute, she switched to her sketchbook.

She hurried to draw a quick picture—a way to calm herself, and a surprise for Lawrence when he returned—then left the house.

Little houses like Lawrence's ran up and down the quiet street behind snowy lawns and big leafless trees. Pausing on the porch, she let herself revel in the tranquil atmosphere. The gentle scene stood in stark contrast to her harried mornings in the city—horns honking, pedestrians grimacing, garbage overflowing in cans along the sidewalks. How amazing would it be to start every morning on this sweet street? A peace she never felt on a workday settled over her, until she remembered she had to hurry.

Her career would take a steep dive if she blew off the meeting. And she couldn't expect Priya and Sarah to face the CEO and Derick without her. Lawrence would understand, and she'd be back as soon as she could. *A few hours*, she told herself, vowed to the closed door, *then I'll be back*.

Once at Sparkle, she took the elevator to the top floor, to the fabled upstairs Derick loved evoking to terrify his staff. Against all odds, the temperature upstairs ran even cooler than on her floor. Her lavender cashmere sweater and wool suit felt suddenly thin. Priya got off the elevator a minute after her. They exchanged a tense glance, then went together to the executive conference room.

This conference room had a high ceiling, all the better for the CEO's commands to echo throughout. Floor-to-ceiling windows provided a majestic view of the city, the cloud-rich sky, but also suggested the possibility of being thrown through one to hurtle to the street below for making a mistake. They took a seat near the end of a marble-top table the length of a football field.

Each place had a binder prepared by an admin, filled with reports and projections, some of which Elena had put together and triple checked yesterday. Next to the binders sat signature Sparkle sample boxes, doubtless holding the special cookie for the New Hope grand opening.

Elena gazed around the room as department presidents, VPs like her, and assistants filed in, all in their best lavender-accented clothing. The mood as heavy as a wake, Elena went over her dad's maxims for success in her head while they waited for the CEO to grace them with her presence. The room at least smelled nice, soothing and familiar in a way she couldn't quite place.

Margaret Zimmerman, the CEO, a conventionally attractive woman in her late forties with expensive blond hair, glided into the room. Derick followed hot on her designer heels, whispering some private tidbit to her. Did he realize how desperate he seemed? Elena would bet he'd waited outside the door like a groupie for the CEO to show, frantic for one extra second with her. Disgusting.

"Everyone, please take your seats," Margaret said, making no apology for keeping them waiting five minutes past the scheduled start time. Elena knew from her dad this was a common, deliberate play to prove one's importance. Superiority. Elena tried to imagine Lawrence making his assistant Carm wait around for him as a flex. She smirked at the idea. Her chef would never need to stoop so low to lead.

Margaret's executive assistant, a cowed young man who looked strangled by his tie, clicked on the projector. Pie charts appeared on the screen. Margaret began a sermon extoling Sparkle's vision for the quarter, for the upcoming new year. Elena's thoughts were a beat behind thanks to no sleep. She strained to remain attentive. Remarks about deliverables and growth slurred together, smearing in her tired mind.

The CFO took a turn, yakked about projects and margins, diagrams taking the place of pie charts on the screen. Elena found it hard to focus, her thoughts drifting to Lawrence and his nana. How long could this meeting drag on for? She needed to make a call, have another cup of coffee. Conserve some energy for tonight so she could drive to the hospital. She fought off another yawn, eyes watering.

"Let's turn it over to Derick Cunningham, president of marketing. He's going to explain his strategy for our latest grand opening," Margaret said.

Elena straightened in her seat. She needed to feign interest at this point. Derick loved to call on his team during these meetings, show off how he'd browbeaten them into submission. Derick stood, which seemed unnecessary, like he was trying to appear more important than he was.

"As you can see, based on my VP's report on page fifteen in your binders," he began. Elena hated it when he called her *my VP*, as if she existed solely in relation to him. *I am not yours.* "We made a big goal for ourselves for the location in New Hope, set to open this weekend on Christmas Eve. I'm sure we can all agree a Christmas Eve opening is a lot of fun."

Elena could disagree. Who wanted to spend the holiday stressing at work? And the minimum-wage bakers and customer service team at the store wouldn't be excited either, she'd wager. Those workers couldn't afford to ask for a day off, and she knew overscheduled managers from other locations were expected to be on hand all day to lend their experience.

"My VP has outlined the steps we've taken thus far," he continued. Did any of the upper management team know her name, or did they think her birth certificate read *Derick Cunningham's Vice President of Marketing*? Dad would want her to find an opportunity to interject here to make sure they learned her name. She cast around for a statistic she could add to Derick's recitation of her work.

"I have come up with a little something special on my own, though," Derick said, cutting her off as she opened her mouth to speak. "We all know that an exclusive flavor makes the grand opening the place to be. Our customers love to collect the experience of tasting these one-day-only cookies."

Why was Derick acting like he'd invented a strategy they employed companywide? *Get to the point already. Let this nightmare end.*

"The test kitchen offered me a white-chocolate pistachio exclusive for this opening, but I think we all can agree that isn't very festive."

Oh, Derick cared about holiday spirit? What a farce.

"Which is why I invented a brand-new cookie. I know, you didn't think I had it in me, but I'm full of surprises." Some department presidents laughed along, though others rolled their eyes. "Open up those boxes and have a taste. I think the test kitchen did a phenomenal job executing my vision."

Elena flipped up the box top, and the room spun around her. Her hands flew out, grabbed hold of the table for support.

"These gingerbread latte cookies will help us meet—even exceed—our ambitious grand-opening sales goal. Messengers are out delivering boxes of them to our top influencers as we speak. By end of day, I expect to see *#iSparkle* trending along with my hashtag *#NewHopeNewCookie*. Everyone within a hundred-mile radius of sleepy little New Hope will be at my grand opening. I am going to send our sales through the roof."

The executives applauded, a sound like thunder all around her. The cookie, a near exact replica of the cookie Lawrence had devised with her assistance, blurred in front of her eyes. She felt a cold hand on the back of her neck, someone asking her in an urgent voice if she was okay.

But how? How had he stolen it? She'd tried her hardest to keep Derick away from Lawrence. Even gone to her dad for help. Stood up to her own discomfort and told her boss straight out not to meddle.

Then she saw it in flash, ears ringing, insides roiling.

Her own careless, foolish, love-drunk error.

Lawrence's handwritten recipe on her desk, Derick with his phone out, and a wicked smile on his face.

CHAPTER THIRTY-THREE

Apart from the granola bar Elena had given him that morning, her eyes soft with a tender concern, Lawrence hadn't eaten anything all day. A Styrofoam container housing rubbery scrambled eggs from the hospital cafeteria sat unopened on a waiting room end table. Mom attempted to persuade him to eat them, but she gave up when he refused for the third time.

Dad snored in the chair next to him, and Lawrence stared at a rack of brochures advertising various medical services and dire conditions. Since Mom left to run home for a shower, Lawrence hadn't stirred once from this rigid chair upholstered in scratchy fabric. The muscles in his low back pinched, yet moving to stretch them felt like too much effort. *How will Nana afford the copays? If our cookie wins the contest, how long until they give us the money? If I can swing giving Nana back the investment money now, at least I'll know she doesn't have to worry about the surgery cost.*

Nana needed to use all her energy to heal.

On the wall above the check-in desk, a clock's hands ticked away. The surgeon quoted a two-hour time frame to add a plate and screws to stabilize Nana's shattered wrist. Nana had been back in some unseen room for almost three hours, without a single update from the doctor. Lawrence wished Carm's daughter had gone into surgery instead of general medicine. She would've been kind enough to let Nana's family know what was going on. This surgeon was young, new, and an out-of-towner to boot.

With Elena tied up in her big meeting, Lawrence had nothing to do but stare, and try to avoid looking at an equally worried man a few rows over. The dude kept sighing, raking his hands through his hair, and generally putting Lawrence even further on edge.

The automatic doors to the waiting room glided open, and Trey walked in, his grandpa a step behind. Mr. Simmons clutched a bouquet wrapped in brown butcher paper and tied with string, the hallmark of Pamela's floral shop.

"Hanging in there, buddy?" Trey asked, taking a seat opposite Lawrence. Grandpa Simmons went up to the receptionist and began loudly questioning Nana's whereabouts while the poor woman tried to explain HIPAA laws to him.

"I'll feel better when she wakes up. I want to talk to her."

"I don't blame you." Trey's attention turned to his grandpa for a second, then back to Lawrence. "Is there something going on between Gramps and Nana? He hunted me down at work and demanded I give him a ride over here. And he's wearing his best bow tie."

Amusement twinkled in Lawrence for the first time since Nana's fall. "You're late to the game, man. Apparently, he already made her save him a dance for the senior center Christmas Eve ball."

"No way! Those sly players." Trey's dimples—the ones girls had waxed eloquent about since fifth grade—showed.

Lawrence's mood darkened as quickly as it had lightened. "Looks like there won't be any dance after all."

"I know Gramps will ask again next year, and Nana will be feeling much better then." Trey wriggled out of his winter coat.

Lawrence smiled too, relieved to have his best friend with him. "You should've seen Gramps at Ms. Pamela's. Everything had to be just right. He must've turned down three bouquets before he found the perfect one. The whole time, he was lecturing me about how I should buy Iris flowers every month for no reason."

"It's not bad advice," Lawrence said, wondering what kind of flowers Elena liked best. He'd give her a field full if he could.

"Obviously, we should all be taking tips from the old man."

At the desk, Mr. Simmons had switched tactics. He now held his wool fedora over his heart as he made a tragic plea for information. He conjured some old-school charm, calling the young receptionist *miss* and a *nice lady* in a gentle, musical voice. She nibbled her bottom lip, eyes darting, and then she offered to check with her supervisor.

"I think he's about to sweet-talk that woman into getting us an update on Nana, so I'm not complaining."

"Oh, before I forget, I checked in on Sugar as long as we were out. She should be okay for a couple hours."

"Yeah, Elena fed her breakfast."

Trey crossed his arms behind his head, leaned back with a low whistle. "Whew, she's giving you the girlfriend treatment. Things are heating up all over New Hope."

"You think so?"

"For sure. You gonna make sure she knows it? Don't pull a Lawrence and clam up; you need to lock it down."

"This from the guy who was all suspicious of her not too far back."

"That was before I got to know her. And before Iris told me I had to like her or else."

"Iris knows what's what." An endorsement from Iris meant a lot, since she didn't suffer fools gladly. She and Lawrence's ex-girlfriend Jen had never gotten along.

Bit by bit, the whole town was beginning to see what he already knew.

But destroyed from garbage sleep, no food, and stress, he didn't know what exactly he'd say to Elena. How he'd tell her he wanted to be exclusive. That might be for the best. If he didn't have a chance to overthink things, he could enjoy the moment, speak from the heart.

The receptionist escorted Grandpa Simmons to the seating area, tugging uncertainly on her badge lanyard. She looked at Lawrence. "My supervisor told me to let you know the surgeon was held up with a previous patient. Your grandma's surgery started fifteen minutes ago."

Lawrence groaned. Why were awful days also the longest?

"Thank you, Miss Molly," Mr. Simmons said, sitting next to Trey. "You're a sweetheart. You let us know if anything changes."

"Thanks, Gramps," Trey said as Molly walked away.

Lawrence thanked him too, then dug his phone from his coat pocket. His sister Lonnie hadn't been able to get a flight home yet. He let her and Mom know about the surgeon's delay on the group thread. How much longer until Elena's meeting ended? He hoped she'd be able to talk for a quick minute soon. This day had no right to go so slowly.

Yawning, he gazed down at his feet, noticed he had on different-colored socks—one white, one blue. Between that detail, his gray sweatpants, and a T-shirt with holes, he must look as wrecked as he felt.

"You want some coffee, bro? I'm gonna take Gramps down to the cafeteria for one."

"Sure, Trey. Thanks."

Lawrence decided to give the brochure rack a break from his concentrated eye contact while he waited for Trey and Gramps to return. Dad snored softly away, sleeping to cope. Lids heavy,

Lawrence closed his eyes. This chair had to be the most uncomfortable piece of furniture ever built. He was going to need spinal surgery after spending the day crunched up in this miserable thing. Useless. He could never rest in this position.

Desperate for something—anything—to take his mind off Nana, off the image of her hooked up to machines, he stood and opened his email. Carm had been replying to customer orders, bless her. He refreshed his inbox, and an email from Sparkle Cookie appeared on the screen.

Fall in Love With Our Exclusive Flavor, the subject line read.

He had to give it to Elena for managing to stay on top of work and make time for him during the week. She really was remarkable. Pleased by this little connection to her when he needed it most, he clicked on the message.

Be the first in line to taste our Grand Opening Flavor in New Hope, PA.

Exclusive to opening day, everyone who's anyone will be trying our Gingerbread Latte Cookie. Snap a pic with it and don't forget the hashtags #iSparkle and #NewHopeNewCookie.

He must've made some wounded sound, because his father woke up with a jolt. Alarmed, Dad asked something about Nana he couldn't quite hear. The screen on his phone had a jagged crack running across it, bisecting it. The screen. He'd snapped it. Blood dripped from a cut on his finger.

A fresh surge of intense fury made him want to hurl his phone against the wall and annihilate it. To sever his link to Elena. She had exploited their relationship to get ahead at work. Cheated him when he'd trusted her with everything, from his heart to his livelihood.

Then he was stalking through the hospital corridors, his fists at his temples, a warm smear of blood from his hand on his face. Outside, no coat, the wind slashed him. But he was already numb. Doubled over.

The Christmas Crush

How could you how could you how could you?

All the things she'd made him feel, all the improbable heights she'd brought him to, just to fling him down to the lowest possible point. Lowest of his life. Desire, lust, admiration, hope, understanding. The first flash of a true love.

And now the cruelest of those galloping, breathless emotions. Sharpened steel, shoved between his ribs, up through his heart.

Betrayal.

CHAPTER THIRTY-FOUR

"I'm going to throw up." Elena burst through the door to the C-suite-level bathroom, barely registering how much nicer it was than the ones down on her level. White moth orchids in golden pots to match the fixtures, cloying fragrance from a reed oil diffuser. Priya caught up, held back Elena's hair as she leaned over the toilet. Away from that horrible room, from Derick's triumphant cruelty, the nausea and cold sweat began to pass. She and Priya relocated to a low faux-leather sofa across from the sinks and a full-length mirror.

Priya opened her arms, and Elena fell against her, sobbing. "I never cry at work. Never," she insisted as fat, hot tears gushed down her face. *Never let them see you cry, Elena.*

"I know you don't," Priya said. "I think you can have a pass this one time."

Elena sat upright, clenched her fists. "I've been robbed. Robbed and ruined. That worthless tyrant stole our cookie. Mine and Lawrence's. The one I helped with to convince him I don't care about this loathsome job. That I cared . . . care . . . about him. Want the best for him."

In the mirror, she saw her skin mottled with angry red patches. She jumped up. "I'm going to ruin Derick Cunningham. See how he likes it."

Priya took hold of Elena's sleeve, tugged her back to the sofa. "Cool off first. You cannot confront Derick in this state. You're going to get fired *and* arrested. Don't give me that look; I am not bailing you out.

"Listen, Elena, I hate him almost as much as you do, but this is not the time to let loose. Stay still, will you? We're going to figure this out. I'm going to help you figure this out."

Elena stood back up.

"Hey," Priya warned.

"I'm going to splash off my face." Elena crossed to the sink; the water ran cold from the tap. She pressed handfuls of it into her skin, makeup ruined. Up here they got rolled terry-cloth towels in a basket instead of the paper towels that always ran out downstairs. She waved a towel at Priya. "This is what I've been supporting; this is what I've been killing myself for. So these people who don't know my name can live in luxury."

She twisted the towel in her hands, almost convinced she could shred it. Wanted the relief of damaging something. She threw it into a basket beside the orchids. Back on the sofa, she cradled her head in her hands. "He's never going to forgive me."

"Derick? Who cares?"

"No. Lawrence."

"Oh, Elena, give him more credit than that. You can explain what happened to him. He'll understand."

The president of product development swung the door open, paused when she saw them. Elena and Priya sat stock still, betraying nothing. While the woman reapplied red lipstick, smiling in the mirror to show bright-white teeth, Elena gulped back tears. Madame President took a tissue from the box on the vanity, blotted her lips, then reopened the tube for a second coat.

"It looks fine, you don't need more," Priya said, words ringing out in the eerily quiet room.

The woman's mouth dropped open. She had the decency to mutter an apology for interrupting before turning on her heel and leaving.

"Priya, are you nuts? That was the president of product development," Elena said, momentarily shocked out of her own misery. "If she tattles to Derick—"

"I got an offer letter this morning. I'm giving my notice."

"Priya, I'm proud of you." Elena's voice caught in her sticky throat. She was proud, of course, and happy for her friend, but now she would be all alone in this hell until she could find a new job.

"You're next. I'm sure of it." Priya tucked a strand of Elena's hair behind her ear. "And talk to Lawrence. It will be okay. I know it."

Hands shaking, Elena pulled her phone from her blazer pocket, turned it on. No text from him yet. He was supposed to let her know how Nana was. "His grandma is still in surgery, I think. They're super close. He was such a mess this morning."

Dad would say to break news this bad in person. Doing so would make her message clearer, more genuine, give Lawrence a chance to read her body language. She could take the next few hours to compose herself. Lawrence would be able to see how blindsided she'd been by Derick's actions. She could show him how much she regretted leaving their recipe unattended. Then Lawrence would hold her tight, and together they would find a way forward. There were several days still before the grand opening—time enough to make this right.

"Is that a smile I see?" Priya asked.

Elena nodded, the pressure on her heart relenting. Then the phone rang. Lawrence!

"Hi, is Nana—"

"Don't you say her name."

Elena's eyes widened. His voice sounded much deeper on the phone, far away and furious. Shock at the force of his anger, when all she'd known of him was endearing uncertainty and mildness, made her sink into the cushions astounded.

"What do you—"

"You proved my worst fears about you true. *Everyone's* worst fears," he spat out. "And I defended you, like an idiot. Worse than my worst fears, actually, because never in a million years did I think you would rip off my creation. I believed we were alike—that you knew how precious these things are. Turns out we don't have a thing in common. And after all that stuff you told me about your dad pushing you to excel, like you didn't want success as much as he did. At any cost."

His anger might make sense, but all she heard was the comparison to her father. A flame of equal wrath shot up in her. She floundered for the control she knew she needed; it eluded her, and her words exploded. "That's what you think of me, is it? Well, let me tell you something—"

"Tell me what? I don't know what kind of a corn-fed country bumpkin you take me for, Elena, but even I know when I've been grifted. The scary thing about you is, you don't seem to realize what you've done is wrong. Remorseless. Like somehow you think things can be fine between us after you cut my throat to get ahead."

All at once the icy self-possession returned, and she nearly gasped with relief. The shield, the protection. She could counter his attack with equal force, and when she did, he would be the one to hurt. What could hurt more than someone you'd thought understood you assuming the worst, thinking you capable of heartless treachery? Her chin trembled, but her voice went flat as she said, "You know less than you think you do. My boss—the one I've told you truthfully mistreats me, the one you alleged you wanted to defend me against—he stole your recipe—*our* recipe—right off my desk.

215

"I can accept responsibility for leaving it there, but I will never accept the things you said about me. That you could even think them shows how little you know me. Shows you don't know me at all and never did, and never could."

A sharp intake of breath on the other end of the line. Priya looked at her with horror, tipped her head toward the door to indicate she was leaving. Elena saw her friend walk away, leaving her alone in this cold room. Welcome cold. She checked the mirror to see her skin back to its normal color.

"How am I supposed to believe that, Elena? Don't try to spin this. Did he also send out the newsletter you told me *you* write? You know it, the one with the subject line *Fall in Love With Our Exclusive Flavor*? Really, Elena? *Fall in love*? Was that some kind of joke? A special dig at me to let me know what a complete fool I've been? All day I'm sitting here, wondering if my grandmother is going to live or die, and now I have to read an email advertising *my* cookie with *your* hashtags."

Derick. She would deal with him the first chance she got. She let Lawrence's accusation land between them. Dad always said let people dig their own graves. Half of winning an argument was knowing when to shut up. If Lawrence claimed she was Dad's clone, she might as well act like it.

"Stop putting New Hope on a pedestal. Real life still exists here, not just in the city. This is my business, my dream, you're helping destroy."

That hurt, enough to crack her facade. Enough to let a single tear escape. She flicked it away with the back of her hand.

She cleared her throat. He wanted confidence, polish, heartlessness? She could give it to him. All her life, she'd trained to take down the competition with precision and lethal accuracy. And she could fake it too; she could stifle everything true about herself to give him what he thought he wanted.

"Listen to me, Lawrence. Hear the calm in my voice and know I'm being honest. It's exactly what Derick did. Which if you had been paying attention to anything I've said would make perfect sense.

"What possible reason could I have to lie to you now? Because I want to salvage this relationship, or whatever this was? That's not a compelling reason to me. According to you, this is the moment I should gloat because I suckered you into giving me what I needed. But that isn't me. And the truth of the matter is, I felt sick when I found out—only a few minutes ago—what he'd done to me, to *us*. I was worried about your grandma, and I was worried how I'd convince you I'm sorry the recipe was stolen."

He didn't respond, the moment endless, all the awful things they'd said forming a concrete wall between them.

"Okay, listen, things are crazy here." His voice wavered, yet she didn't care. He'd compared her to all her father's worst traits. "I'm sor—"

If you can't strike first, Elena, then strike hardest.

"As long as we're being brutally honest here, do you know what you are, Lawrence? Not what I *think* you are, but what you've actually proven yourself to be?" She waited a beat, heard what sounded like a strangled gasp from him. She had to rip out her own heart to make her point, to make him feel as badly as she did. "Another man who expected the least of me. Another man I won't be able to make happy and who isn't worth my time. Like my dad. My brothers. Derick. I thought you viewed me differently than they do. But you're no better. At the end of the day, what you are, Lawrence Higgins, is just some guy I never want to see again."

With that, she hung up, not giving him time to respond. Because Vosses were bosses, and they always won, no matter how bad it hurt.

CHAPTER THIRTY-FIVE

One final whack with the sledgehammer, and the last rotten board splintered. Wood chunks flew around him. When he turned to his tool chest, he saw Pamela's front door open across the street. The florist stepped onto her porch and rubbed her arms to warm herself, craning her neck to look at him. Twilight made the temperature dip even lower, and Pamela shivered with theatrical flair.

"Everything okay over there, kiddo?" she called. Fantastic. Soon all of New Hope would know Lawrence Higgins was having a breakdown while breaking down Nana's crappy steps.

He took a pair of screws from where he held them clenched between his lips like cigarettes. He inspected the fresh lumber he'd picked up after leaving the hospital.

"Fine," he said.

"Your mom called and told me the surgery went well. We're all so relieved."

Dad hunting him down with the good news about Nana's operation was the only reason he could function. Overwhelmed, regret like a stone in his stomach, he'd called Elena back right after she hung up on him. Twice he got her voice mail, his mind a jumbled mess, his words stuck to his tongue, unable to leave a coherent message.

There had been no sympathy from her for the fact that he'd been having the worst day of his life. She'd spoken right over him as he tried to admit fault, made sure to let him know exactly what she thought of him.

He might've been wrong about the recipe fiasco—despite all logical signs pointing straight to her; who could blame him for thinking two plus two made four?—but he wasn't wrong about her unsettling ability to freeze him out. How she'd used the same superior tone she'd pulled on him the night of their town hall. He never should've chased after her. She could've gotten new gloves, and he could have spared himself this heartache.

"Is there anything I can do for you, Lawrence? Do you want some wassail?"

"No," he said, his tone sharper than he meant it to be. Wassail reminded him of Elena. She'd ruined his favorite holiday drink on top of everything else. "I'm sorry, Ms. Pamela. I'm exhausted."

"No worries, kiddo. Don't stay out here too long. Frostbite won't make anything better."

Remarkable he hadn't gotten frostbite from Elena on the phone this morning. Like everything they'd shared meant nothing, like she'd forgotten it all. He'd put it all on the line for her, for her to treat him like a stranger at his lowest moment.

Pamela went inside—probably called his mom the second she shut the door to express her concern for his sanity. Maybe he'd get lucky and his phone couldn't receive calls anymore. It looked pretty rough. Over the course of the afternoon, cracks had spider-webbed, and a big portion of the screen had turned into a pixelated blur.

Didn't matter to him if he could never take or make another phone call.

Crouching, he shifted past screwdrivers and hammers in his banged-up toolbox, searching for the tape measure to calculate the cuts for the stringers. The wound on his finger throbbed beneath the bandage they'd given him at the hospital. Where was that damn tape measure?

Irrationally angry at the missing tape measure, he dumped the contents of the box on the salted path to Nana's house. They rattled to the concrete, his best screwdriver rolling away toward the sidewalk. Who cared?

Ah, the tape measure. He measured the drop from the porch, felt around on the ground for the pencil he kept with his tools. When he found it, he saw the lead was mostly worn away. For some reason, this sad excuse for a pencil made him think of Elena again. Of her cup of pencils, how they flew across a page in her expert hand.

How she'd captured him exactly. Elena wouldn't let a pencil get worn down and useless.

Even if she was telling the truth about the recipe theft—and, as time passed, a sick suspicion he'd overreacted, that she had been honest, gnawed at him—things still wouldn't work between them. Elena, precise and professional, a gifted artist, and Lawrence, the overreacting, on-the-verge-of-not-being-able-to-afford-rent baker, didn't make sense.

And how could he move forward with someone who wouldn't give him the benefit of the doubt on a terrible, unusual day? Didn't she care he'd been tired, hungry, and beyond worried?

He jotted his measurements down on a scrap of paper he found in his pocket, chewed on the eraser. Not that he'd given her the benefit of the doubt. Why hadn't he? What corrupted, hidden part of himself had made him assume the worst? Not merely assume it but act on it. He, who never spoke without thinking first. Where had that come from?

He reached for his phone to make the calculations for the stringers. The screen looked worse than ever, and he couldn't find the calculator app. Looked like he'd gotten his wish, couldn't make a call even if he wanted to.

No choice but to end the night here. He'd have to go home to cut the wood anyway. Darkness was fast replacing the remaining daylight. Nana wouldn't be home tomorrow or the next day. Might not even be home before Christmas. He could pick this project back up after work tomorrow.

He collected the tools he'd scattered like a petulant child, his lower back complaining, still in knots from that stupid chair. Exhaustion launched a fresh offense, and he rubbed his eyes, walked on heavy feet to his truck.

What difference would it make if he took responsibility for how he'd acted, for the thoughtless things he'd said? *Worse than my worst fears. Remorseless.* Words that stung as badly as slaps. The dig about her being like her father, when Lawrence knew her complicated relationship with him. Words designed to hurt.

Her words clawed through his memory, sharp as paint-stained nails raking his skin. *At the end of the day, what you are, Lawrence Higgins, is just some guy I never want to see again.* She was the one who'd yanked away any hope of reconciliation, the one who'd stated her refusal to forgive before he could even ask her to. She was the one who wouldn't answer the phone, give him a chance to apologize. His stomach grumbled. No matter how terrible he felt, he'd have to make himself eat something when he got home.

Back at the house, the rooms felt emptier than he'd ever known them. Trey and Iris had taken Sugar for the night, unsure when Lawrence would make it back. No friendly paws padding toward him, no jangling collar tags. The only sounds his own breathing, the floor creaking.

He turned on the overhead light in the kitchen, and a lightbulb popped, went out. In the semidarkness, he found a slice of bread, smeared some peanut butter on it with a spoon. He swallowed a lump, tasting nothing. He pushed away images of Elena in this room, wearing his T-shirt, standing on tiptoe to fetch a mug from the cabinet. A pain he hadn't noticed before pounded in the back of his head, his neck tight.

He rolled his head to loosen his muscles. On the table, he spotted a large piece of paper. Thick paper, sketch paper. Artist's paper. He crossed right over, saw a note in the upper corner.

When the other girls send nudes, but you're an artist and you have to do it one better.

With a speed he didn't know he possessed, he flipped over the paper. Elena, lithe limbs, luxurious curves, the fall of her hair over her shoulder. Desire, immediate, painful, shook him from his days-long stupor. There was that higher eyebrow she didn't like but he adored because it conveyed all her mischief, the pleasure she took in a clever remark. The full cheeks that fit perfectly in his palms.

His hungry eyes sought hers, the way she portrayed them looking up. Looking for him. How he looked down into them as he lay over her. The eyes she called too big.

Those eyes got him more than anything else. Vulnerable, confident, trusting, bold, afraid. Complex and confusing. Raw, and now outside his reach.

Under the portrait, another note. *Remember you have me with you, even when we're apart—Your Elena.*

He'd hurt this beautiful, caring person. Hurt her like she meant nothing to him. Like he hadn't held her all night while she slept, like he didn't know the feel of every inch of her. The woman who'd come to comfort him when he needed her most, the one who wanted to do her job and fight to help his bakery survive. How could he fault her for her voice going cold? For saying hurtful things back?

His fingertips ran over the words *Your Elena*.

My Elena, how could I how could I how could I? Please come back one more time and be mine again.

He ended up falling asleep at the table, face on its unforgiving surface, hands on the drawing of her.

CHAPTER THIRTY-SIX

In the past, Elena had thought a whirlwind romance sounded enviable. A goal. The kind of transcendent experience you might long for all your life and never have.

Tonight, whipped in that whirlwind, she found herself shipwrecked on a lonely shore. Battered, wet from her own tears, alone in all the places he used to be. She lay on her living room floor, her hair spread out on the braided cotton rug. Candles almost burnt down, flames flickering, reflected in the glass of a half-drunk bottle of red wine. A canvas streaked with gray on the floor beside her. Paint drying to the palette and brushes submerged in dirty water.

Some hollow comfort, at least, in knowing she'd been right. Right to be scared. Right, but for the wrong reasons. It would've been better to rush things with him, to not allow herself to get invested, to care. If she'd gone with her initial plan to treat him like a meaningless fling, she would've spared herself this piercing discomfort. In all her life, she'd never lost her way so completely.

Elena, Dad loved to say, *you have to be strong to be safe. The world is unkind, and you have to protect yourself. I have to worry about you more than your brothers, because it's twice as unkind to women.*

She rolled to her side, the silk fabric of the green robe Lawrence liked pooled around her. Leaned against the TV stand was one of her sketchbooks, open to his portrait. She squinted at it, searching for imperfections, in him or in her work. Broad shoulders, lean waist, that inverted triangle the old masters loved to paint. The body type the ancient Greeks sculpted, trapped in marble to steal breath from observers for millennia. Timeless. Primal, it called to her through the fog of her anger.

A testament to his beauty and her talent. In college, she'd used up all her electives on art classes, forming a strong student-teacher relationship with her gifted instructor. Professor Megan O'Neil would love this drawing, the use of light and shadow. How Elena's skill had developed with regular practice. The way the paper seemed like it would be warm to the touch, warm as him. Her hand reached out, brought the sketchbook to her.

She rolled onto her stomach, looked down into his eyes. Why had she believed she understood anything about him when she drew them? The arrogance, the foolish naïveté in thinking she'd seen something special in him. Something real, and worth recording. Worth keeping.

Without a second thought, she tore the picture down the center, a long, languid rip, fibers fraying.

"Think I'm my father's daughter, huh? I don't know you any more than you know me," she told the left side of his face. She crumbled all of him up, dropped the pieces in the murky water, stirred them with a paintbrush. The paper began to further break apart. It was difficult to imagine in the midst of this pain, her body tired with it, bruised all over without a mark on her, but one day soon she would have a new job, and this ordeal would sting less. Next time she would stick to her convictions, to the guidelines her father gave her, and never mix her professional and personal lives again. It wasn't worth the disillusionment.

Much as she hated it, Dad had been right to teach her to keep her guard up. Alas, the world wasn't the pastel-hued Monet landscape she wanted it to be. Rather, it was a place made of legal briefs, reports, suits and countersuits, and romance gone wrong.

Her phone sounded an alert. Her heart jumped to answer before her hand could even lift it.

She would answer this time—if it was him, she would forget everything she'd ever been told and respond. Logically, she knew he deserved to be ignored. But her heart, oh how it abhorred logic.

Turn off All Too Well (10 Minute Version) (TS), Priya's text said.

> *I'm not listening to it.*
> *Liar.*
> *How's your brother?*
> *Don't change the subject. Change the song.*
> *But I really do think I left my scarf at his place this morning.*
> *Did not. I saw you in it today.*

Elena lifted the record player's arm, cut Taylor off mid savage burn about broken promises. No, she had left something far worse at Lawrence's. That self-portrait. She'd give anything to have it back, to have never trusted him enough to give it in the first place. She slipped the album back into its cardboard sleeve. Flipping through her collection in a milk crate she'd covered in painted flowers, she made a new selection. A moment later, guitar chords wavered into the room.

> *Back to December is no better FYI. Turn it off.*

Uncanny. She stopped the player for a second time.

> *Kiaan agreed to talk to a counselor, so progress.*
> *That's good.*

Did he try to call again?

Who?

Lawrence!

I don't know anyone by that name.

Ouch.

And I know, you told me so. You were 100% right. Bad idea.

I feel no pleasure in being correct.

Elena pulled herself up to sit cross-legged, took a sip from the bottle. Why had she thought her life would be better if she got involved with some guy she'd met through work? That place brought nothing but misery. Tomorrow, when she felt stronger, she would send out more résumés. Any reluctance to leave the area for a new job had gone up in smoke following the implosion of her relationship with Lawrence.

She could move across the country, and what would change in her life anyway? She'd still see her family a whopping twice a year. Still spend the holidays alone.

Picturing herself still sitting on this rug on Christmas Day ignited a fresh round of tears.

A secret piece of her had dared to hope she'd spend Christmas Day with Lawrence. That all she had to do was tell him she'd be alone and he would swoop in to rescue her, to bring her to his charming town full of people who adored him. To a place with fresh white snow, pine trees, lights, pretty decorations. Where the air smelled like cinnamon. To a place she'd imagined many times as a child but never thought she'd find in real life.

It might as well not exist. She had never belonged there like he did. He was right: she was a visitor, a tourist in his town. And now she was back in her place, by herself on the floor.

Another mouthful of wine, dry and sweet on her tongue.

What had he wanted to say when she'd spoken over him? He'd been about to apologize, she understood that much. And why did he call back twice but leave no message? The savage glee she felt when ignoring his calls had long since disappeared, replaced by a pensive mood. Might he have given a compelling explanation for his actions? Over the years, Dad had talked about mitigating circumstances, reasons a person didn't deserve the harshest punishment.

Would Dad concede Lawrence should have his say? Didn't the law require both sides to speak? Perhaps even Dad would want her to listen, hear Lawrence out. It might be the right thing to do, not only in her eyes, but objectively. Shouldn't she, of all people, know the world wasn't black and white? Something artists, lawyers, and even bakers could agree upon.

She traded the wine bottle for her phone, clicked on his contact.

Straight to voice mail. Fair enough. "It's me. I'm willing to talk if you are."

Late into the night she waited up, pining for a return call. While she waited, she drew, brought him back to her on the page. Over and over again. Until her hands were coated in charcoal, until it lodged under her fingernails in a way she could never wash fully away before work.

Let Derick complain, let him write her up. She welcomed any opportunity to clash with him. It might take some creativity, but she would find a way to best him.

On her fourth portrait of Lawrence, as she drew, recreating his tantalizing eyes, she started to believe this Christmas might still be different and, against the odds, she might not have to spend it alone.

But then he didn't call, not that night, or into the next day.

CHAPTER THIRTY-SEVEN

"Geez Louise, you gave me a fright. Pumpkin, you look awful."
Nana pressed the button to raise the hospital bed. She fumbled for
her glasses, put them on, then gave him a full inspection. "Sheesh.
Even worse with my glasses. What on earth is wrong with you,
dear? Are they admitting you next?"

"I slept face first on my kitchen table, having nightmares about
the worst mistake of my life." He sat on the edge of the vinyl armchair next to Nana's bed, still wearing yesterday's gray sweatpants
and ripped shirt. A night at the table and a morning spent cutting
and hammering boards from the new steps had pushed his outfit
into full-scale disheveled territory. He'd forgotten to shower for the
second day in a row, making him downright pitiful to behold. Not
that he cared what he looked like.

"My goodness, I am out of the picture for less than two days,
and I wake up to my grandson looking like he's been through the
wringer. And you've made a terrible mistake to boot. This better not
be about my stairs again, because I told you I could've called your
dad myself. It was not your fault."

"Accept I'll never forgive myself for that one, Nana, and you can't talk me out of it either. Bad as that was, I did something even stupider." He fiddled with the bandage on his injured finger. The wound beneath stung. How could he begin to explain the situation to Nana?

"Well?" Nana asked.

"In the heat of the moment, thanks to a big misunderstanding, I flipped out on my . . . on Elena."

Nana clucked, gestured to the pink plastic water cup on her tray. Lawrence sprang up, held the cup while she took a long drink from the bendy straw. "My mouth is as dry as if I'd spent the night drinking gin. Which would've been more fun."

"Nana," he chided, returning to his seat.

"Why don't you start at the beginning. I have a very difficult time imagining you 'flipping out' at anyone, especially that lovely young lady. I'm sure it's not as bad as you think. You do have a tendency to be hard on yourself, especially when it comes to relationships. I've never heard you so much as raise your voice."

"No, this time I went ballistic. I don't know what came over me. All these crushing, um, emotions all at once." He proceeded to give her the full rundown of his blowup with Elena. Each word he spoke made him feel worse, the pit in his stomach deepening. He'd forced down plain toast for breakfast, but he felt like he'd swallowed a lead weight.

"This is a fine pickle!" Nana snapped the fingers of her good hand, shook her head, disgust plain on her face. "I thought you were exaggerating, but this is really awful. What can you have been thinking, Lawrence?"

"I don't know. So many things were going on, and I was shocked, and I guess I kind of expected her to not really care about me, for it never to have been real to begin with. Oh, I don't know; it made sense in the moment."

"Goodness gracious, when I told you to trust your instincts and be yourself, I didn't mean the worst version of yourself.

Well, call her, you big dope! You kids are constantly on your phones."

Lawrence's eyes shifted to avoid Nana's. He watched the fluid drip from the IV down the line to Nana's arm. "I kind of can't do that at the moment."

"Trust me, you don't want to be too proud. Call her, say you're sorry, give her a chance to apologize for the things she said back. Not that anyone can blame her for taking you to task. It pains me to say this, pumpkin, but you were way out of line."

"I know, Nana."

"So call her. I'll wait." Nana made a move for a magazine on her tray.

"I was so upset, I . . . a little bit broke my phone."

"Broke your phone? Lawrence Benjamin Higgins, have you forgotten all your home training? And what does a 'little bit'"—here Nana made air quotes with her uncasted hand—"broken mean?"

"As in it's completely ruined. It won't even turn on or charge anymore. I can't get her number off it to call from a different phone. I'll have to go into the city to get a new one and hope they can transfer my contacts."

"I missed everything during that stupid surgery."

Lawrence didn't know what to do short of calling to beg for forgiveness. Brilliant ideas eluded him. Nana hummed, which meant she was deep in thought. "Why don't you go see her?"

"I considered that, but I know she's working a ton right now leading up to her grand opening—"

"You better not have done anything to mess up the grand opening, young man. Especially after you roped all of New Hope into going."

"I'm not a complete psycho. I came to my senses before I told anyone else what happened."

"Finally, a good decision. I guess you can't very well wait out in the cold for her to return home." Nana pursed her lips.

"Plus, there's something menacing about a guy my size loitering outside her place after she told me she never wanted to see me again."

"And certainly you can't go in your present condition."

He combed his fingers through his hair. It felt gritty from the recent lack of showers. He suspected he didn't smell too great either.

"She really said she didn't ever want to see you again?"

Lawrence flinched. Nothing pained him more than the finality in Elena's voice when she'd said that. Unable to speak, he nodded his head.

"That's good," Nana said.

"What? How?" he asked, sitting up straighter. It wasn't like Nana to kick him when he was down, but maybe he deserved it.

A nurse in blue scrubs walked in, gave a perfunctory greeting, then began typing rapidly on a computer in the corner of Nana's room. Seconds later he came to the bed to check Nana's blood pressure. "One thirty over eighty five. Borderline high, but an improvement."

The fact that Nana's blood pressure was stabilizing alleviated some of Lawrence's uneasiness. He waited while the nurse took Nana's temperature—normal—and then asked Nana again what she meant as soon as he left.

"I must've told your grandfather I never wanted to see him again at least three times."

"You told Pop Pop you never wanted to see him again? But you were in love. You were married fifty plus years." The whole family had gathered at a banquet hall for Nana and Pop Pop's golden anniversary a few years before he passed. Lawrence's parents kept a picture from that night in the family room.

"And no one could get under my skin like that man. One time I said it was when I was in labor with your auntie Arlene. He fell asleep while I was writhing in agony. Can you believe that? Who cares if he'd been awake for thirty-six hours at that point?"

"When else did you say it?" Lawrence asked, fascinated.

"I know I said it early on, because after we'd been on two dates, I saw him walking down Main Street with Gladys Martin. Well, she was Gladys Campbell then."

"Oof. Pop Pop. Bad move." The tempest inside him calmed a fraction as Nana reminisced.

"I said it that time for the pleasure of watching him grovel his way back into my good graces. And grovel he did. Gladys Campbell-Martin never did hold a candle to me, if you don't mind me being so vain as to mention it."

"What did Pop Pop do to convince you to see him again?" Lawrence scooted further to the edge of his seat, his fatigue lifting slightly.

"Now this is a story. I can't believe I've never told you this. Every night I came home from teacher school to find different specialty ingredients waiting for me on my parents' front porch. You see, even back then, I loved to bake. Pop Pop knew that. He went to the city and got me all sorts of fancy things we didn't have here at the local market. Marzipan, pink sugar for decorating, vanilla extract imported from France."

"How long did this go on?"

"At least a week. It would've gone on longer, because I wanted to see how many wonderful things I would get, but my mother persuaded me to take pity on him and return his calls. I was twenty at the time, and she was very worried I'd end up an old maid."

"And the other times? What did he do then?"

Nana sighed. She tried to rearrange her blanket one handed. When Lawrence noticed her struggling, he got up and tucked it around her.

"Isn't that funny? I can't remember anymore, all these years later." She took Lawrence's hand, her wrinkled skin soft and warm. "What I do remember is that I always forgave him. Do something special for your young lady. She'll forgive you. After all, you didn't even stoop to taking out that hussy Gladys Campbell."

Lawrence laughed for the first time since his fight with Elena. "Nor will I."

What to do for his Elena? He didn't know her favorite flowers. There was no place outside her apartment building to leave her tokens like Pop Pop had done for Nana, that legend. An idea glimmered in the back of his mind. A creative idea, to show his creative sweetheart the depth of his regret. The height of his hope for their future.

He whispered the idea to Nana.

"Oh, pumpkin," she said, "that will be perfect."

CHAPTER THIRTY-EIGHT

Once eighteen hours passed without a word from Lawrence, Elena despaired. He would never call back, and she'd have to live forever with the consequences of her ugly words. How had a version of herself ever existed who didn't want to see Lawrence? Her comments rang in her head every unoccupied minute, bats in the rafters waiting to swoop down to remind her how she'd thrown everything away over a stupid misunderstanding.

Her body toiled at Sparkle Cookie HQ, meticulously preparing for the grand opening she still intended to knock out of the park, but her mind stayed stuck in that fateful, heated conversation. Remembering how she'd kept waking the night before, foolish and sleep dazed, reaching out her hand to touch nothing.

In the dark hours, disgust at him for thinking her traitorous had given way to wondering how she would've reacted in his place. She probably would've been far more furious than he, since she hated being outplayed. She would've steamrolled over him with a verbal assault to gain the advantage, never giving him the chance to explain. The chance he'd given her.

Late at night, she began to wonder why it had been easy to badger Lawrence when she found it a challenge to speak up to those who wronged her on a daily basis. It was a low blow to go hard at Lawrence when she knew full well he'd hit rock bottom, that he struggled to articulate himself on a good day.

Those thoughts pounding her, she couldn't make herself fall back asleep. She kicked the covers off, overheated, then caught a chill and wrapped them back around her. They still smelled like his soap and his skin. For more than an hour she couldn't find a single comfortable place in her whole bed.

She might have lain awake all night, eyes stinging, save for the sudden comforting thought that she could take steps to do better. To be better.

"Voss, give me good news about tomorrow," Derick sneered over the cubical wall, jarring her back to the present. He'd gone into full-blown delusion since the recipe theft. Based on his cocky posture and extra-abrasive attitude, he believed he had the advantage, that he had scored a coup against her. How little he knew.

She narrowed her eyes at him. Didn't respond.

He wacked the top of the cubical wall, sent the papers pinned to it flapping. "Voss, hello? I asked you a question."

A thousand bitter recriminations he richly deserved sprang to mind, but she had something even worse in store for him. She wouldn't ruin the surprise by giving him any warning. She could delay her satisfaction for a bigger payout in the very near future.

"Everything is in place per the metrics you laid out. I am taking the rest of the afternoon off."

"No, you're not," Derick said. He smoothed his already too-smooth hair with the flat of his hand. "I want specifics."

"I've already supplied you with my daily report, which, per my official job description, is all that I owe you on a day-to-day basis."

"C'mon, Voss, you know I have to go upstairs before an opening and give them the razzle-dazzle." He fanned out his fingers into jazz hands. "You're my right-hand woman. Help me out."

She swore she got a literal bad taste in her mouth at his insinuation they were in this together. Sourness on her tongue.

"I'm not able to provide anything further. I have unused sick time—all of it, in fact. Remember when you insisted that I come in two months ago when I had the flu? I had a fever and chills right here at my desk. Today I will not be doing that. I will be taking my contractually owed time."

"You're not sick."

"I have a headache."

"Prove it."

"Prove I don't," she sniped back.

He looked around, as if he expected a chorus of people to support him. A performer hoping for an audience's cheers. What did he have? Next to nothing, and less than he thought. Priya had given her notice, Alan was long gone, and Sarah was too busy avoiding him by ducking into corners to offer any aid.

"Looking for someone?" Elena asked.

His eyebrows lowered, eyes narrowed to match hers. "Where's the rest of the team?"

"Not much of a team left."

"Watch your tone with me, Voss."

"As you wish. However, I've emailed HR, who approved the sick time. They cc'd you. I'll see you later." She stood from her chair, put her arms into her coat sleeves as Derick crossed his arms, moved to block her exit.

"Keep your phone on, check your emails." He didn't sound as terrifying as he used to. In truth, he sounded more scared than scary.

Elena regretted using her combative skills against Lawrence, but Derick presented the perfect opportunity to put a deserving person in his place. "I will not be available by phone nor email until normal work hours tomorrow. If you contact me, that would be a violation of the HR manual, page seventy-six, aggressive and/or harassing treatment."

Derick shifted his weight to let her pass, giving her barely enough room. In her high-heeled boots, she stood an inch taller than him. She would not shrink against the wall to shimmy past him. Instead, she strode in his direction, and at the last possible second she saw it dawn on him she wouldn't change course. Unwilling to collide with an employee and end up on an incident report, he had no choice but to clumsily dodge.

"Elena, what's wrong?" he asked, voice low with pain and confusion. He really had no clue how much everyone disliked him, what a mean, self-serving person everyone believed him to be. In his world, he was in the right and she was in the wrong.

"Oh, Derick," she said lightly, "everything is fine."

She didn't look back, left without letting him protest further. The near-constant agitation she felt in that place lessened the moment she got to the street. Even the sorrow soaking her over the loss of Lawrence abated a fraction. Outside, the wind and bright sky wouldn't let her wallow. She'd been straightforward and professional, not a bully like Derick, but she'd still managed to get her way. A sense of freedom, of accomplishment, swelled in her.

What's more, she had a mission to power her forward. A purpose and a plan.

First, she ducked into the café, purchased two coffees, and gave Mel an extra-big holiday tip. The barista—who'd dyed her hair a festive red and green—wished Elena luck. Said Elena would kill it.

From the café, she walked five blocks, coffees balanced in a paper holder. She traveled past the frigid river and under the skyscrapers' shadows until she came to an imposing concrete-and-glass tower, fifty stories high.

"Elena, what a lovely surprise," said Tonia Greene, Voss, Voss & Voss's longtime administrative assistant, coming from around her desk to give Elena a hug. "Looking for your parents? Your mom is out getting her roots done before the trip."

"I'm here for Dad. Is he busy?"

"Never too busy for you, of course. He's in a sit-down, but just with Alexander and Oliver."

"I should've brought more coffee," Elena said, wishing she had enough to offer Ms. Greene and her brothers.

"I've seen their assistants go in with pots twice in the last hour. The boys will be fine. You go ahead."

Dad only scheduled sit-downs in his own office, where he could control everything from the temperature to the height of the chairs. Elena went down the familiar hall, past the open doors of her brothers' offices to the one at the far end. The largest and the best. She didn't knock.

"Hi, Dad," she said, walking right in. She smelled French cologne and Italian leather. Her brothers were in full suits, Dad in shirt-sleeves, a tie, and suspenders. His suit coat hung on his desk chair. "Hi, guys."

"Elena! Isn't this lucky. I didn't think I get to see you until after vacation." Dad got up from a chocolate-brown armchair next to a bookcase full of legal tomes, gave her a kiss on the cheek. Both brothers stood to give her dutiful hugs. Oliver wore his typical annoyed expression, but Alex gave her a genuine squeeze. "And a coffee for the old man? To what do we owe this honor?"

"Let's sit down. I have something I need to say."

"All right . . ." For the first time ever, Dad looked thrown, as if the last thing he'd expected was Elena with an agenda.

An out-of-body anxiety stole her breath. As long as she could remember, she'd wanted to have this conversation with her family. Would she have the guts to actually have it?

Blinking, her eyes flitted to find her painting on Dad's wall, right where he'd said he put it. Then she looked at her brothers; they each had one eyebrow slightly higher than the other. Like her, a trait they all got from Dad. These were her people. She could, and must, say her piece.

"Alexander and Oliver, this is for you too. It's something I've needed to say for some time. I know you all love me and want the best for me, but the questions, concerns, and advice about my life in general and my career in particular must stop. It—"

"We ask because we wor—"

"Dad, you taught me never to let someone speak over me. I must ask you to refrain from responding."

Dad snapped his mouth shut; a small smile danced on his lips. He swept out a hand in a *You have the floor* gesture. Oliver took out his phone, but Dad gave him a stern look, and he quickly returned it to his suit pocket. Alexander nodded, and she remembered him doing that once before, years ago, when she forgot her lines in a school play. Encouraging.

"It undermines my confidence and invalidates my choices. I work hard, have always been able to take care of myself, and I will ask you directly if I need advice. All of you."

"Dramatic much, Elena?" Oliver said, rolling his eyes. She would not let him faze her. "This could've been an email."

"I came here to meet you on your level, Oliver. Communicate in the way you understand. Directly."

"We appreciate that, E," Alexander said.

"I thought I was being helpful. I've seen a lot, you know; I want to protect you from mistakes," Dad said, shoulders drooping, the closest to crestfallen she'd ever seen him.

"I know, and that means the world to me. But I need you to trust me. Don't second-guess every choice I make."

Her brothers looked to Dad for confirmation. Dad bowed his head to her. "We will respect your wishes, Elena. Thank you for telling us. For being straightforward. Clearly, you can apply my advice. That should be all the proof I need that you can look out for yourself."

Awkward silence began to creep into the room. Time to throw them a bone, bring up the second item on her list. "With that out of the way, I want it understood I have also come here to ask a favor as a professional woman who has been wronged. Not as a daughter or a sister running for help."

"What can we do?" Dad asked, shoulders squaring.

"I need you to use all your legal acumen to utterly and completely annihilate a formidable archenemy who has done his utmost to ruin my life in every possible way."

Oliver's eyes took on a wicked, hungry shine. Alexander clapped, and Dad smiled ear to ear. Pushing himself out of the chair again, Dad came over and put his arms around her. "Elena, I think I speak for your brothers too when I say we'd love nothing better."

CHAPTER THIRTY-NINE

The secret to a showstopping cookie bouquet lay in the foundation. All the decorating skills in the world didn't mean a thing if the base cookies spread or domed on the pan. To achieve clean, accurate shapes, the dough had to be the right consistency, not too crumbly or too sticky. Bake them until just set, no browning on the edges. The trick was getting a dough that not only held a shape but tasted delectable as well. Good thing Lawrence was the undisputed sugar cookie master.

He lined up his cutters next to the rolled sheet of dough. Over the years he'd collected dozens and dozens of cutters, many from Nana. He selected an oval, a square, two different flowers, a book, a Christmas lightbulb, a paintbrush. A heart.

Crouching at the workbench, he got eye level with the rolled dough, verified the height across the near-perfect rectangle. His lower back pinched again as he stood. Although it had improved, it still bothered him off and on. He wore a latex-free glove over his injured hand to keep the fresh bandage in place and avoid contact with the ingredients.

"What's all this for, boss?" Carmen asked, stopping at the bench, hands full of flat boxes to restock the front counter. After this shift, Sweet L's would be closed for the next few days for the holiday. Today would be a relatively easy day devoted to customers picking up completed orders. No new baking was on the schedule until Monday.

"Making something I've never tried before."

Carm's brow crinkled in confusion. "You make sugar cookies all the time."

"These are special. These are an I'm-sorry-please-forgive-me-I'll-do-anything-to-make-it-up-to-you apology cookie bouquet."

"My, my. Well, I hope they turn out."

"So do I." Deep in his bones, in the beats of his heart, he wished this creation would impress Elena, soften her. Something for all of her senses, to know how much he cared, how much he ached for her forgiveness. No recipe contained directions for infusing emotion into dough; no ingredient could mimic genuine feeling. For that, he had to rely on the magic that came by making something delicious for someone special, where ingredients and method mixed with the inexplicable so that a cookie could convey as much as any other art form.

"I'm glad to see you looking refreshed, mijo," Carm said, backing into the swinging door to go out front.

Last night his body had given up when his mind wouldn't, forcing him to sleep in spite of himself. He couldn't sleep in his bed, since his pillows smelled like Elena's shampoo, but he'd gotten decent rest on the sofa, even through Sugar's snores. Morning brought excitement; Nana would come home tomorrow, in time for Christmas Eve. Today he could go to his happy place to make Elena the most spectacular cookies on earth. Didn't hurt either that he'd finally showered and eaten a full meal.

While the cookies baked, he got to work on the royal icing. Powdered sugar, meringue powder, water. Simple ingredients, but he varied the ratio to make multiple consistencies for different decorating techniques. Thin to flood the shapes with background color, medium for boarders and letters, and stiff for three-dimensional elements.

Out front, Carm powered on the sound system, and he heard an orchestra begin the *Nutcracker Suite*. He spun from oven to workbench to pantry shelves, stepping over a snoozing Sugar, who had stretched as much out of the office as she dared to reach the kitchen's warmth. Unperturbed by baking sounds and Lawrence's movements, Sugar dreamed away, paws twitching.

He kept his gel food dyes, sanding sugars, sprinkles, edible glitter, and gold flakes in a tackle box. The box rattled when he plopped it on the bench. Mixing icings had a lot in common with mixing paint. He divided the royal icing into multiple glass bowls, then used toothpicks to add dots of food coloring until he had a color scheme he hoped Elena would find pleasing. Gold, pale pink, sky blue, rich green, ivory.

Once the cookies had cooled completely, the fun could begin. He filled icing bag after icing bag with a medium consistency in each color, then piped borders on all the cookies. Next came the waiting. Wait, wait, wait, all the while tempted to bite his nails as the borders dried. When he felt confident the borders were secure, he filled more bags with the thinnest icing. He flooded the surface of the cookies, tapping them until the icing looked smooth as glass.

"Nice start," Carm said, peering around him to get a look. "What are you going to do while the flood dries?"

Drying the flood layer could take hours. Crucial hours. The icing flood had to be set to make the decor details stand out, to keep the different icing colors from melting together into a swampy mess.

"Probably panic that she's going to throw these right straight in the trash. I hope I'm making the right choice spending the day doing this and not hunting down a new phone to call her."

"I know your decorated sugar cookies are worth the twenty-four-hour wait. Let her worry a little too, mijo."

"What does she have to worry about?"

"Come on, now, you weren't the only one who behaved badly. A little time to cool off will be good for both of you."

Lawrence had reached the point where he would gladly accept one hundred percent of the blame in exchange for five minutes with Elena. Carmen could be right, though; Elena might be more receptive once she'd had sufficient opportunity to miss him. A dangerous game of chicken he would have to white-knuckle his way through.

Unwilling to wait too long for the flood to dry, he lugged the fan they used during the summer from its place in the supply closet. He dusted it clean, then set it on full blast aimed at the cookies to speed the process. To keep himself sane during the delay, he went to the front to help Carm fulfill orders.

"You going to be at the tree lighting tomorrow night?" Pamela asked when she arrived to fetch her order.

"Yes, ma'am," Lawrence said, handing Pamela a box filled with peppermint biscotti and delicate pizzelle. If everything went according to plan, he would be there, and he wouldn't be alone. Best not to let Pamela know his intentions, because then Mom would know, then Nana, then the whole town.

He felt slightly confident his plan would work, but not confident enough to have everyone in New Hope staring at him on Christmas Eve. Potentially witnessing his utter humiliation. Best to keep everything close to the chest for the time being.

The next several hours offered a welcome break from obsessing about Elena while he and Carm rang up order after order. From nine AM to two PM, they didn't have a second to catch their breath. If they weren't boxing up orders, they were accepting payment or filling coffee cups. Carm had stocked the bakery case full with impulse cookies, and customers who didn't want to wait until the holiday for something sweet ordered cookies for the road. Even without the magazine contest prize money, he might be able to pay January's rent. And who knew what the New Year would bring? Maybe good things, maybe the best things.

"Boss, I need to tell you something," Carm said as Lawrence locked the front door. The rush of customers had subsided a couple of minutes ago, and now they were done for the day. Carm was, at least; Lawrence would stay to finish the cookie bouquet.

"Sure thing," he said. Carm's tone let him know she had something important on her mind, so he held off on washing down the front counters, gave her his full attention.

"You know how much I love working here, right?"

Oh no, here it came. The moment he'd been fearing.

"I do, Carm. And you're awesome at your job."

"Working here makes me really happy, but . . ." Carm straightened a pile of paper order forms that didn't need it. She didn't meet his eyes, kept looking down at the papers.

"But," he said, prompting her to continue.

"But I'm not as young as I once was, and these grandkids, they take it out of me. My Isabel and her husband still haven't been able to find reliable care for them. And we don't want them to grow up spending half their time with strangers." Again she paused, tapped the papers on the counter to line them up.

Lawrence had been dreading this for so long it felt surreal. And yet he didn't feel as petrified as he'd feared. An unexpected calm bolstered him. He felt he would be able to handle the bakery in Carm's absence. Remembering Nana's encouragement to trust himself more, he tried to hone in on the belief he'd be all right, no matter what life threw at him.

"Spending time with them is more important than anything else," he said. "Can you imagine where I'd be without Nana?"

At this Carm gave him a wan smile. "It doesn't have to be right away, you know. I want to give you plenty of time. As much as

I hate to say this, I think you need to start looking for someone to take my place."

"No one can take your place, Carm. You've put up with me from day one."

"We've had fun, mijo," Carm said, putting her arm around him.

"We have. Don't forget the employee discount is a lifetime discount. You better come see me all the time. And bring the little ones too."

"I wouldn't take them anywhere else. Except for one visit to Sparkle Cookie. We should still come tomorrow, right?"

"You absolutely should."

"It's going to work out, boss. I can feel it in my bones."

"Well then, it's as good as done."

Carm went through the swinging door to the kitchen, tossed her apron in the hamper for the linen service. Lawrence didn't let himself wonder when the last time Carm wore the Sweet L's apron would be. He stayed brave for her. Carm gave Sugar a belly rub and then wished Lawrence a merry Christmas before leaving.

He stood alone with his uncertainty—the unknowns about the bakery, about Nana's recovery, about Elena. He made himself reflect on it all until he felt certain he could face it, that he wanted to try even if it would be difficult.

"What do you say, Sugar? Should I get to work on the decorating?" Sugar rolled on her back, paid him no mind. "Aw, you know you miss her too. Let's make her the most spectacular cookies she's ever seen."

CHAPTER FORTY

Half infuriated, half intrigued by Lawrence's unbroken radio silence, Elena toyed with the idea of finding him after her grand-opening shift. As hours, then whole days, passed without contact, she wondered if she'd mistaken his interest level, his ability to overcome an unfortunate disagreement. Perhaps he didn't think her worth the effort, had opted to dip out when the going got tough. Childish. Forget him, then.

Eventually, however, she became downright worried. Surely he wouldn't ghost her after weeks and weeks together, forget her despite their electric connection? Unless he had become an *actual* ghost. Had a terrible fate befallen him that prevented a return call? Her mind painted vivid, frightening pictures. Lawrence's truck flipped over on an icy back road, the choking smoke of a raging bakery fire, violent kidnappers who somehow overpowered him despite his superior strength.

She recognized such dramatic visions were unlikely, but perhaps a more ordinary peril had intervened. For all she knew, something dire had occurred with Nana. Conceited on her part to assume nothing short of tragedy would keep Lawrence from returning her call. But empowered by her recent foray into honest conversations, she guessed it couldn't hurt to see him face-to-face to offer a respectful explanation of her actions that terrible day.

Except everything about returning to New Hope hurt. The exit sign on the highway seemed like a memorial marker. The snow on the roadside had turned mud-stained since she'd last driven through. Sky overcast. Sidewalks hadn't been cleared, and stamped-down ice patches ran in uneven paths. In the full daylight, no one turned on their holiday lights, of course, making houses and businesses seem pointlessly wrapped in ugly wires. Deflated Santas lay prone on front lawns, hollow until nightfall. Dismal to the core.

Getting to stay on the new side of town offered a shred of relief. She couldn't face driving down Main Street yet, seeing the bakery. Dipping her toes in might prepare her for a nighttime visit. Meanwhile, she'd have to hope to stay busy.

She went through the employee entrance into the New Hope Sparkle Cookie. Instantly, the smell of gingerbread latte cookies hit her, heavy enough in the air she could almost taste them. That scent pulled her into the past, brought her back to making them the first time with Lawrence in her kitchen. The night the snowstorm let her keep him, to the day they made the cookies with Nana and Elena got a glimpse of what it would be like to be part of his life for real. To know his family. The ingredients written in his hand, stolen by Derick.

She shook her head, couldn't allow herself to dwell.

"Hello, I'm Elena Voss from corporate, here to oversee the opening," she told the manager, a man about her age wearing the required lavender polo shirt and dark-gray slacks. "Are you excited for the big day?"

"Kenneth Scultz," he said, offering his hand to shake. When she took it, she caught interest in his eyes, in the curve of his mouth. Seeing someone look at her the way Lawrence first had made her miss him all the more. She gave a firm handshake, then got right to business, giving Kenneth a hint she wanted to keep it professional.

She put him to work rearranging tables, then went to the kitchen to introduce herself to the bakers. Since Sparkle cookies came from a mix, most of the kitchen staff were high school students. A girl with wide-set blue eyes seemed impressed by Elena's title, too shy to say much, while a boy baker cracked a few jokes. Getting to work was helping; the ache in her stomach and the racing thoughts of earlier disappeared.

Back out front, she checked to see a growing line waiting for the store's opening in thirty minutes. Not as many people as she needed to earn her bonus, the cushion she wanted while looking for new work. Had word gotten around about her poor treatment of Lawrence? It seemed unlikely he would all out sabotage her work, but maybe people knew they'd fought and figured they didn't need to attend the opening anymore.

A sudden possibility thrilled her. Would he show up? Might he make a kind gesture, forgive her even when she didn't deserve it, hadn't said sorry? Hope batted in her chest. "Time to open the doors, Elle," Kenneth, the manager, said.

She bristled at the unwelcome nickname. If she'd been more compassionate when Lawrence called, she might be able to name-drop her boyfriend, get the point across clearly. What could she say now? *I have a situationship I ruined because I don't have a clue how to be assertive and not downright aggressive?*

Be assertive, not aggressive. Not her dad's voice this time, but her own. In her heart, she knew she did have a clue. After all, hadn't she spoken up to her family without resorting to barbed words and scare tactics? "Please call me Elena," she said.

"My bad," Kenneth answered. There, she'd done well. She could find a compromise between her dad's values and her own. Kenneth seemed none the worse for wear, and he switched to a businesslike demeanor, giving her space and sticking to opening-day issues.

Even if Lawrence didn't accept her apology tonight, she vowed to remain respectful to him. She wouldn't let disappointment or anger overwhelm her this time. She suspected she would feel better about herself if she stayed truer to herself, to the gentler, artistic side. If she found the balance between not getting walked on and not walking on anyone else.

Maybe all I'll have to show for this is a better sense of self, but please, let me have him too.

Time to let the influencers in the back door after they pretended to wait in line, so they could take their pictures without crowds messing up shots. A woman wearing a blinding amount of highlighter posed kissing the gingerbread latte cookie. In another corner, a mommy influencer fed some to her daughters in matching cranberry-red velvet dresses and hair bows, who screamed and kicked because they didn't want to be there.

Same, girls. Same.

A third influencer took a bite for the camera, then promptly spit it out into a napkin.

I can't wait to leave this place behind.

Elena's phone rang. Derick. Perfect; she couldn't wait for his reaction to the letter sent by her dad and brothers on Voss, Voss & Voss letterhead. Dad had promised they'd messenger it straight to Sparkle Cookie HQ's in-house counsel by nine in the morning. She ducked into the kitchen as Kenneth opened the doors to the general public. Leaning against a shiny stainless-steel refrigerator, the metal cool through her shirt, she answered.

"Voss, what is all this? Some kind of a joke? You sent a cease-and-desist for a stolen cookie recipe? You know how the culture is around here; I have to produce. When I saw your recipe, I figured I could get the jump on it for us both." His words flooded out, his pitch high, almost squeaky.

"My lawyer is confident we can prove wrongdoing. We have witnesses who can testify to the recipe development predating your supposed invention of gingerbread latte cookies." Nana and Carm were the witnesses; she also had a text from Lawrence asking her if she knew where he'd left the recipe. At the time, she hadn't, and he'd had to rewrite it. Dad doubted this strategy could hold up in court, but he was also sure Sparkle Cookie wouldn't want the bad press of a scandal. They'd settle.

"You're asking for commission on every unit sold in addition to your bonus? I have to go upstairs to explain all this, and I need you to make it make sense."

"Derick, in all honestly, it should make perfect sense to you. You know that you use bullying and shaming to make us work harder so you can take the credit. You know in your heart you stole that recipe from me, didn't even attempt to acknowledge my contributions in the quarterly meeting."

"But . . . but . . . Voss, we're a team," he spluttered.

Elena bit her tongue to keep from all out laughing at him. "We were never a team, Derick. That would imply you valued any one of us. You only care about yourself. I hope you've updated your résumé. Now I need to focus on this grand opening. Happy holidays. Bye!"

Her mouth widened into a full smile, her heartbeat fast with excitement. Derick would get his just desserts, and she would find a different job. She had a lot to offer a company, and if this opening went well, she could put it on her own résumé.

Nervous energy jittering in her veins, she left the kitchen to find a stream of people gushing in the front doors. The most she'd ever seen at an opening. She rose on her tiptoes, looked out the front windows. The line stretched forever, people in thick jackets and scarves, chatting and taking pictures. There was Mr. Martinez the bookseller, Pamela the florist holding what looked like a bouquet wrapped in butcher paper. Even Carm and her daughter with a trio of little kids who jumped about, throwing snow clumps.

Tears, happy tears, on her cheeks. He hadn't told everyone to stay away; he hadn't stood in the way of her success. Did he possibly still support her, want to see her win? Her eyes flew from face to face, hoping to spot the one she wanted most. Nowhere in sight. Trey and Iris held hands, joined the line. His best friend, but where—where—was he?

"Elena," Pamela said when she stepped out of the cold into the store. "These are for you."

"Thank you, Pamela. How thoughtful." Should she ask Pamela if Lawrence planned to come? If she'd seen him, or how Nana was doing?

"They're not from me, hon." Pamela handed her the flowers.

Adrenaline fizzed like champagne inside her. She forgot to say another word to Pamela, or even to say hello to other people from New Hope she recognized. She had to get alone as fast as possible to tear off the paper, to see what he'd sent. Skidding on her high heels through the kitchen, she rounded the corners at a fast clip until she made it to the back office. Thankfully, Kenneth was out front assisting customers.

Hands shaking so intensely she feared dropping the bouquet, she set in on the manager's desk. The paper crinkled as she tore it away. Not flowers, but cookies! The most beautiful cookies in the world. Paintbrushes, crème brûlée, a little open book with miniscule words in icing: *You have bewitched me body and soul. Pride and Prejudice*, the book they'd looked at on their first date. A glove, like the one she'd left in the town hall, the one he'd run after her to return. A square with exact portraits of Lorelei and Rory Gilmore, a frame around them like they were inside a TV.

She extended a shy finger, gently touched a large square cookie covered in writing. Not another book quote. A long explanation, and a plea for forgiveness.

First of all, I broke my phone like a fool. If you've tried to call, I haven't been ignoring you. Nana is feeling better and I've come to my senses. I should never, never have thought the worst of you when you've shown me many times how much better you are than that. I can't forgive myself, but maybe you can find it in that sweet, kind heart of yours to cut me a break. I suck and I'm sorry. I can do better, much better. I hope you have the best grand opening. If you can still—

Here an icing arrow indicated she should turn over the cookie for the rest of the message. She plucked the cookie out by its cardboard stem, twirled it to see the other side.

—stand the sight of me, please meet me tonight at the gazebo by town hall at nine o'clock and we can work things out. Yours, Lawrence

She put her face in her hands, crying and laughing at the same time. Who cared about crying at work in a moment like this? The best moment, maybe ever, in her whole life up to now. Gulping in a breath, she dried her face on her lavender sleeves.

She put the apology cookie back in the bouquet, traded it for a decorated rose cookie that shimmered with fine glitter. Elaborate and as artistic as anything she could paint. And it smelled delicious, buttery and sweet. She took a big bite.

He'd been right all along. She could taste love.

CHAPTER FORTY-ONE

What's the worst that could happen? Lawrence asked himself as he waited in the pressing crowd gathered for the tree lighting. Total and complete disgrace for one. No doubt every single person at tonight's ceremony knew who Lawrence hoped to see running toward him. Sure, he'd told a limited few, but word had a habit of getting around New Hope in no time flat. Well, that was the price he had to pay for what he'd done. Even if she stood him up, he had to be proud of himself for taking the chance, for refusing to retreat into his shell to avoid disappointment.

Too bad Nana wasn't up to the tree lighting this year. She would've stood by him, preventing him from fleeing. On this, her first full day out of the hospital, Nana had opted to rest at home and watch *It's a Wonderful Life* on her ancient TV with Trey's grandpa in the uncomfortable chair beside her.

Lawrence had picked them up split pea soup from the diner and brought them a plate of cookies, including Nana's favorite: crisp molasses cookies. Nana drank her soup clasped in her working hand; Mr. Simmons helped her dab her mouth with a paper napkin.

Meanwhile, Lawrence sat on Nana's stiff sofa, knees bouncing with anticipation, forcing himself to watch the first half hour of the movie.

With each minute that passed, he tried to shore up some nerve for the night ahead. He couldn't concentrate on the movie; though he'd seen it many times, the plot confused him. He could barely respond to Nana's questions. Her voice sounded like it came from deep underwater. Everything seemed distant, like he was watching his own life from a remove, preoccupied with a dozen scenarios of how the night might play out.

Elena happy to see him. Elena standing him up. Elena coming to see him to announce to the entire town how terrible he was. How he would have to change his name and relocate.

Here at the tree lighting, he felt glad the temperature sat at twenty-eight degrees, because then people weren't chatty. With his scarf wrapped high and his hat pulled low, he could be somewhat incognito, give off the impression he didn't want to talk. He helped Carm set up a folding table outside the gazebo with cookies for the kids. Every time footsteps approached, he twisted around, expecting Elena.

"Mijo, take it easy," Carm said, giving a little boy a candy cane cookie. "If you have a panic attack, you won't be able to enjoy yourself."

"I have to walk around." Getting his body moving in the hopes of dispelling some energy was his best option for not dropping dead. He looked to the clock tower where he and Trey had once suspended the poor Santa decoration. Neither had lived that down, but maybe the legend of Lawrence Higgins getting dumped at the gazebo would take its place. Then he'd have to wait another almost decade until some new embarrassment made people forget about him and Elena.

A throng began to descend as the time for the lighting grew nearer. Yep, pretty much every person he'd ever known crowded into the square.

Voices grew louder the more people piled in, and he tried not to be bothered by all the talking, by the people jostling into him. A DJ on the town hall steps fiddled with a laptop, and then "Santa Claus Is Coming to Town" blasted from speakers. A tangle of cords trailed down the stairs; the music shook around him.

His poor eyes got a break at least, since the lights were kept to a minimum to make the moment when Santa lit the tree more magical. He tipped his head back to look at the starry sky. Focusing on the points of light in the clear sky, he debated if this had been the worst idea ever. Would she even be able to find him in this horde? Was it too late to change the plan? Of course it was. Without the ability to call her, the odds of finding a way to tell her to meet at his place instead were beyond low.

Giggling children ran by him. One knocked into his left leg as they raced to see who could get to the live reindeer in a pen by the gazebo first. Poor animals. They usually enjoyed a peaceful life at the Christmas tree farm north of downtown. But they more than earned their keep when hundreds of children—sticky with candy, reeking of peppermint—descended on them at this event. He and Trey used to race to the reindeer every Christmas Eve. Thanks to his long legs, Lawrence always won. Maybe he could run through the streets, hope to catch Elena parking.

Parking. Dread sank his stomach. Why hadn't he thought of it sooner? It became a complete nightmare parking for the ceremony. She'd end up spending the whole night looking for a spot, give up and go home. He wouldn't be able to call for two more days, since he couldn't get to the city for a phone until after the holiday. Stupid, stupid. This whole plan sucked. He'd gotten hung up on the idea of how romantic it would be to see her as the tree came to life, and he'd forgotten all the logistics.

Music wailed from the DJ booth, and he saw Mayor Montgomery taking a microphone. "Friends, neighbors, and visitors, New Hope welcomes you to our annual tree-lighting ceremony," the mayor said. Frantically, Lawrence looked around, desperate to catch a glimpse of Elena. He saw a young woman with dark hair, but when she turned to listen to the mayor, it wasn't Elena. Trying not to trample anyone, he pushed toward the gazebo. People ducked away from him when they saw him marching forward, a singular purpose plain on his face.

"We're going to count down now. Kids, close your eyes. We need your magic to make this work. Eyes closed? Good. Now, please, make an extra-special wish to see Santa before he flies off in his sleigh to deliver presents," Mayor Montgomery said. She turned to a village worker in tan coveralls, nodded. "Lights, please."

The entire square went pitch dark; the music lowered, as he'd known it would. Somehow, he'd expected he would've found Elena before this moment. That fate would lead them together. Let him hold her hand and see her face when the lights came on. She loved holiday lights.

"Ten, nine, eight . . . ," the mayor and the crowd chanted. The only illumination now came from the fire truck as it crawled down a closed street to the center of the square. Children shrieked when they saw Santa in the swirling red lights. Applause broke out. Lawrence used the advantage of his height to try one last time to find Elena. Rose to the balls of his feet, stretched his neck until the muscles pulled.

Nothing.

No one.

Although he'd been a bundle of nerves, he'd still believed deep down that she would be here. He wished he'd had time to pump Pamela for information on how the cookie bouquet delivery had gone. Had the bouquet been discarded uneaten? No. He'd seen Elena with desserts. Even if she didn't want to forgive him, she wouldn't let good treats go to waste.

Santa waved to the crowd and mounted the steps to the gazebo, pausing to catch his breath on the second one. If Santa collapsed, even greater chaos would break out and he'd lose all hope of finding Elena. Not to mention the trauma for the children.

The man in front of Lawrence lifted a little girl with pigtails sticking out from her knit hat onto his shoulders, effectively cutting off Lawrence's view. Lawrence wove around him, stubbed his toe on a loose cobblestone.

"One more countdown now that Santa is here," Mayor Montgomery boomed. Lawrence knew they liked to whip up the audience with a second countdown, but he needed the lights on already to get a good look around.

His heart beat in his ears with each number. *Ten, nine, eight, seven, six* . . . Was this taking way longer than usual? *Hurry up, let me see her.* More clapping, cheering, loud as a stadium during a play-off game. *Five, four* . . .

Where are you, Elena?

Three, two . . .

One.

A gloved hand took his and the lights burst on, filling the square with color and warmth. He looked down and there she was, looking at him with big, dark, hopeful eyes. Everyone forgot the cold, cheering too loudly for Lawrence to be able to say any of the things he'd planned for days. Her cheeks and the tip of her nose were red from the cold, and he put his hands on her face to protect her from the chill. To feel her again.

She reached up, wrapped her arms around his neck. He pulled her up and in. He didn't need to say anything, and neither did she. What could either of them say that could say more than this kiss? Frosting-sweet lips on his. Many times in his life, he'd lived the magic of the tree lighting, buying into it less as he got older. This time, it felt truly enchanted in a way it never had before. He'd been wrong about a lot lately. For the first time, Elena in his arms, body against his, he realized he'd been wrong about New Hope. With Elena back beside him, it *was* a fantasyland. Better than the best dream.

"I'm sorry," she said.

"Not as sorry as me." She couldn't possibly be as sorry as he was, or as happy. No one had ever been this happy. No one else had ever gotten to hold Elena like this, see the colorful lights flickering in her bright eyes.

"I missed you," she murmured, her breath warm in his ear.

"Not as much as I missed you." In truth, he had never missed anyone more. He breathed her in. He didn't have to miss her anymore, or ever again. She was here, here in his arms. To stay.

CHAPTER FORTY-TWO

Elena felt like a kid on Christmas morning. Even better than a kid, in fact. Her childhood Christmases had often been spent in some sunny location, sitting at formal hotel brunches before Dad golfed and Mom disappeared to the spa. This Christmas morning, she sat at Lawrence's kitchen table, coffee in hand, watching him make pancakes. Sugar lay over her bare feet, keeping them perfectly warm while she waited. Through the sliding door to his diminutive back-yard, she saw more snow had fallen overnight, icing an old oak's branches. Paw prints in curlicue patterns disrupted the snow on the ground, yet everything still looked dreamy and wonderful to her.

"Are you sure your parents won't think I'm a crasher? I wish I had a gift to bring." She accepted a plate from Lawrence with three fluffy pecan pancakes in a neat stack, topped with butter and a generous pour of fragrant maple syrup.

"Everyone will be grateful I'm not sitting around like a lonely mope dragging down the mood. That's gift enough for them. Anyway, my mom would never forgive me if I let you go back to the city alone while your family is out of town. You have to promise not to laugh at my little league pictures all over the hallway wall. Or believe any stories my sister tells you."

Elena cut a chunk of pancake with her fork. She'd seen the entire process as he made breakfast but didn't quite believe anyone could make pancakes this light and flavorful without sorcery. They melted on her tongue. "Is your sister a liar?"

"No, not at all. I just know she's going to bust out all her most unflattering memories to give me a hard time. Remember, it's all from her perspective. I was actually much more with it than she gives me credit for."

"I can only imagine the embarrassing stories my brother Oliver would tell about me if he had a chance. He'd probably bring up that time I became truly convinced the basement was haunted. Wouldn't go down there for months."

"Kids. Such imaginations." Lawrence added more syrup to his pancakes in amber drizzles. He pointed his fork at her. "Basements are pretty creepy when you think about it. I think Oliver is wrong and you were onto something."

"Thank you! No one believed me. I swear I heard whispering down there." She shivered.

He reached over to pinch her cheek. "I promise to go into all the basements with you."

"I will use you as a human shield if a poltergeist comes for us."

"Tough, but fair." He got up to retrieve a mini nut-free pancake for Sugar. Torn between the promise of food and her spot on Elena's feet, she lay there sniffing the air until he placed it right in front of her. "This one. She's got the soft life. Wait till you see her at my parents'. I swear they're happier to see her than me. Even their cat likes her. Go figure."

Happiness billowed in Elena. She hummed between bites. A holiday with family and pets and him. Best of all, things didn't feel awkward between them. He'd accepted her apology and she'd accepted his. Last night, after the splendid tree lighting, they came back here to talk everything out. They vowed to give each other the benefit of the doubt going forward, to be careful not to say hurtful things when they were upset. To cut each other slack.

She'd sat on his lap in front of the fireplace, shadow and light playing on his handsome face, amazed that she could have a conflict and things could turn out okay. That she could have a second chance and be willing to give one, despite everything she'd been taught to the contrary. Even Priya had admitted it sounded different from the fights that had torn her and Arjun apart. They'd often got madder at each other as time passed instead of wanting to reconcile.

Elena realized she had never been as alone as she felt in her lowest moments, because she'd always had her friend. Priya had been the sweetest to answer texts late last night, especially after Elena learned Priya had finally managed to meet up with her brother. Priya shared her brother's confession that he was being bullied and that his out-of-character behavior had been his response to peer pressure. Thankfully, Kiaan had agreed to see his counselor again to find new ways to confront his problems. Yes, things might not be ideal all the time, but when people cared for each other, when they were willing to try, solutions existed.

Elena wiggled a foot free, petted Sugar's cottony fur with her toes. "To be fair, she's really, really cute."

"Hey, if you only hang out here to see Sugar, I'll take what I can get." He shrugged those broad shoulders, a half smile on the lips she loved to kiss.

"You might be a smidge cuter."

"Plus I don't eat off the floor."

"That is a mark in your favor."

When they'd finished the pancakes, Lawrence took Sugar for a walk while Elena got ready to meet his family. Yesterday she'd been optimistic enough to pack clean clothes and her cosmetics pouch in her tote bag. Today she wouldn't have to wear Sparkle purple; she could wear a cardinal-red angora sweater with gold jewelry. She bit at her lips as she surveyed her appearance in the bathroom mirror. Poised to minimize the difference between her eyebrows, she dropped her brow pencil in the sink. It had been a few years since she'd been at the meet-the-parents relationship stage. That relationship had ended after six months—not for any dramatic reason, just life.

How could she tell if what she and Lawrence had would last? She wanted this to be real. Needed it to her very core. Wanted their relationship to grow, to have more holidays with him. Was that why she felt like she was about to go on a job interview instead of a holiday meal? She twirled her hair around her finger as she mulled over what it would mean if Lawrence's family didn't like her. Would they hold a grudge about the fight, even if he didn't? He was close with his family, and if she and they didn't get along, he might question her suitability too.

No matter how they treated her, she would not fall back on her old ways. They weren't that old, after all. Nothing could make her take the easy way and put up her protective barriers. She had to show Lawrence—and herself—that she didn't have to resort to patronizing behavior to cover self-doubt.

But being vulnerable was unknown territory, left her fluttering with uncertainty. The hair coiled tight around her finger now, and she unwound it before she cut off circulation. She kept her hands busy putting on gold hoops before she pulled out all her hair.

"Beautiful," Lawrence said, watching her descend the creaky stairs to the living room. She folded her hands together to keep from tangling them up in her hair again. "What's wrong?" he asked when she got closer.

"Are you sure I shouldn't go home? It's not the first Christmas I've spent on my own, and it won't be a big deal. We could see each other tomorrow." His parents might like her better once some time had passed. Though she tried to be nonchalant, she couldn't look him in the eye.

"Getting cold feet?"

"What? No. Not at all." He snaked an arm around her waist. She adored that move, loved to be pulled into him. Caught up in her hopes and the excitement of the tree lighting, she'd jumped at his holiday invitation. Now she worried he felt he had to include her out of pity.

"Is it my plaid shirt? Do you not want to be seen with me? Nana got me this shirt, so I have to wear it."

"Nana will be there?" Nana liked her. If Nana put in a good word, that could help. "Besides, you look good in everything."

"Then why won't you look at me?"

"It's nothing. I'm being silly." Dad had taught her negotiating skills and Mom had taught her etiquette, made her practice at the country club and charity luncheons. Since Lawrence's mother had accommodated the unexpected addition, it would be unspeakably rude if Elena backed out. "I feel . . ." What did she feel? Something she wasn't used to. "I feel shy."

"Aw, baby, I'm an expert at shyness. Awful feeling. But you'll be great. Follow Nana's advice and be yourself. Everyone is excited to meet you, by the way. Mom stopped by while you were in the shower and asked what your favorite food is."

"Oh no!" Elena leaned back, gave him a horrified look. "She's not going to extra trouble for me is, she? I hope you told her I'll eat anything. I'll eat dirt if she serves it."

"I did not say you eat dirt. Let's save a little of your weird for the second time you visit."

She pursed her lips. "They might not ask me back."

"Come on, now, we don't get too many new faces around these parts. They'll want to get to know you."

"Well, if you promise they won't hate me."

"Elena, sweetheart, no one could hate you."

Not true. She'd hated herself since their disagreement up to the moment he kissed her at the tree lighting. But could she find the fortitude to trust him, to put herself out there? Her tongue stuck to the roof of her mouth. She swallowed to compose herself. "Okay, if you say so. Can I hide behind you if I get too scared?"

"My family aren't poltergeists, I promise you. Guess what? I think you're going to have fun. And we're out of time. Sugar, get your leash. We gotta head over."

A blind jump, then, and a faint faith for a safe landing.

CHAPTER FORTY-THREE

A nervous Elena might be the cutest version of Elena. Endearing, if a bit strange, to see her facade drop. She kept combing her fingers through her long, dark hair until he took her hand to encourage her to relax. It was weird to be on the other side of social anxiety, in a place where he felt totally comfortable. How could he ensure she had a good time?

"Are you sure I can't help in the kitchen?" Elena asked, perched next to him on the sofa. Mom bustled past in her wreath print apron, paused, a casserole dish containing macaroni and cheese in her oven-mitted hands. Through the kitchen doorway he saw Nana sitting on a barstool at the stove, stirring one handed since she refused to let anyone else near the gravy. Nana's other arm was in a sling that made him blue each time he saw it.

"No, no, dear. Lonnie and I made most of the dishes last night." Mom had her ways when it came to hosting guests, and Lawrence knew nothing could induce her to accept Elena's assistance. Maybe in time. "And you two brought dessert. Just a few finishing touches left, and then we can eat. You enjoy your punch."

Mom hurried toward the dining room, and Elena tensed beside him.

He rubbed the back of her neck. She sighed like she'd been holding her breath, then seemed to regret sighing and covered it with a fake cough. "Be careful with the punch," he whispered. "Nana spikes it like crazy every year."

Elena's eyes widened, and she carefully set her glass on a coaster atop a round end table that still bore the floral skirted tablecloth his mother had bought on sale in 1993.

"Elena, I love your sweater," Lonnie said, stretching out on the love seat across from them. He and Lonnie might troll each other—as siblings must—but he could hug her right now for making an effort with Elena. No introvert could deny the value of someone who initiated conversation. Elena might be far from an introvert, but she clearly needed a lifeline today.

Lonnie's boyfriend had been conscripted by Dad to help find the dining room table leaf in the attic. Lawrence could hear the creaking all the way down here. He expected one or both of them to fall through the ceiling at any moment. Usually, Dad made Lawrence help set up the table, but everyone was treating him like a VIP today because of his special guest.

"Thank you," Elena said to his sister.

"Where'd you get it?"

"Um . . ." Elena shook her head slightly, like she needed to clear her thoughts. "It's actually from this boutique by my apartment. They make garments from salvaged fabrics. To be sustainable."

"I love that. I'll have to check it out the next time I'm in the city." Lonnie had the Higgins bright-blue eyes, and they shifted to Lawrence to make sure he noticed what a thoughtful sister she was being. He nodded to keep her talking.

"Sugar seems to have taken quite the liking to you," Lonnie said, indicating the dog, who hadn't left Elena's side. Sugar must've sensed Elena's need for an emotional support animal. A lifetime of soothing Lawrence's jitters had honed the dog's skills. "Do you have pets?"

"We weren't allowed to have them growing up, because my mom worried about fur on clothes and furniture. I love animals, though, and always wanted a cat."

Lawrence got a pang of sadness at the thought of Elena's pet-free childhood. "You like cats?" he asked, and her chin dipped in a nod. There was no shortage of kittens needing homes in the New Hope spring thanks to all the barn cats. A seed of a plan began to take root in his mind. He envisioned the look on Elena's face if he handed her a kitten. Or a whole basket of kittens.

"You have to meet Chuckles," Lonnie said, snapping her fingers. "I'll be right back." She left to search for their parents' ancient tortoiseshell cat.

"Doing okay?" Lawrence said softly.

"Everyone is so nice." She looked at him with astonished eyes, as if she'd been expecting the opposite. Again, he felt that tug in his heart, this time wishing she'd never be treated with indifference again. She wouldn't be if he could help it.

Earlier he'd wondered what she would think of his childhood home, a well-kept but aged farmhouse, no neighbors for a mile. From everything she'd told him about her childhood, she was used to the finer things. He thought the Higgins family home one of New Hope's prettiest, but he knew it was humble. The floral wallpaper here in the living room bore traces of mistreatment from when he and Lonnie were little. Crayon that never quite came off, nicks where they'd tossed toys. The wood floors had been scratched by various family pets.

He followed Elena's gaze as her eyes fell on one of Mom's doilies. Mom had a serious doily addiction; they were under every lamp, every dish displayed in the china cabinet—she even had a long one under the TV. Used to drive him nuts when he was a kid because he always got in trouble for spilling juice on them. They did make the place look homey. Elena kept looking around the room, asking him in quiet tones about this and that, interested in the artifacts of his life. Just as he liked seeing New Hope through her eyes, he realized he liked seeing his family home reflected in them as well.

Her hand felt cool in his, and he brought it to his lips to warm with a kiss, thinking how she loved holiday decorations. "Look behind you."

Elena turned to see the sofa table, which held a porcelain Christmas village atop a thick layer of fake snow. LED tealights flickered in miniature shops, homes, and Santa's workshop. She brightened, eyes lighting up to match the festive display. She dropped his hand to run a fingertip over the rooftops.

"Don't look too closely at the bed-and-breakfast. I cracked off the chimney when I was seven, and we had to glue it back on." Poor Mom; she'd really put up with a lot over the years.

"The bakery is my favorite." Elena pointed to the little red brick building, a fair dupe for Sweet L's.

"Mom found that the year I opened." Should he tell Elena the peril the bakery faced? Would that automatically make her feel guilty because he couldn't enter the contest? Because Sparkle Cookie had jacked up rents? He intended to give this relationship his best—last night he'd made sure she knew he wanted to be exclusive. She wanted the same. Did that mean he had to find a way to tell her about the rent increase? His natural instinct told him not to mention a word. That felt like keeping her at arm's length, though. And she had just started to chill; he couldn't distress her now. He didn't fear they'd have another argument, but he didn't want to put a damper on her day.

Mom called everyone to the table, and he forgot about the bakery as he enjoyed Elena's reaction to the food. She hit her stride asking questions about the different dishes, delighting Nana and Mom as they boasted about their recipes for green bean casserole and corn muffins. Even Dad had something to say, telling Elena how he himself had concocted the turkey brine. It was the only thing Dad could cook besides peanut butter and jelly sandwiches. Who could blame him for wanting to show off?

Elena oohed and aahed over the Christmas tree plates and matching napkins Mom had collected over several years. He suspected she'd never had a real family Christmas in her life. What did the Vosses do on holidays? Say bah-humbug and go their separate ways the first chance they got? Grim.

An hour or so after dinner, everyone began to agitate for dessert while playing Uno. "Okay, okay. I'll get it," he said.

Lonnie glared when he held out a hand to Elena. "You're not taking her away, are you? I wanted to tell her about the time you and Trey put dish soap—"

"Let me stop you there," he said, before Lonnie could shame him with his preteen indiscretions. Happy Elena and his sister were having fun, he nonetheless wanted to keep her for himself. He stole her away to the kitchen.

"Yay, more coffee!" Elena said. He refilled her Christmas tree mug, then looked over his shoulder to make sure no one was watching. He stole a long kiss. How wonderful to have her here, to see her happy. This was the kind of moment he'd feared was lost forever after their fight.

"I'm going to set the cheesecake out to come up to room temperature, and we're going to make some cherry sauce to put on top."

"Anything you say, chef," she whispered for his ears only, wrapping her arms around him from behind. He gripped the refrigerator handle.

"Or we can go back to my place right this minute, and they can get their own dessert."

"And miss the cheesecake? You are delicious, but you're no cheesecake."

"How can you be so fickle?" He took the plastic-wrapped cheesecake and set it on the counter, checked again for privacy. He grabbed her and whispered, "Lay off the flirting, then, trouble-maker, or no dessert for you."

He lived for the way she curled against him, giggling. "Only till we leave. Then I'm going right back to it."

"I consider that a promise. I'll hold you to it." The burner clicked, then the flame burst on. "This cherry sauce is to die for, sweetie. Although I would still choose you over it, it's a close second. Can you get the bag of cherries from the freezer while I juice the lemon? Those cherries come from an orchard in New Hope, by the way, so you know they're the best. Only the best for you."

"I'd expect nothing less."

He spun back to the stove, furiously whisked sugar and corn-starch into the lemon juice and water.

"Add the cherries slowly," he instructed. "Don't want hot water to splatter you."

"The whole bag?"

"Believe me, people are going to want to eat this by itself. It's best if we have extra." As the fruit began to warm and soften, sweet, tart cherry scent overtook the kitchen.

"It smells sensational. Look at that color. Like garnets. I think this sauce would go well with my second-favorite flavor."

"Well, I know coffee is your first favorite. What's the second?"

"Chocolate, of course."

"Ah yes, of course. You're right, chocolate and cherry go together like . . . like Lawrence and Elena."

At the same moment, they looked into each other's eyes over the simmering pot. His words stuck in his throat; he couldn't quite think straight when she looked at him like that. But was she think-ing what he was thinking? Would she be willing? Was it too tender a subject to suggest? No. He pushed past his reservations with almost physical force, heart speeding up, as he resolved to be up front with her.

"The contest," he began. She lowered her eyes. "We said we'd give each other the benefit of the doubt going forward—please believe me, I'm not bringing it up to make you feel guilty, or that I still blame you for what happened with the gingerbread latte recipe.

"The truth is—the whole truth I haven't told anyone else, not even Nana, or Trey—the bakery needs a cash infusion. Rents are rising—"

"That's Sparkle's fault," she said, still not looking at him, her tone hard to decipher. He heard her swallow hard. He put his hand on the small of her back, on the downy sweater. Hoping he could transmit through touch how much he wanted her to know none of this was her fault, he gave her a second to absorb his words.

"Rent is part of it, and Sparkle isn't the only new business interested in this area. Rents are going to increase, and not all because of one chain bakery. That's the reality. The one I didn't want to face."

The sauce began bubbling out of control, threatening to rise out of the pan, create a huge mess. He twisted the knob, lowered the flame, and stirred off some steam.

"And Carm told me she's going to have to retire soon."

"Oh no," Elena said, eyes flashing back up.

"I know. It's been a while coming. Don't know what I'll do without her. Anyway, I need to make sure the bakery is doing well financially so I can attract a replacement employee."

"Wow. That sheds new light on why you were angry the other day. I'd be stressing out too."

"It's an explanation, not an excuse. I had no right to take it out on you, especially when you had no idea how serious the stakes are. But please, can we not go over it again?" This was going off the rails; he wasn't making his point right, it was upsetting her, he—

"Go on," she said. She kissed his cheek, slowed his swirling thoughts.

"More than anything, I want to be able to . . ." He looked at the doorway yet again, not to sneak a kiss but to make a confession. He lowered his voice. "To be able to pay Nana back her investment in the bakery."

Elena hooked her arm around his neck, kissed his cheek a second time. "You are the absolute sweetest. Do you think we can do it? Create a new cookie in a few hours? The deadline to submit the recipe to their email is midnight."

He looked at the stove clock. They would leave here in a few hours. He had more frozen cherries at home, and plenty of cocoa powder. "I think we deserve a second chance. I want to give it my all."

"Do you even need me? You're the brilliant baker."

He put his hands on her hips, moved her to face him. "Elena, I need you. More than anything."

Then he kissed her, deep and sweet, without reservation, forgetting anyone else existed.

CHAPTER FORTY-FOUR

Congratulations, Lawrence Higgins and Elena Voss! Your contest entry Cherry Chocolate Christmas Sweethearts has been selected as a finalist. Home Baker Quarterly cordially invites you to the Snowcap Inn on New Year's Eve for the final round of competition. Please bring one dozen freshly baked cookies for the judges to sample. New Year's toast and dance to follow the contest. Formal dress requested.

Elena reread the email for the zillionth time since they'd received it three days ago. The party would begin in an hour, and she still expected their invitation to be rescinded. Why she thought so, she couldn't put her finger on. A lingering fear that Derick would pop up like a horror-movie villain to spoil everything again, perhaps.

Witnessing Derick being walked out of Sparkle Cookie HQ by security had left her elated yet shaken. Would he come back for revenge? In the end, it was his own fault he'd gotten fired. He ambushed CEO Margaret Zimmerman as she attempted to leave her office, followed her around the C-suite level babbling about "false accusations" and "cookie conspiracies." Elena hadn't expected such a dramatic end to his employment. She'd assumed they'd write him up, give him an action plan, and he'd have a chance to course correct or change jobs. They might have if he hadn't stood outside the ladies' room when Margaret ducked for cover inside. Rumor had it everyone in the C-suites witnessed him crying about "that liar Elena Voss." Elena harbored a minute degree of sympathy at his unexpected proof of human emotion, but not enough to think he deserved to keep his job and subject more employees to his problematic behavior.

Keen to avoid any further unpleasantness, Margaret had promptly offered Elena the percentage of sales on the gingerbread latte cookies Dad demanded, in addition to the bonus Derick had promised. Elena had collected a tidy a sum in record time, which lessened the blow of Derick's unhinged accusations. Dad called from the Caribbean to congratulate her, and even took it in stride when she said she didn't plan to apply for Derick's job. The C-level executives all knew her name now, and the prospects for promotion had never been better, but she still wanted out.

What if Derick showed up at the Snowcap Inn, looking for a fight? She leaned against the wall in Lawrence's living room, the scene playing in her mind. No, she didn't have to worry about that, because Derick wouldn't have a snowball's chance in hell of winning a fight against Lawrence, especially since she would pitch in. It was possible tonight would go smoothly and Lawrence's cash-flow issues would be solved without her help.

She adjusted the strap of her one-shoulder plum-colored silk dress. The fabric glided over her in a curve-flattering bias cut. The floor-length hem accented her height and made her feel good about herself. Mom had flown home this morning, on an earlier flight than Dad, to help her shop, a stunning development.

They spent the whole day together, assisted by Mom's personal shopper to find the perfect gown. Elena smiled remembering her mom asking questions about Lawrence, about Elena's feelings for him. When had they last had a deep conversation like that? She wasn't sure, but it had been a while. Mom insisted on paying for a salon blowout and lash application. The expression on Lawrence's face when he opened the front door to see her in all her glory would live in her heart forever.

"Ready, sugarplum?" he asked, trotting down the stairs in a well-fitted black suit with a black tie, looking for all the world like he'd stepped out of an Old Hollywood movie, heartthrob gorgeous. She drew in a breath, mouth open, at a loss for words. "What, you thought you were the only one who can clean up nice?"

Lawrence looked amazing in jeans and a flannel, tasty in a towel after a shower, was pure snuggle-bait in his sweats, but nothing—nothing—could compare to the sight of him in that suit. Dashing.

"I want to paint you," she said at last, taking hold of the jacket lapels to tug him to her.

"Someone should paint you, sweetie." He traced the contours of her face. Careful not to muss her lipstick, he gave her the gentlest kiss.

"You have the cookies?" she asked when they parted. "I have the recipe copies with our story."

"Sounds like we're all set, then." They walked to the door; he opened it, paused. "No matter what happens, tonight is already the best New Year's Eve, because I get to spend it with you. Let's have fun, not worry too much about the competition. Something will work out, I know it."

She had an idea for an alternate plan to ensure the bakery's success, but she wouldn't tell him yet. She wanted to see how the night went first. She swooped up her dress to keep it from dragging on the ground, and he gave her a hand to keep her steady in her heels as they stepped out.

Once they arrived, Lawrence escorted her up the stairs to the inn with sure steps and his shoulders squared. She couldn't stop looking up at him, couldn't stop feeling just as lucky as he did that they were together. That she could call him—this handsome, caring man—hers. The porch boards creaked under their feet. Dozens of flameless candles in different sizes graced the entryway, flickering like fairies. From inside antique punched-tin lanterns, more candles cast patterned shadows on the inn's facade. One final glimpse of Christmas.

"Wow," the innkeeper, Marilyn, said when they walked into the lobby, surprise tinged with confusion on her face. "Can I help you?"

"We're here for the contest," Lawrence said.

"My goodness, aren't you two glamourous? Come right this way." She bustled toward the ballroom, and they followed, arm in arm. Marilyn looked at them again, pointed at Lawrence. "I remember you! The baker from New Hope, right? Yes, and I thought you were here about the snow removal, since you're rather . . . um . . . a . . . rugged baker. Silly me! And you also attended the cookie swap, miss, am I right?"

Happiness flooded Elena, warmed her blood, at the memory. It seemed like yesterday and forever ago at the same time. How much things had changed since that day, when she'd rushed out to avoid getting too close to Lawrence. She squeezed his forearm where she held on to him, the wool suit jacket sleeve smooth under her fingers. "Yes, that's me," Elena said.

"I wish you both good luck. As pretty as a picture, you two."

Inside the ballroom, the Christmas tree had been moved from the center to a corner of the room, and a parquet dance floor took its place. The string duet was back, playing "Greensleeves." Elena and Lawrence swept into the room on the melody's repeating chords. The tune carried her heart away with it as she reveled in the refined atmosphere. Real candles in crystal jars on high-top tables draped with ivory cloths, tulle swags laced with white lights on the walls, and the curtains open to reveal the snowy grounds, well-placed floodlights throwing the ancient pine trees into relief.

Everyone was beautifully dressed—a few more men in suits, though none quite as gorgeous as her own man. The women wore a jewel box of colors, cocktail dresses and long gowns. Sequins sparkling.

"Champagne?" a waiter in a burgundy vest asked, lifting a silver tray. They each took a glass, clinking them together. Elena sipped the dry, pear-and-floral-flavored liquor.

At the judges' table, Lawrence gave them the box of Cherry Chocolate Christmas Sweethearts, and Elena provided them with the printed recipe, which included a short origin story for the cookies.

"I'm a little nervous. Are you nervous?" she whispered to Lawrence as they circulated the room. She didn't think she could stand to see him disappointed, even if she had a secret strategy to help the bakery regardless.

"Not with you by my side." He shrugged his shoulders as if he'd never had symptoms of social anxiety a day in his life. She liked that she could be a calming source for him, and her own agitation relented.

A flash went off nearby. A grandmother and a teen in a pleated skirt smiled at the photographer as she took a second picture.

"Here, let's get a picture for the magazine." Any good marketing executive knew the magazine would print Lawrence's picture even if he and Elena placed dead last in the contest. She straightened his tie as she gave the photographer's assistant their names, careful to stress the name of the bakery as well. Then she showed him how to pose and leaned against him, letting the dress slit fall open just enough to catch the eye.

"Photogenic," the photographer said, tipping her camera for Elena to see the preview screen.

More like scorching hot. Lawrence looked so good, and her clear infatuation lit her up, making her not mind her full cheeks or wonky brow. Step one in the plan to promote the bakery complete.

Elena asked the photographer to please take a picture of them using her own phone. Once she saw that photograph, she knew it would bring traffic to the social media site she'd get Lawrence to start for Sweet L's. Step two well under way. Add a few videos of him stirring dough in a Henley, and they'd have a million followers.

The sound of a spoon tapping a champagne flute caught their attention. They both looked to the sound and froze. The magazine's editor tapped once more, and the chatter died down. Tonight the editor wore a stunning black velvet dress.

The editor cleared her throat, traded her glass for a microphone. "Ladies and gentleman, I'm pleased to announce the results of *Home Baker Quarterly*'s Spirit of Christmas cookie contest."

CHAPTER FORTY-FIVE

Lawrence's heart leapt into his throat. He stroked Elena's shoulder to center himself. If the contest didn't go their way, what would he do? What would Elena think of his alternative plan to bolster the bakery's business? No matter what happened, he intended to share his idea with her. More than an idea, a dream, a deep hope. He blew out a wavering breath. *Everything will work out, one way or another*, he promised himself.

"This year's entries astounded us. You are all a very creative, talented bunch." The editor unfolded the paper a judge handed her. "This year was especially tough for our judges, given the stories you shared along with your recipes. We loved the stories from the Choi family, about how their little ones helped and created havoc in the kitchen while Mom and Dad worked on their entry. And we have a grandmother-and-granddaughter team here, Janet and Winter Clark, who told us how Christmas is their favorite time of year. Winter is even named for the season! And then we have a precious story from Elena Voss and Lawrence Higgins.

"They shared with us that their cookie symbolizes the importance of forgiveness and hope for a future. Elena wrote: *This cookie combines our two favorite flavors so that each can shine and complement the other. Lawrence makes me want to be my best self, and he says I inspire him to do the same. For us, the Spirit of Christmas means seeing the good in ourselves and others.* That's lovely, Elena and Lawrence, thank you.

"Without further ado, the judges have tasted the finalists' scrumptious cookies, and have come to a decision. I know we can agree all the cookies are winners. Now, to name our grand-prize winner. Envelope, please." She held out her hand to the judges' table. One of the judges, a woman in her midthirties with red-framed glasses, paused before extending the envelope to the editor.

Everyone held their breath—the room quiet, devoid of even the smallest sounds, like an exhalation. The night Lawrence met Elena, the only path forward he'd seen was to beat Sparkle, to have enough money to be sure the bakery would survive. Tonight, amid the glistening lights, with Elena beside him, he knew the bakery would survive, because he would never give up on it. Because Elena supported him and believed in his dream too. Because she hadn't given up on him, or on the bakery, despite disagreements and setbacks. He'd never experienced a feeling like this, the feeling of excitement without a sour note of anxiety.

The envelope crackled against the microphone as the editor opened it. Lawrence laced his fingers with Elena's and found himself looking at her face instead of the editor's, as if no one were in the room but he and she.

"Ladies and gentlemen, please give a round of applause and join me in congratulating the winners of the *Home Baker's Quarterly* Spirit of Christmas cookie competition. Give it up for Janet and Winter Clark, our grandmother-and-granddaughter team from Pittsburg!"

Lawrence saw Elena's shoulders drop as they clapped along with everyone else. He winked at her to let her know he wasn't concerned, and a slow smile lit up her pretty face. "Like me and Nana back in the day," he said to Elena. He hoped winning the contest inspired Winter to keep baking all her life, as he had been inspired by his grandma.

Once everyone had an opportunity to congratulate the winners, the string duet broke into an instrumental cover of "All I Want for Christmas Is You."

"We have to dance to this one," he told Elena. She beamed at him as brought her onto the dance floor. His hands at her waist, on the slick silk fabric, fingers on the curve of her hips, they moved together.

"It's going to be okay, don't worry," she said. Before he could say he wasn't worried, she continued. "If you want, I have ideas, lots of ideas to promote the bakery. To make sure everyone gets to taste your amazing cookies."

"I have a plan too," he said. Elena's arms were around his neck, her head tipped back to study him. "My idea is a little crazy, but I think it will work."

"Really? I'm intrigued. Do tell."

Would she think it was more than a little crazy? Maybe insane, even? Or rushing things? "I know the most talented marketing vice president, but she hates her job. They treat her poorly; they stifle her creative spirit. And I know a guy who lost his assistant and could really use a brilliant partner."

"Me?" she chirped. She stopped swaying to the music.

"You and me, sweetie." He touched the tip of his nose to the tip of hers. "And this new job would give you time to paint. No more burning the candle at both ends, painting all night and working all day."

He saw her throat bob as she swallowed, eyes round and bright. "I'd have to be a real partner, though, not an employee. That's part of *my* plan."

He raised an eyebrow. Their separate plans overlapped? She didn't think he was out of his mind to suggest they work together? "Okay. Tell me your plan."

"I've recently come into some money, as you know," she went on. "Also, I've saved up some capital. Let me be a full partner and buy in. The cash infusion can go to rent and to fund my marketing strategy. I know a good lawyer, and he can draw us up a contract to make everything legitimate."

He'd offered the job on blind faith they'd be able to survive somehow, never expecting her to have a ready solution to the money problems. He lifted her, twirled her in an embrace. Breathed in her dusky, floral essence, gloried in the sensation of her glossy hair brushing his cheek. An older couple on the floor next to them both smiled. Infectious happiness that spread to everyone around them.

"So, you think we can do this? Work together and have a relationship?" she asked, still pragmatic as he set her down. It was a big request, he knew, to ask his beautiful, talented new girlfriend to throw her lot in with him.

"I can't imagine anyone I'd rather try to conquer the world with. You make me feel like I can do anything." He'd lived too long second-guessing himself, only feeling confident in his physicality. He was confident in Elena and in their feelings for each other. "As long as we're being fearless here, can I say something else?"

Now he felt a tiny burst of nerves, static in his chest, close to his heart.

"You can tell me anything."

His pressed his lips to her ear so only she could hear him. "I love you. Some people might think it's too soon to say that, but I think I should have said it sooner. I love you, and I know I'll prove to you in time how true my love is."

She slid her hand down to rest on his heart. He wouldn't allow himself to worry if she would say it back or not. He would be his best self, and his best self, his truest self, loved Elena. No part of him, good or bad, could survive without her. Who cared what the future might bring? Even the next second. Right now, for this breath, this heartbeat, he lived in her eyes, and that was all he needed.

EPILOGUE

Two Christmas Eves later . . .

"Ginger, no. You have to stay home, little one. Sugar, show her how it's done." Elena grabbed the orange tabby kitten as the furball lurched for the door. She kissed the spot between Ginger's ears, closing her eyes to savor the fact that she finally had a kitten after years of wanting one. Lawrence had surprised her with Ginger two nights ago, opening his winter jacket to reveal giant golden eyes peering from the smallest orange face. A pink nose tinier than an eraser.

She set the kitten next to Sugar on a crumpled blanket under the Christmas tree. Sugar snuggled up to Ginger, promising she would babysit until Elena and Lawrence got back from the tree lighting.

"Are the cookies in the truck?" Elena asked Lawrence as he walked into the living room, looking unfairly sexy in a fitted red sweater. More than two years together, and her heart still caught when he walked into a room, her cheeks still heated, and she had to cross the distance to touch him at once. Hands on his strong forearms, she repeated her question, since he seemed strangely distracted.

"Yes, sweetie, everything is loaded up. No New Hope kids will be without cookies because of us." He opened the front door, blanched, and then grabbed his coat from the closet. "I can't believe I almost forgot this, though."

An extreme reaction to forgetting his coat for a second, but he could get in his head sometimes, and she was too occupied with the upcoming ceremony to question him. Since she'd bought in as a partner, Sweet L's had been flourishing. Between Lawrence's unmatched baking skills and her ability to tempt new customers through the door, they'd been making steady profits for over a year. But success didn't keep her from switching into full-on business mode when they had a special event like the tree lighting.

She locked the front door with her own key, which hadn't gotten old in the eight months they'd been living together in Lawrence's (her) house in New Hope. Some might think seeing each other all day, every day at work and then spending most of their free time together would dim the glow, but loving Lawrence was easy, and it grew on itself. The more she had, the more she wanted and needed.

Sure, sometimes they disagreed, but they were both committed to being honest when they felt upset, to giving each other space before anger could make them say things they regretted. Ninety percent of the time, they managed to give each other the benefit of the doubt. And the ten percent of the time they didn't, they'd built up enough goodwill with each other that forgiveness came naturally, if not always easily.

As Lawrence drove to the town square, Elena watched snowflakes floating in the air. The night felt extra cold, and she pulled on her leather gloves. Wind snapped around them when they exited the truck, but she warmed up rushing around setting out cookies on a table near the gazebo. Cookie duty meant a prime view of the tree lighting.

Kids began to crowd the table, chubby hands and red cheeks. Iris came over, gave Elena a hug, then chose a cookie for baby Milo, who watched the scene with serious eyes from the carrier on Trey's chest. Iris and Trey stuck close by, even as Lawrence and Elena got too busy to chat.

"Is that my mom?" Elena asked, rising to her tiptoes. Yes, here came Mom and Dad, wearing designer overcoats, looking a bit lost, weaving through the crowd. "Honey, look! My parents are here."

"I know," Lawrence said, attention focused on a family of four as he handed them cookies. "You always wish they were around for the holidays, so I begged them to give up the Caribbean for the Snowcap Inn this year. Merry early Christmas, my Elena."

"Oh, thank you! Thank you! Figures they'd do it to make you happy." Mom and Dad were kinda obsessed with Lawrence ever since they'd seen how much Elena loved working at the bakery. Her new job gave her a steady income plus the time to freelance illustrate for *Home Baker's Quarterly* and work on her painting. She waved wildly, excitement pumping. "Mom, Dad! Over here."

"This is delightful," Mom said, leaning in to kiss Elena's cheek.

"I'm wondering why we even planned to spend Christmas on the beach in the first place," Dad said. Elena gave him a long hug. "Who knew there was such beauty this close to home?"

Elena knew, but she was too thrilled to have them here with her to point it out.

"Mayor Montgomery said we can come up by the tree this year," Lawrence said. "I guess they're starting a new thing where a local business gets to be by the tree to highlight them."

"Hey, they should've reached out to marketing for that, not you," she said, giving him a sly smile.

"What can I say? The local boy still has an edge around here."

"Go ahead. We'll pass out the cookies," Mom said, pushing Elena toward the gazebo. Elena turned back to protest, but Lawrence grabbed her hand right as Mayor Montgomery began the first countdown and the lights dropped.

Inside the gazebo felt less frosty than the open square, and she had to admit she was eager to be close to the lighting, even though she knew Santa was Mr. Martinez. In the pitch dark, she felt Lawrence pulling off her left glove.

"It's cold," she said, yanking her hand away. He caught it, removed the glove, then kissed her fingers. The fire truck lights whirled red across the square, and children clapped for Santa.

"I'll keep you warm. Anyway, can you blame me for wanting to remember the night I met you, love?"

His hand and lips heated her, and she flushed at the memory of him running after her to return the missing glove. What if she hadn't forgotten her glove that night? Everything might be different. She might still be suffering at Sparkle Cookie, hating her job, spending Christmas alone in her old apartment. She opened her palm to him; he pressed a kiss inside her hand. The lips she loved against her skin.

Santa climbed the steps, and the throng began the second countdown.

Ten, nine, eight . . .

Lawrence stepped back, maybe to get a better view.

Seven, six, five, four . . .

Her left arm stretched out behind her, hand still clasped to his.

Three, two . . .

One.

The lights exploded to brilliant life. Elena squealed in joy, voice echoing. The rest of the square stayed completely silent. Her gaze flew around the crowd. Where were the cheers? Mom made a twirling motion with her finger; Dad laughed about something. Elena's brows knit, confused.

What . . .

"ELENA, TURN AROUND," the entire population of New Hope shouted as one. Santa—Mr. Martinez—pointed behind her, eyes merry.

She spun. Then her mouth fell open, warm tears clouding her vision. She blinked them away. Lawrence, on one knee behind her, blue eyed and breathtaking. Picture perfect. Lawrence holding her left hand in his, a red-velvet ring box in the other. An *open* red-velvet ring box, an emerald solitaire the color of evergreen trees inside. Snow swirled around them, and a thousand lights glittered.

"Elena, sweetheart, I want you—I want everyone—to know, the last two years have been better than anything I could have wished for. I never could have imagined you, or dared to dream you. Under the most unlikely circumstances, I found my best friend, my partner, my true love." His voice rang out—fearless and honest. His signature shyness was nowhere in sight as he declared what she meant to him, unworried by all the expectant eyes. "Every good day is better with you in it, and every bad day is endurable because you are by my side. Will you marry me and be my Elena forever?"

They stood in the town hall's shadow, steps and a world away from their first meeting. Since that cold, confused night, everything had changed. All the risks had paid off. All the chances she'd taken had brought her to this moment, with the love of her life on his knee in front of her. Her heart was the fullest it had ever been. The crowd—these people who'd become friends and family—watched, waiting for her answer. Elena could dazzle them with an eloquent response, but instead she leaned down until her lips grazed the ear of the man she loved. Her warmth to his. And she whispered for only him to hear, "I will love you all my days. Yes, Lawrence, my darling, I will marry you."

Best Christmas ever.

CHERRY CHOCOLATE SWEETHEARTS

Taste the love for yourself using the recipe Lawrence and Elena developed for the Spirit of Christmas cookie contest. While you mix, bake, and assemble these window sandwich cookies, be sure to think loving thoughts.

Cookie Dough

1 cup butter, softened
1½ cups sugar
2 large eggs
2 teaspoons vanilla
3 cups all-purpose flour
⅔ cup unsweetened cocoa powder
1 teaspoon baking powder
½ teaspoon salt
Red and white sprinkles or decorating sugar

1. In a stand mixer fitted with a paddle, combine butter and sugar. Cream at medium speed 1–2 minutes or until fully combined. Butter should have a lighter appearance.
2. Slowly add eggs to the butter mixture, mixing well between additions. Stir in the vanilla.
3. In a separate bowl, sift the flour and cocoa powder. Add baking powder and salt; stir to combine.

4. With mixer on low speed, add the dry ingredients in three parts. Scrape sides of bowl between each addition. Mix about 30 seconds or until fully combined.
5. Wrap dough in plastic wrap and chill for 1 hour. While dough chills, preheat oven to 350 degrees.
6. Roll dough to ¼ inch. Use a 3½-inch heart-shaped cookie cutter to cut the dough. Use a 2½-inch heart-shaped cookie cutter to cut a window out of half of the 3½-inch hearts. Now you have a top and bottom for your window sandwich cookies.
7. Decorate top cookies with sprinkles or sugar.
8. Bake 9–12 minutes, rotating pan halfway through (just like Lawrence!). Bake until edges are set and centers are still soft.
9. Cool on a wire rack.

Cherry Filling

4 cups frozen cherries
¼ cup water
1 tablespoon cornstarch
1 tablespoon lemon juice
2 tablespoons sugar (use more if cherries are tart)

1. Combine all ingredients except cherries and whisk over medium heat.
2. When the base has thickened, carefully add the frozen cherries.
3. Bring to a light boil, stirring often until thickened, 15–20 minutes.
4. Remove from heat, and use a large fork or potato masher to crush the cherries.
5. Allow to cool completely.

Assemble the Cookies

1. When all ingredients are cool, spread 1–2 teaspoons of cherry filling on the bottom cookies, then gently press on the top cookies.
2. Store tightly wrapped in the refrigerator and let come to room temperature for serving.

ACKNOWLEDGMENTS

First thanks must go to my agent, Shannon Snow, who found my writing in the slush pile and was the first person in publishing to believe in me. Shannon and the team at Creative Media Agency have gone above and beyond to bring my writing to readers.

Thank you to my editor, Melissa Rechter, for allowing me to tell this story to the world. I loved writing it with all my heart. I appreciate the hard work of everyone at Alcove, especially Thai, Mikaela, Dulce, and Rebecca. Lucy Davey, I love the beautiful cover. Rachel Keith, I appreciate your careful copyedits.

I'm grateful for the community I found in #momswritersclub and the support from Jessica Payne and Sara Read. Thank you to #ThrillsandChills group, especially Tobie Carter and Kelly Malacko; you keep me motivated with sprints and support.

Thank you to the Squad: Carrianne, Rachel W., Rachel P., Dana, and Giuls. You ladies hype me up.

Matt . . . hmm . . . I'm sure you did . . . something. Love ya, bestie. Sabrina, thanks for helping me keep Matt in line. Dawn, we will always miss you.

Love and appreciation to my second family, Jill, George, Emily, Danny, Mike, and Karen.

Mom, thank you for reading all my stories with an excellent eye, always helping me make them better with your wise suggestions. Dad, thank you for proofreading my early work, even the handwritten stuff. I know how blessed I am that you both encouraged me to hone my craft while I lived with you. Bless you for never doubting I would achieve my dream.

Anna, your opinion means everything to me. I hope I've made you proud. To you and Joe, thank you for Jonathan and Vera; they make every day better. Much love to you all and Mom and Dad.

Emmett and Archie, you are the greatest part of my life. You made the world new again. Believe in yourselves and work hard. I can't wait to see what the future holds for my bright and brilliant boys. I love you forever and always.

Nick, my best and truest love, the kindness in your eyes changed everything for me. I couldn't write a single romantic word without you to inspire me. *Je t'aime à jamais.*